THE REBIRTH OF MISS FLOSSIE MAE "BETTYE DEVINE" DUPONT

M. J. Hart

Kingdom Builders Publications LLC

Printed in the USA

ISBN 978-0-692-87121-8
Library of Congress Control Number 2017938411

Authored by
Mildred Juanita Hart

Editor
Batina L. Dawson

Visual Artist
Alfreta Ross

Photographer
John F. Hart

Cover Colorization
Eric Quzack

Cover Design
LoMar Designs

ACKNOWLEGEMENTS

As always, I thank God first and foremost for doing just what He has promised; never has He ever left or forsaken me. He has kept me through the storms, valleys; through fire and flood. I thank Him for making crooked places straight, opening and closing doors, directing my path, and for allowing me to partake in His salvation. In spite of it all, You have been so good to me. Through Him, all things are possible. And I believe these things have helped to sharpen my creativeness. Therefore, He's working them out for my good. I thank my dear family for their love, encouragement and support. I am extremely blessed to have you all in my corner, believing in me as I believe in myself. You have walked with me through my dreams and desires; ran with me toward my vision. Go team: Alfreta Ross, Felicia Hart, James Jr. and Anitra Hart, John and Monica Hart, Henry and Batina Dawson. I sincerely thank each of you for always so lovingly and so willingly—taking the journey with me, at times, both literally and figuratively. And to my partners in laughter, venting, encouraging, shopping and entrepreneurship, you all are my "Ride and Let's Ride" crew! My sisters and brothers, I look forward to us continually growing older together. Pat, I thank you for your, "Let's do this! Let's get it done" nature. I want to extend a special thank you to my eldest daughter, Alfreta for her artistry. You are a precious Jewel. My prayer is that someday, I will see your artwork on display. A very sincere and heart felt thank you to Mrs. Dorothy H. McLeod, who has encouraged me more than you'll ever know. You have come to know several of my creative works depicting the lives of characters from Miss Flossie Mae "Bettye Devine" DuPont to Miss Pearlie Mae Freshwater Crippins. Anytime I've asked you to read a story or a manuscript, you have been generous with your time. You never hesitated. I value your knowledge and direction. I am ever so grateful for your compassion. And to my Daddy and my sister, Cookie, this year and last began and ended with a few obstacles, but we know that there is nothing too hard for God! And by faith, we believe that He has got that thing too because our God is indeed a Healer!

DEDICATION

This Book is dedicated to every dreamer, dream catcher, dream holder, and dream conqueror. It is most especially to those who have had and has the courage to step out, sometimes, by faith alone to attain them. May we continue to press, thrive, and achieve. And may God forever bless the gifts and talents which He has instilled in us that we will be awakened, believing that all things are possible, and our dreams will be made manifest.

THIS BOOK BELONGS TO

CONTENTS

M. J. Hart

DREAMER OR SCHEMER

BY M. J. HART

Is it really a *dream* if you are willing to cheat and scheme for it?

Is it worth the price you have to pay—
Looking yourself in the mirror everyday—
Knowing that the shortcut you took or the bad choices you made—
Cost you far more than the pain you now feel—
Cost you more than the shame you are constantly dealing with—
Almost cost you your good name—
Made you settle for less than you deserved—
Leaving you with less coming out than you had when you went in—
Made folks look down upon you—
And you know—you were raised to believe that a good name is
EVERYTHING.
Yet, you spent much of your integrity trying to gain fortune and fame—
When reality set in and you finally came to yourself—
You realized that you had lost far more than you had ever hoped to gain—
Because what you got in return could have cost you substantially more than
that—
You could have had to pay with every ounce of dignity and grace you had—
Perhaps, could have been made to pay with your very life—
So, you eventually made the choice to pick yourself up and try to rebuild—
If not from scratch—from the fragments and broken pieces left—
And then, you decide to hold your head up—
Cause you finally have a plan that doesn't sell yourself short—
And you tell yourself that you will never again allow anything take you down
so low—
Leave so distraught that you believe you have nowhere to go—
That there is no redemption for all of the mistakes you've made—

Dreaming with no vision—

Feeling trapped inside your mind—
Trying to reach a place, to achieve something without light or clear
directions—
Following after someone or something that's even more lost than you—
Trying to contrive and connive yourself into a place that was never meant for
you anyway—

But was it really ever a *dream* if you have to cheat and SCHEME, trying to
attain it?

CHAPTER ONE

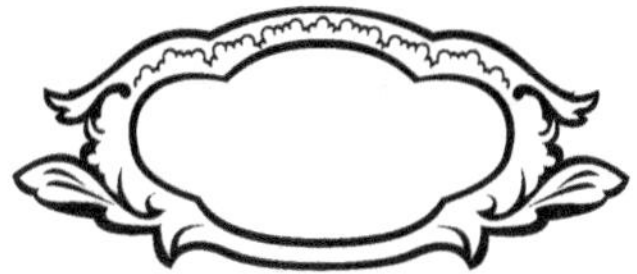

Mrs. Bertha had cooked all morning and it wasn't even Sunday. Fried chicken, turnip greens with corn meal dumplings, baked sweet potatoes, field peas, sweet tea and chocolate cake were some of her baby girl's favorites.

Still, she was sort of torn between two opinions. She was glad—in fact, overjoyed that Flossie Mae was coming home. However, a part of her also regretted that things hadn't worked out like her baby girl had intended. Nonetheless, she believed, they had still worked out in Flossie Mae's favor.

Like most mothers, she wanted her children's hopes and dreams to come to something. Lord knows, she didn't agree with Flossie Mae going way up yonder, singing that old devil's music. Mrs. Bertha believed there was a strong chance of her child getting caught up in who-knows-what, with who-knows-who all in the name of fame and fortune. Howbeit, she was of age. They couldn't hold her back.

"That Boy." Augustus Atwater had enticed her. Howbeit, Flossie Mae had messed around and got the big-head. She had gotten too full of herself. Folks were always telling her how good she could sing and all. It hadn't done a thing except swell that head of hers up. Mrs. Bertha had to admit, her baby girl could *sho'nuff* sing. But, if she had her way, Flossie Mae would use that voice of hers to sing God's praises.

In her mind, Flossie Mae had everything figured out. She expected things to work out just like she wanted them to, just because she wanted them to. That was her young'un up and down. She never stopped to consider that sometimes the ins and outs of life have a way of altering our plans.

It won't no telling what had happened up there in the City. And hadn't nobody mentioned anything about "That Boy" coming back with her either. Mrs. Bertha couldn't put her finger on it. Still, she knew that something won't right. Didn't a soul have to tell her that.

She didn't know the real story and probably wouldn't for some time to come. She had promised herself and her Frederick that she wasn't going to pry. "In due time, our young'un will tell us what she wants us to know," he had said.

Unless Flossie Mae had done a whole heap of changing, 'due time' would probably come around about the same time that chickens started having pigs. Regardless, Mrs. Bertha was bent on keeping her word. She wouldn't pry. Above all else, her baby girl was almost home—home where she was still loved by her folks. And with the help of the Lord, everything was going to be all right.

Mrs. Bertha was standing, ringing her hands, looking out of the kitchen window when she saw her Frederick running up from the fields like he was coming to put out a fire. About the same time, she saw a car coming up the road, leaving puffs of dust behind that reminded her of dark, dirty clouds.

She had prayed for this day! She had waited! She had prayed some more! And she had shed some tears too. But she kept on waiting. And she kept on praying, knowing that the Lord had heard her and would answer her prayers. Finally, the answer had come. Her baby was home again!

She wiped her hands in her apron. It took everything in her not to run out the back door like a streak of lightning and meet them before they could get up to the house. Her young'un being so close and yet so far away was certainly like labor, pressing. Thankfully, a lot less painful than the day she had entered into the world. And just like that day, when she finally laid eyes on her, it was worth every minute of her suffering or at least, had managed to overshadow it.

CHAPTER TWO

Flossie Mae was the seventh daughter born to Bertha Mae and Frederick Douglass DuPont. She entered into this world on September 20, 1937 around 12:00 noonday or about as close to it as can be recollected. At least that's what Aunt Eva, the midwife put down on her paper. So that's what the record shows.

The natural or the first birth of Miss Flossie Mae DuPont occurred on an unusually hot day for late September. The sun was having its way. The wind seemed to be on a holiday. And Mrs. Bertha sure won't having herself no picnic.

She had been in labor since supper time, the day before. She was more than ready for something to happen. But it appeared, her young'un couldn't decide whether it wanted to *hee* or to *haw*. Like her Mama used to say, "A young'un ain't gonna come 'til it gets good and ready." And it appeared, this child won't nowhere near ready.

It would take a real stretch of the imagination to assume that even then, long before it became apparent to anyone else, Flossie Mae had a strong desire to be the center of attention. It looked as if she was waiting for the perfect time to make her entrance.

However, Mrs. Bertha was more than ready after nine long months that seemed to drag into twelve, counting June, July, and August twice. Being hot and sweaty, tired, and full of child in the midst of the heat, and the flies, and the misquotes made her hope the more that she would give her Frederick a son this time. If possible, she was ready to shut the door on her childbearing years.

Her mother had managed to bear and rear up eleven, four girls and seven boys. Howbeit, she was quite willing to let her mother have her glory all by herself. She could also remember the few misses her mother had. In spite of already having more young'uns than that little house could hold comfortably, her mother had shed tears as if the one she lost was her first and only child. Now, Mrs. Bertha more than understood a mother's love as well as a mother's pain.

Flossie Mae's birth took place in Coley's Corner, North Carolina. She was born on the property of Mr. Earl Robert Russell and Mr. Robert Earl Russell IV. They were the twin boys and only heirs of Mr. Robert Earl Russell III. It was also where she got her first glimpse into what this sometimes cock-eyed, twisted up, bent-out-of-shape world had to offer folks who looked like her.

The elder Mr. Russell was a tyrant, a thief and/or a real good business man, depending upon who you asked and which side of the red line you happened to be standing on at the time. If he saw anything wrong with the practice of—'all -for-me-and-none-for-you'—you sure couldn't tell it by his actions.

It didn't seem to bother him none that Mr. DuPont whom he referred to as, "boy" had a wife and a house full of young'uns to feed and clothe with his settle-up money that always amounted to less than a rough week's pay.

Mr. Russell took full advantage of Mr. DuPont's inability to read and write well. His poor counting skills seemed to always work out in his favor too. Still, his advantage went far beyond that. Exactly who was the "boy" going to address his complaints to? Mr. DuPont hadn't realized just how much he had been cheated out of until his daughters got some schooling. They became pretty good with figures, especially Fannie. She could put figures together in her head better and faster than most folks could on a piece of paper.

More than anything else, that helped to change his mind about the importance of an education. He didn't want nobody to come along and take advantage of his daughters just because they didn't know any better. It was still necessary for them to work the fields, but it was not above all else.

He didn't ever want to see or even envision either of them walking behind their man, dropping seeds into ground that would never belong to them or working hard to harvest crops just so they could bearly manage to stay as poor as they had been the year before.

His Bertha had done all of that and more. And he knew it. He couldn't have asked for no one better, but sometimes, things got really tight. At times, he wished that she had given him a couple of sons. He often felt guilty about how he had to work his daughters, but it couldn't be helped.

One day, Mr. DuPont walked ten miles to Mr. Russell's nice house with its big, well- kept yard, with his shiny, new car parked in the driveway to get the money due him, his money.

He walked around back, took a deep breath, removed his hands from his pockets, and knocked on the door. A colored lady, dressed in a maid's uniform opened the door.

"Can I help you?" she asked. Her nose was turned up and her face was frowned as if Mr. DuPont was the first colored man she had ever laid eyes upon.

"I come to see Mr. Russell on some business," he answered.

"Wait here!" the woman said, shutting the door in his face. Mr. DuPont must have stood outside that door—waiting for better than twenty minutes before Mr. Russell finally decided to show himself.

"What can I do for you, boy?" he asked, knowing full well what business Mr. DuPont had with him.

"I come to collect my money, sir," he answered.

"Boy, I don't owe you nothing! Now, git on 'way from here 'fore I call the law!" he shouted, pointing his finger in the direction of the roadway.

"But sir," Mr. DuPont tried to explain.

"Boy, I told you to git on 'way from here! Now!" Mr. Russell said before slamming the door in Mr. DuPont's face.

Not looking for trouble, just his money, Mr. DuPont walked the ten miles back home with his pockets just as empty going back as they had been when he came. His mind was full of wondering. He wondered about how he, how (they) were going to make due. He had learned a long time ago that a body can do a whole heap of praying when its' got such a long way to walk. He thought about some other things as well on that long journey home, but he wasn't going to allow Mr. Russell or the devil to make him stoop so low. Somehow, they were going to make it, with the help of the Lord.

Flossie Mae had no idea what she was being born into. No special entrance was required. If she had really known, perhaps, she would have taken a tad longer to get here. She didn't know it yet, but she would come to despise the place, the hard work, being poor, and at times, the hardships of being colored.

She would love her family dearly, but sometimes, her feelings would get all tangled up inside of her worse than her long, thick hair after a good washing. And, at times, it would be difficult to keep her feelings of love and hate separated in her heart. One day, Flossie Mae would leave Coley's Corner, vowing to never look back. However, sometimes, it becomes necessary to take the long and bumpy road in order to get us to the place we need to be.

It was during a time prior to the commencement of World War II. Franklin D. Roosevelt was the U.S. President. Segregation was rampart. Black Americans were referred to as, Coloreds, Negroes, and much worse. They were called just about any and every other thing, except a 'Child of God'. And though they were citizens, they were constantly denied the rights written in the

Thirteenth Constitutional Amendment, still, eighty-six years after the fact. If those on the other side of the fence knew of or had even heard of 'The Emancipation—most acted otherwise.

In and during slavery, you could both literally and figuratively work a man, woman, boy or girl to death, for free. In sharecropping, you could for all intents and purposes, basically do the same. The exception being, they worked. They got paid. But their share of the proceeds from the harvest was not enough to survive on. It appeared to be a cooperative effort. However, the efforts of the family who actually worked the fields meted them little cooperation or pay from the family who actually owned the fields. The system was set up in such a way that made it almost impossible to get out from under.

Flossie Mae had also been born in the throes of hardship. Howbeit, it was also a time when folks like her Mama and Papa couldn't tell much difference.

Bertha Mae and Frederick Douglass DuPont were newlyweds and not much more than young'uns themselves when hard times began to pinch, tug, and choke even the well-to-do. They had heard far too many stories of folks doing ungodly things to themselves because they didn't have any more money, but they could never understand it. They suspected, if they had looked to money to be their end-all, they wouldn't have lasted a single day.

All in all, the DuPonts were hard-working, honest folk who lived simple, God-fearing lives. In their own way, they found a level of contentment that their baby girl could not grasp.

To imply that Flossie Mae DuPont was not born with a silver spoon in her mouth would neither be a stretch of the truth nor take a stretch of the imagination. And to say that she had difficulty coming to grips with her lot in life would not be an unjust statement or a rush to judgment. It was quite visible to all who knew her or heard her speak.

Flossie Mae came into this world with her eyes shut and her mouth wide open. From the moment she arrived, the DuPont house was forever changed.

Aunt Eva, the Midwife and Mama Victoria, grandmother to Flossie Mae and the other DuPont girls were with Mrs. Bertha. Her father, Mr. Frederick Douglass DuPont was out in the fields, plowing behind Napoleon, the mule. Ophelia, Joanne, Ruby, and Fannie walked behind their Papa, picking up 'taters as he turned the ground.

Mable and Betty played on the front porch. It would be another year or two before they became fully acquainted with the hot, scorching sun and the hard work that would blister their little hands and make their feet ache. And a few years thereafter, they would come to understand far too well what sharecropping really meant.

Sharecropping sure wasn't any kind of life for anyone who aimed to get ahead. Yet, it was the only kind of life Bertha Mae and Frederick Douglass DuPont knew at the time. It was the only kind they had as far as they could see. And it was the only kind of life they had to offer their seven daughters.

CHAPTER THREE

SEPTEMBER 20, 1937—ABOUT 12:00 NOONDAY

"Oh Lord , I don't think I'm gonna make it this time!"

"It hurts so bad!"

"I'm so tired!" Mrs. Bertha cried out.

"Child, you gonna make it just like you done with the rest of your chirren!" Aunt Eva, the midwife assured her.

"UUUUUHHHH, LORD! OOOOOOHHHHH, LORD!" Mrs. Bertha continued to moan.

"Here Honey, pull on this here sheet when the pains grip you," Aunt Eva commanded while tying the sheet to the iron rail at the foot of the bed.

"OOOOHHH, LORD! PLEASE TAKE THIS YOUNG'UN OUT OF ME!" Mrs. Bertha cried out. In her mind, she wanted to be strong, but the pain along with the heat was snatching away every effort toward that.

"Shugar, this cool rag on your head gonna help ease up some of the pain," Aunt Eva promised.

As a midwife, she did all she knew to do. It won't no easy thing watching other womenfolk suffer the pains of childbirth. She knew from her own experiences, those pains will make you do a heap more than moan and groan. When she birthed her own chirrens into the world, it felt as if the weight of her suffering along with a few more had been laid on her to bear. And she knew, no matter what she said or done, won't a thing gonna ease up the pain for Mrs. Bertha except that young'un bringing itself on out of there.

Mother Victoria sat in a chair by the window, trying to suck up every little breeze that dared to blow. "This here is a bad sign, a *sho'nuff* bad sign. This here young'un ain't gonna bring nothing but trouble," she said as if it was a matter of fact. She spoke as if it was the truth simply because it came out of her mouth.

"Mercy! Mercy! Mercy!" Mrs. Bertha cried out even louder than before. Her mother-in-law was almost harder to take than the pains of childbirth. She was suffering something terrible, but if she had to bear one more word from Mother Victoria, she just might be forced into getting up from that bed and doing or saying something shameful.

"Push, child! Push!" Aunt Eva commanded.

Mrs. Bertha and Aunt Eva both took a deep breath. Then she pushed with all of her might. She pushed until her eyes bulged and her face resembled a plump, fresh tomato. Nonetheless, she kept on pushing and kept on hollering until the last of Flossie Mae's nine pound self was out of her.

From birth, Flossie Mae had real strong lungs. Right after Aunt Eva spanked her bottom, she pitched a fit. There was no way to tell whether she cried so because she had to squeeze herself through such a narrow door or because she looked at her surroundings, asked the Creator where in the world had He sent her, and received an answer that didn't quite suit her high hopes for life on this side.

Either way, there was no going back, especially, not if Mrs. Bertha had anything to do with it. Hadn't a soul asked her nothing before she came. So, much like the rest of us, she really didn't have no say so about the how, what or who she came through. At best, all she could do was what she was doing—holler.

"I reckon somebody ought to go tell your boy he done got his self another gal," Aunt Eva said.

"I told y'all, nothing but trouble!" Mother Victoria repeated.

Aunt Eva didn't have nothing to say. Mrs. Bertha was way too tired to have her say. And Mother Victoria liked hearing herself talk. So, like always, she had plenty to say.

"The last thing we needs on this place is another gal. Bertha Mae keeps spurring 'em out all right, but we needs some sons to carry on the DuPont name and to do some of this work 'round here. Sho' hope you get it right the next time."

She already had a full-grown grandson carrying on the DuPont name. He lived in Upton with his family. He was the son of her dearly, departed daughter, Odessa. But Victoria DuPont never acknowledged his existence. She blamed him for all of his unwed mother's troubles. But, he didn't ask his mama to take up with his pappy or to be born—no more than Flossie Mae or anyone else had. Nor had he asked to have Victoria DuPont for a grandmother.

Mrs. Bertha laid on that bed, admiring her young'un, thinking at the same time how folks wanted and needed a whole heap, but that don't mean they gonna get it. She wanted and needed her mother-in-law to mind her own business—just one good time. And right now, was as good a time as any to start.

—◦—

FLOSSY
MAE

CHAPTER FOUR

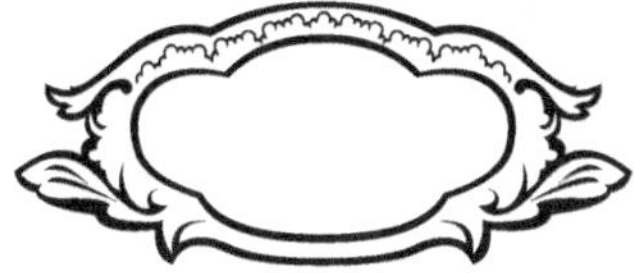

As Flossie Mae grew, so did her folks' troubles which were not due to anything she had or had not done. There were just so many mouths to feed, too little money, and like always, so much work to be done.

She often overheard her mama and papa talking as they sat around the eating table at night, trying to figure out how to stretch a dime into a dollar. Of course, it was an impossible task, but that never stopped them from trying.

In her mind, she didn't see that it would hurt nothing if she possessed the things and the kind of life style that folks like the Russells managed to have. She figured, it was through no fault of her own that she had been born colored and poor.

Flossie Mae didn't see nor did she believe that her skin color ought to be the determining factor in how big her slice of life's pie should be. And she certainly didn't see nothing wrong with hoping for, even expecting at least an in betwixt kind of life or the kind of life to fit how she felt on the inside.

Everything around her seemed to be based upon color. She didn't see nothing wrong with her wanting a taste of the good. In her mind, Flossie Mae imagined the change starting with her riding the bus to the school house, especially on those real cold mornings, instead of having to duck into the woods, out of its way. However, that privilege was only granted to the white children who attended the nice brick schoolhouse across the way.

She and her sisters had been subjected to name calling, spat upon, and dusted up when it was dry—splashed on when it was wet. All they were trying to do was get to their separated and far from equal schoolhouse on time. Everybody knew of the unfairness and inequality of it all. And everybody saw the differences and the end results thereof. As far as she could see, everybody seemed to look pass it or did the best they could with it. But, from her vantage point, it appeared that nobody was trying to change it.

Then there was the matter of those hand-me-down clothes and wired-up shoe soles that didn't seem to bother her sisters in the least, but made Flossie Mae stew. It was hard for her to understand why life had served her such a terrible hand.

"Bertha, we got just enough left over for one pair of shoes," Flossie Mae overheard her Papa say one night after he had settled up with Mr. Russell.

"But you knows we can't get by with just one pair this time. Ophelia or Joanne can wear my shoes to school, but what about Ruby and Fannie? They need shoes too. Mable, Betty, and Flossie Mae gonna soon need shoes," her Mama said.

"All I can figure, everybody who don't have shoes to wear got to stay put. I need the oldest ones here working anyhow. Least 'til we get the crops in. School and shoes just got to wait for a while," her Papa said.

"Maybe come Christmas, we can see our way to get the chirren something nice," her Mama said, knowing that it was more a hope than a reality.

"Look here woman! I'm doing all I can! When Mr. Russell settled up with us the last time, we bearly had chicken feed money left over. This time, we got even less than that. If I had a boy or two amongst this house full of gals you done gave me, maybe things would be different. We just might come out ahead sometimes instead of always being two steps behind," her Papa said, raising his voice.

"I wish you could just be thankful for what you got rather than supposing on things that ain't never gonna be," her Mama said, lowering her voice in a way that made it clear to her husband that he best lower his voice too.

In her mind, Flossie Mae always hoped for something different from the life of a sharecropper. She wondered about and desired a life far beyond the corn and cotton fields. She wanted something much easier on her back than picking up 'taters, picking cucumbers and beans, or whatever else her Papa happened to plant.

Howbeit, Frederick and Bertha DuPont gave their children the best of what they had to offer. Mrs. Bertha would use printed feed sacks to stitch up little dresses for her daughters. Whenever she could, she would buy a piece or two of cloth. The newness of it along with the fact that no other living soul had worn that garment seemed to satisfy Flossie Mae for a while. But it wasn't just about school buses or clothes or houses or hard work. It was life in general, hers' in particular. Flossie Mae didn't like hers' one bit—no more than she liked the name, Flossie Mae.

Her folks saw nothing wrong with her having dreams, but it saddened them how she took her dreams to the extreme by denying her reality. She wanted to be who she was not. She longed for the things she felt lots of money could buy along with the places she believed it could take her. She had neither money nor any idea how to come into it. Nonetheless, she desired a life she had not while hating the life she had. Needless to say, "She was one discontented sister!" While at the same time, she was also one stubborn, determined sister!

Discontentment festered on the inside of her like a bedsore, getting bigger and bigger until she began to despise the pain and ugliness it caused. She wanted it to go away, but it wouldn't. She couldn't let go of it because it wouldn't let go of her. Though she wasn't altogether certain what she was so desperately trying to hold onto or where it might lead her.

Besides the pain she carried around with her, Flossie Mae had been gifted with a beautiful singing voice. Whenever she sang in church which she had done since the age of four, folks would stand and clap and shout. At times, even fall out. The trouble was, she liked the attention, but she didn't necessarily believe in what she sang about.

Sure, she believed in God. She believed that He was out there, "Somewhere." looking over and taking care of folks who had more than they were ever gonna use up. She felt that her family and all of those like them had been forgotten or overlooked. Seemingly, they had been left to endure the misery of it all, the best way they could while He allowed the Mr. Russells of this world to get away with treating them like less than dirt.

In her eyes, all of those pretty sounding words didn't seem to make a bit of difference. After folks quit grinning and clapping, shouting and being slain in the Spirit, they would have to leave the church house. Come Monday, at the crack of dawn, they would be making their way right back into the fields, plowing, picking cotton, pulling weeds or whatever else that causes the skin to burn and chafe. It also caused calloused hands, swollen ankles and made the back ache—the very same back that Mama Victoria said she won't old enough to have yet.

It never entered her discontented mind that maybe, possibly, perhaps, for a time such as this, she, Miss Flossie Mae DuPont was put in place to bring those folks some joy. For a while, she was put in place to sing them right out of their misery, to help them escape the drudgery, to take their minds off the hardships of life.

Perhaps, it would have made a difference if she had understood that faith was keeping these people in a place where hard times and seemingly heartless tyrants could not take hold of or get the best of them. Their faith helped them to endure the pains of misery. Maybe, if she had known that folks like her Mama could keep right on grinning and clapping and shouting because they knew that their God had neither left nor had He forsaken them. Their faith kept them looking up and seeing those things which were not yet, but would one day be.

Who Flossie Mae did think about constantly was Flossie Mae; and what she thought about after that was how she was going to escape.

"Baby, I sure did enjoy that piece you sang this morning," Mrs. Annie Mae, the Reverend's wife said, after Sunday Service.

"Honey Child, ain't a bird nowhere got a thang on you! You're just a natural-born song bird," Mrs. Sarah said, taking hold of Flossie Mae's hand.

"You just keep on singing, you hear," Mr. Leander told her.

"That song of yours done something for me this morning. Child, God done gifted you in a special way," Mother Frances said.

Flossie Mae had heard compliments such as these often. She began to take them to heart. The truth is, most often, they went to her head. The older she got, the more she saw her singing voice, her gift as her ticket out of Coley's Corner. But, where was out? And how was she going to get there? She had asked herself these questions countless times. The notion of leaving Coley's Corner made her feel restless. Some days, hopeless, other days, desperate. Yet, until now, no answer had come.

On more than a few occasions the Reverend's sermon had touched on the matter of discontentment. If Flossie Mae had really been listening, she could have possibly seen the light though the Reverend had no particular person in mind.

"Anytime and anywhere you find discontentment and/or a willingness to use what The Good Lord done gave you—for His glory—for your own glory, Satan is not going to be far behind.

He will make it his business to help you along. Whatever or whoever we choose as our "deliverer," we best hope that it will be able to *keep* us. If not, we will have to *keep* it. And if we aren't mindful, before it's over, we will end up paying more than we figured. It could cause us our very life! Children, Satan is no friend of ours, never was, never can be. He's out to kill, to steal, and to destroy!"

On this particular Sunday, she couldn't hear because her attention was leaning in another direction, focused on other matters. Augustus "Gussie" Atwater, Mrs. Lucy's nephew from up North had come for a visit. Flossie Mae wondered why someone, anyone in their right mind would ever leave anywhere else to come to Coley's Corner?

To her, he appeared to be city-sharp and snake-oil slick. Nonetheless, he was somebody different. At church, all of the girls were eyeing him, especially, Flossie Mae. And he was eyeing her as well as the rest. Throughout the Service, some of them kept looking back at him snickering.

They didn't know it, but Mrs. Bertha was eyeing them too. Not one of her girls had gotten themselves in "trouble". And she sure didn't intend for her baby gal to either. Won't no smooth talking, here today and gone tomorrow, hard-knot of a boy gonna come along and fool her young'un if she had anything to do with it.

Mrs. Bertha didn't know, but her daughter had already begun to make her own plans for Mr. Augustus, "here today and gone tomorrow, hard-knot" Atwater! Flossie Mae figured—if he knows the way in—he knows the way out. And that's where she aimed to be—out!

Of all the things Augustus Atwater would eventually tell her (some truths, but mostly lies), he would neglect to mention how he was on the run, hiding out at his Aunt Lucy's until the heat died down. From the time he was in short breeches, if trouble was anywhere around, it could single him out in a crowd.

Mrs. Lucy, herself, didn't know too much about her nephew except that he was lazy, thought that hard work was beneath him, wanted to saddle somebody else with his troubles, and was always looking for the easy way out. He also thought that her door should swing on welcomed hinges, opening up to him whenever he decided to knock. Howbeit, he was family just the same, her very own dead sister's child. Her sister was the only reason she did all she could do to help him out during his *many* times of need.

It wasn't the first time. And she doubted if it would be the last. Some folks were just prone for trouble. Augustus happened to be one of them. Her nephew usually came without warning and left in the same manner. Except, a piece or two of her belongings always managed to walk out with him.

On his last visit, Augustus had walked off with Mrs. Lucy's brooch. Till this day, the incident continued to puzzle her. That Dime Store brooch didn't hold one bit of value to a soul except her. She imagined some unsuspecting woman wearing it. Undoubtedly, she had been fooled into believing that he had bought it especially for her.

Besides her patience, her kindness, and her respect, she wondered what it would be this time? Which one of her belongings would stick to his fingers, take legs and walk out with him? Except this time, he was eyeing something that already had legs, Miss Flossie Mae DuPont.

Mrs. Lucy didn't want to go 'round bad-mouthing her own kin, but the truth was the truth. That boy had grown up to be just like his Pappy. He and his wayward self, had taken her dear, sweet sister through the muck and the mire. It appeared the man didn't have the common sense of a horse fly. At least, a fly will try to get out of the way of the fly swatter. But, he would run slam into it.

Augustus had latched onto his same worldly ways, lying and thieving and looking for the easy way out, anything except making a living for himself the honest way. As far as she could see, Flossie Mae wasn't doing a thing except grinning herself up on a mess full of trouble. And she was going to tell Bertha so.

Flossie Mae grinned all over herself every time she saw Augustus Atwater. He in return, was always full of pretty sounding words or whatever he thought a woman or some young, 'don't know much yet' gal wanted and needed to hear.

The more he saw and heard of Flossie Mae DuPont, the more familiar he wanted to become with her. Likewise, the more she saw and heard of Augustus Atwater, it appeared the more partial she became to him—but, not really.

Augustus thought that Flossie Mae was too country, much too country for his usual taste. She was pretty and all, had a real nice smile, and was real sassy, but in an attractive, yet crafty kind of way. She was also real dumb and far too curious for her own good. She asked a lot of questions about how things were up North. Her questions led him to believe that she was ready, had been ready for a long time to see what life had to offer her outside of Coley's Corner.

For her taste, Augustus didn't look as good as he tried to make himself out to be. He wasn't really her idea of what she imagined a citified fellow to be either. She had overheard his Aunt Lucy, telling her Mama how he laid up in bed half of the day and how she could hardly get him to do so much as sweep the yard. So amongst all of his other flaws, she reasoned, he was lazy to boot.

One thing she did know, you can't expect to get far in this life if you won't even help yourself. If she could get out in the fields as soon as daylight hit and pick a hundred and fifty pounds of cotton, dig taters 'til her back could hardly straighten, stack wood with the best of them—the least he could do is get his lazy hindquarters out of the bed at a decent hour. And if his poor, old Aunt Lucy could still take in washing, he can surely pick up the yard broom every now and then to help earn his keep. She doubted if he would ever become rich unless someone was foolish enough to just dump a pile of money in his lap.

She grinned at him, but she had no intentions of taking it any further than that regardless of what he said, did or thought. She just wanted him to point her in the right direction—show her the way out. And that was all she wanted from him. After that, he could go on about his business!

Mr. Frederick Douglass DuPont didn't have any kind words or thoughts toward Mr. Augustus Atwater. He didn't take to his kind, and even less so when they happened to be looking in the direction of one of his daughters. Apart from being much too old for his Flossie Mae, he looked on him as being akin to and on a par with a weasel. He looked harmless enough. Nonetheless, looks can be deceiving. Weasels tended to cause harm to everything they touched. Usually, foxes, weasels, snakes, and the like eventually met up with the barrel of his shotgun.

It appeared, the more he and Mrs. Bertha talked, the more Flossie Mae grinned. And the more she grinned, the more Augustus Atwater schemed. When it came to the ways of the world, Flossie Mae was still in the nest, waiting to be hatched while Augustus was already a full-grown rooster.

However, the DuPonts had experienced enough of life to know that there were some folks who looked on an apple tree fully content with picking their apples up from the ground, without stress or strain or worry. Some folks want their fill, but are only willing to reach up to the lowest branches. Some folks stretched and climbed, and filled their buckets from a little further up. There were others who set their sights on a much higher level., expecting and accepting nothing less than the best pick of the crop. And then there was Flossie Mae. Apparently, she didn't just want to pick apples from the tree—she wanted the whole tree. But there were also the Augustus Atwaters of this world who wanted the apples and the tree. However, they wanted someone else to pick them and then set them down at their feet.

As far as Mr. Frederick Douglass DuPont was concerned, his daughter was going to wind up with a big bucket full of nothing if she was looking to that Atwater boy to fill it. Still, since she was a little-bitty thing, his daughter had been about as headstrong as Napoleon, the mule. She was too old to be chastised like a ten year old. The way Flossie Mae carried on at times, he suspected a ten year old might be angered by the comparison. And he had just about talked himself out. Short of tying her up in the cellar or running that snake off with his shotgun, he didn't know of anything else to do that would sway his baby gal. Though he knew, his Bertha would never stand for such a thing as that.

Generally, Mr. DuPont was a quiet man. Lately, he tended to get more than a little teed-off whenever anyone approached the subject of Flossie Mae and Augustus Atwater. It was that very subject that caused him to raise his voice and say what he did to Mrs. Bertha one night.

"Honey, it appears, Flossie Mae done got that mind of hers made up to take a liking to that young man," Mrs. Bertha began.

"Over my dead body!" Mr. DuPont said in a way that surprised his wife,

Sweetin', now, that ain't no kind of way for you to be talking. We done taught our chirren to find their way in this here world. Flossie Mae is set on rushing out there and finding hers. I don't like it either, but she is of age," Mrs. Bertha said.

"Bertha, I declare, that gal of yours is more like Victoria DuPont than I would ever care to admit! I don't rightly know how she did it. She sho' didn't take up much time with them. But my Mama, rest her soul, managed to pass those stubborn ways of hers onto Flossie Mae. Trying to talk to Mama after she done got something in her head did as much good as dashing a cup of cold water onto a forest fire," Mr. DuPont said, his voice still rose though it had grown a tad bit lower.

Mrs. Bertha sat in silence. She didn't want to get into the subject of her mother-in-law. She didn't care to add her two cents worth. Victoria DuPont had gone out of her way to make life as miserable for her as possible. Still, she didn't wish to speak ill of the dead.

Throughout her marriage, she had bent over backwards, turned the other cheek, turned a deaf-ear, forgave and tried to forget, trying to keep the peace. Victoria DuPont was just as determined to have her way or nothing. So, in the end that's exactly what she got—nothing! But that was of her own choosing.

Like her own dear Mama, Flossie Mae Nichols used to say, "Baby, you can't make folks like you no more than you can make a rabbit cuddle up to a porcupine or a lamb snuggle up with a wolf. Nevertheless, no matter how folks go to treating you, you can't allow them to change you. Whether we put on a show of being as sweet as honey or as sour as lemon drops, don't a one of us hold a claim to this here world. Can't a one of us make it all by ourselves, alone. Some things hold true for each and every one of us. We all got to meet our Maker. We will have to answer for the bad as well as for the good. And won't a soul be able to stand in our place and answer for us. No matter what we got or what we lack, none of us will escape."

Mrs. Bertha had no intentions of getting into it with her Frederick over Augustus Atwater or Victoria DuPont. Nor did she want to remind him again that his stubborn streak was pretty good and wide too whenever he wanted it to be. Then again, he could be as sweet as puddin'. She would just approach the matter at another time.

CHAPTER FIVE

Bertha Mae and Frederick Douglass DuPont wanted their daughters to dream big dreams, to have a desire for something above and beyond sharecropping. Regardless of how things looked to Flossie Mae who acted as if they were squashing her last chance at happiness, they wanted them to meet the *right* man, fall in love, and live good lives. And they suspected that it was going to take a miracle for that to happen with "That Boy" Augustus Atwater.

For that reason, it did not trouble them in the lest when he left town without so much as a whisper. Way in the back of his mind, Mr. DuPont had hoped to be proven wrong by that boy, but it appeared that he hadn't been. He had hoped that he would turn out to be all that he believed his Flossie Mae had seen in him. Plain, old common sense had caused him to seriously doubt it though.

Still, he had to do everything in his power to keep from grinning all over himself when he heard the news. As he saw it, the only thing left to do was bid him goodbye and good riddance. And he did, but not before his baby girl. Mr. DuPont was certain the day would come when Flossie Mae would look back on everything and see Mr. Augustus Atwater for what he was—a snake in the grass.

Truth is, Flossie Mae thought far less of Augustus Atwater than anyone else realized, including Augustus Atwater. On one hand, her true feelings would have been a great relief to her folks. On the other hand, her true feelings would have caused them great upset. There was no way to look them square in the face and admit that all of her show of affections toward him were just bricks being laid on the pathway to her freedom.

Howbeit, she was determined. Augustus Atwater or no, one day, she was leaving. Flossie Mae felt that she would burst wide open if she didn't. All she had seen behind her and all she could see before her was a life filled with misery and woe. Yet, she wasn't in any hurry to tell her folks. She didn't see any need in hurting them more than she had already. It would be hard enough to tell them when the time came. And rest assured, it would come. She was as certain of that as she was of anything she knew to be so in her nineteen years of living.

Besides, her Mama believed that she had gone blind and foolish to boot when it came to "That Boy" as she always referred to him. And Mrs. Bertha did not bite her tongue when she told her daughter as much. She had wasted so much time and effort trying to convince Flossie Mae that the Lord already had her a good man picked out. "When He is ready, He will bring him out in the open so you can see him too," she had assured her.

Oftentimes, Flossie Mae tried not to be so bold as to back talk her Mama, especially when it came to the Lord, but she couldn't help wondering to herself about where the Lord was hiding this man He done picked out for her? And she sure hoped He didn't plan on hitching her up with none of these nappy-headed cotton pickers in Coley's Corner! Cause they didn't want nothing more for themselves except to stay put, meet some foolish gal, get hitched, have a bunch of young'uns, and work hard 'til the day life leaves their natural bodies. But she, Miss Flossie Mae DuPont, wanted no part of them or that kind of life.

Her Mama had said, "Baby Girl, sit down. I got something I want to tell you. The Lord has a different way for you to go. He never intended on you being hooked up with the likes of That Boy. Anybody as trifling as that, in the long run ain't gonna spell nothing but trouble to anybody foolish enough to get themselves all tangled up with him."

Mrs. Bertha was a sweet, God-fearing kind of women who loved her family. She would go out of her way to help anybody. But, she didn't believe in Shugar-coating what she saw as the truth. Neither did she bother with biting her tongue or closing a blinded-eye to wrong doing.

Flossie Mae was always respectful to the Lord and most of the time to her folks. She didn't dare utter her thoughts aloud. In her mind, she told herself that if this man her Mama was talking about didn't hurry up and get there, he won't gonna see hair or hide of her. If this 'made just for her man' intended on staying 'round Coley's Corner, living the same kind of life as her folks, he best stay put; and she wondered why was it that the Lord was always seeing fit to talk to her Mama about her?

While Augustus Atwater was off doing his usual—getting into trouble, Flossie Mae dragged around worse than someone who had just lost their closest and only friend. It grieved Mrs. Bertha and Mr. Frederick Douglass DuPont that one of their young'uns was in such a broken state. It appeared that that old love bug had come along and choked down a heaping mouthful of Flossie Mae's hide. Surely, it hadn't been an easy task. Their youngest loved herself so—there was hardly any room for anyone or anything else.

Flossie Mae's feelings were hurt sure enough, but only because her dreams had been interrupted. She was certainly no smitten, love-sick puppy as her Mama and Papa supposed. Her moping around was because she couldn't figure out a way to leave Coley's Corner like she had planned. She had hung all of her hopes on Augustus Atwater.

She told herself over and over, "If I ever lay eyes on that big-eyed, pear-toed, egg-headed Augustus Atwater again, I'm gonna tell him a few truths about himself!"

The nerve of him—leaving her behind! 'Specially, after he had told her that he loved her. Undoubtedly, she had meant it about as much or far less than he had, still, she had blushed and told him that she loved him back. Then he bent down, hugged her tightly, and attempted to give her an opened-mouth kiss, but she had no intentions of returning his brazen show of affection.

When it came down to it, Flossie Mae knew she had just as much blame to bear in their lopsided, deceptive, so-called courtship as Augustus Atwater did. Yet, at least in her mind, it was somewhat different. No one expected it from her—a woman. Certainly not Augustus Atwater, he considered her to be little more than some dumb, country bumpkin.

In Flossie Mae's mind, Mr. Augustus Atwater could do one of two things for her. He could be the avenue or the road out of Coley's Corner to anywhere else. Or he could just stay put and point her in the right direction. As far as she was concerned, he had only one thing working in his favor—judging from his comings and goings—he apparently knew where Out was and how to get there in a hurry.

Several months went by without so much as a word from the man who had dashed cold water on her dreams. In the meanwhile, Flossie Mae continued to sing in the choir, work way too hard on the farm, make new dreams and rehearse in her head all of the things she was going to say whenever she saw Augustus Atwater again. For whatever reason, she never doubted that she would.

Although Flossie Mae's experience with men could be summed up with one word—none, she felt that she knew Augustus Atwater well enough to bet that he would show his face again. The day would come when he would either be running to something or running from something; possibly, both. And as long as his Aunt Lucy was willing to provide him with free food and shelter, he would be back on her doorstep before too long.

Whether she would admit it or not, something had changed in Flossie Mae. It was like she had been reborn. In outward appearance, she still looked the same. She was still just as sweet as she could be whenever she wanted to be. Howbeit, there was a different kind of look in her eyes. Mrs. Lucy, seeing it and believing that her nephew was the reason behind it, saw it as her obligation to try to set things right. She had told Mrs. Bertha that it was all for the best because her nephew was full of mess. "He came along and done filled that gal's head up with it too!" Mrs. Lucy concluded.

Mrs. Bertha had agreed. She would try to be a bit more particular with her words to her young'un though. The heart was such a tender thing—so easily hurt, and takes so long to mend.

"Shugar, you keep your head up now. That boy better be mighty glad that I can't get to him! I would try to knock his big head slam off! Child, I'm so sorry 'bout everything," Mrs. Lucy had told Flossie Mae after the Sunday Morning Church Service.

"That's quite all right, Mrs. Lucy. There's no need for you to be sorry. And it certainly ain't your place to be begging my pardon for something that won't none of your doing," Flossie Mae said.

"Honey, you don't have to pretend with me. I know how it is to have your head turned by some no count, good-for-nothing-but-lies somebody," Mrs. Lucy continued.

"Truly, Mrs. Lucy, I" Flossie Mae began.

"Girl, I tell you, there's no need of trying to pretend with Mrs. Lucy. I done been taken with a young man or two myself. Of course, that was all in my younger days. I tell you, my first man was some kind of trifling. If he had been born a dog, he would have been too sorry to lift up his own leg to scratch his own self," Mrs. Lucy testified.

"I don't mean no harm, Mrs. Lucy, but I ain't thinking about no Augustus Atwater! I'm glad he's gone," Flossie Mae insisted.

"Uh huh," Mrs. Lucy grunted in disbelief. She had too much tack to say all that was on her mind, though you couldn't tell it from her conversation thus far.

Her nephew or no, she was sick and tired of seeing gals trip all over themselves every time a fresh face showed itself. It made her skin crawl to see young gals who had been born and raised up with one another go to falling out over some sorry, here-today, gone-tomorrow somebody.

This won't the first time she had seen them back-biting and casting one another's name on a sign board over somebody who ain't got nothing but a pocket full of lint balls. They go to falling all over themselves for somebody who ain't got a thing to offer them except a bunch of empty promises.

True enough, Augustus Atwater was her nephew, but if it wasn't for her dear, sweet sister, Maggie, she wouldn't even give him the time of day. The boy won't nothing but a plum, nappy-headed thief who done took from her for the last time. She had no earthly idea what use he had for an old, tarnished ring and a time piece with a broken stem. Sadly, he probably didn't either.

Truth being told, (and that was her habit) that old ring had been tarnished ever since the day that old, long-legged bean pole, Leroy McKindle slipped it onto her finger. He was a thief too. He took her affections. All she got in return was red eyes and an aching back.

When it came to how she had felt about him—he had only gotten what she had stored up in the top bureau drawer. There was plenty more loving lying there—just waiting to be unfolded.

Nonetheless, she had continued to love him even after she realized that he didn't mean her no good. Sometimes, love can be so blind.

Mrs. Lucy often laughed at her own self over how foolish and blind she was. Someone had told her that they could see how taken was with her man because she was looking at him like he was a big plate of molasses and she was the biscuit waiting to sop him up. For a year or two, he was so sweet, she could have eaten him up. By the time he left, she wished she had. But she also knew that innocence and youth had a whole lot to do with it too, along with only seeing what she wanted to see.

Her sister, Della tried to warn her. At the time, she didn't want to hear nothing contrary about Leroy McKindle. In her eyes, he was the sun, the moon, and the stars that brightened up her day as well as her nights. And she soon learned, giving somebody that much privilege over you sure can cause you to have many a dark day.

"Lu, you knows the sun don't shine on none of us every day. Some days are sort of cloudy. Some days, the sun doesn't want to show itself none. No matter how bright it shines, sooner or later, night is bound to creep in. Y'all best have enough to hold you in the dark times. Child, y'all gonna need a heap more than sitting 'round, looking at one another all cock-eyed," Della had warned.

Mrs. Lucy remembered how she had told herself that Della was just jealous. There she was, three years younger and about to marry while Della didn't even have herself a steady beau yet. She supposed the fear of being an old maid was causing her to say mean things about Leroy, her intended.

Intended what? She often wondered. Cause, he never was cut out to be no suitable husband. Soon, her days were filled with more clouds than sunshine. And it didn't take her a month of Sundays to see many a dark night. Nor did it take long for her to regret ever hearing of a Leroy McKindle. The man sho'nuff took her through the motions. Yet, for a long while, there was a part of her that still missed him or in the least, missed the man she wished that he'd been.

Mrs. Lucy didn't want to go 'round bad-mouthing nobody, but she had a strong feeling—call it that womanly intuition—one day, Flossie Mae would come to regret ever having done so much as looked on an Augustus Atwater.

But like her, it appeared, even the warnings of old folks who done already seen and lived through a heap more than many folks will ever even hear about, won't gonna be able to tell Flossie Mae nothing. As much as Mrs. Lucy hated it, it looked as if life would be forced to teach her a lesson too. Life—and at times, life sure has a way of not showing us no pity.

CHAPTER SIX

Miss Flossie Mae hoped if she told herself often enough, she too would begin to believe her own lie—she was glad Augustus Atwater had moved on. Like everyone else, she bid him good riddance.

Trouble was—before she could totally convince herself—Augustus Atwater reared his head by writing her a letter. As clear as she could make out from his chicken scratch, he was trying to explain that he had to go back to the city to take care of some important business.

Flossie Mae's hopes soared though she couldn't help but wonder what sort of important business a man as lazy as Augustus Atwater could possibly have. In spite of everything she knew and believed to be so about him, she allowed her desires to get in the way of her common sense.

The fact that he was a man full of smooth talk and sweet lies didn't seem to matter as much now. She saw the return of Augustus Atwater as another chance for her to escape. And she was determined that he would not leave again without her.

Who Augustus Atwater failed to mention in his letter was a female in the form of a Miss Pamela Staton Delmar. She had finally become wise to his ways. She wanted nothing more to do with him, and in no uncertain terms, she had told him so to his face. Though she fought back tears while doing so, he was certain those tears stemmed from her anger rather than the pain of breaking it off with him.

Miss Pamela S. Delmar was as mad as fire! He knew it. And so did anyone else who happened to be within earshot.

"Augustus Atwater, you will never get your grubby hands on another dime of my daddy's money! And I hope that two hundred dollars you stole will last you a lifetime! I begged my daddy not to have you thrown in jail, but you better leave before I change my mind!" she fussed. He knew that she was as serious as the solemn look on a dead man's face.

Being who he was, he couldn't help but give it another try. He was willing to plead if he had to. "Baby, you know that I would never do anything like that. This is just a great, big misunderstanding. That's all it is. Come on. Give me another chance to prove myself to you," he pleaded.

Miss Pamela Staton Delmar was through with Augustus and his empty promises. "Gus, how can I put this? Your gravy boat is empty. It once flowed freely. Now, it's all dried up. You will have no more opportunities to use me," she stated as a matter of fact and rather too calmly for his taste.

Augustus Atwater had no doubt that Pamela had plenty of money or at least her old man did. She hadn't really missed a meagerly two hundred dollars. Yet, he would say whatever it took to keep her. The girl had been good to him.

"Puddin', you know that it was never like that. I love you. I have from the very first time I laid eyes on you. Please give me another chance. Baby, please don't give up on us over something like this," he unashamedly begged.

With every word that came out of Augustus Atwater's mouth, Pamela wanted to scream, scratch, hit, and kick him until she couldn't see him! Besides, she was sure that she had heard those some of same words just a few days ago. They were being sung by a recording artist named "Lil' Red".

"I wouldn't give you the shed skin off a snake's back! If I owned a beach, I wouldn't give you a grain of its' sand! If this entire block was mine, I wouldn't give you permission to stand on the sidewalk! Now get off my stoop! I NEVER want to see you again!" she shouted.

Miss Pamela Staton Delmar slammed the door so hard, all of the windows shook. Augustus shook a little himself. She might have a strange way with words, but he knew she meant every last one of them. There was no mistake about it—this time she was mad! This time—she was through with him!

Augustus Atwater hadn't seen a woman that mad since the night that pretty, little gal chased him into the woods with her shotgun. As best as he could recall, her name was Lorraine. She had that thing cocked and ready to shoot. She could run too. If he hadn't been running shine at the time, undoubtedly, his hide would have been laden with buckshot. Good thing he knew those woods like the back of his hand. That time, much like this one, could have been resolved if he'd just been given a chance to explain.

He knew his women. But—he never gave them a chance to really get to know him. Actually, women knew him better than he suspected. Problem was—he didn't know himself very well. Overtime, he had put on so many different faces, had told so many lies, and had made so many promises—it had become difficult for him to separate fact from fiction.

One thing he did know, it was becoming very necessary to take things at a much slower pace. It was time to return to his Aunt Lucy's. First, he would have to beg her pardon. He would get down on his knees if he had to. He would say that he didn't know why he had stolen from her. She had been like a mother to him, taking him in and all. He would top it off with how he had lain in bed night after night, listening to her send up prayers on his behalf.

Just in case none of those pleas worked, he would end with, "Aunt Lucy, I know those prayers of yours done reached the ears of God. One of these old days, I'm gonna make something out of myself just like you and my Mama always wanted me to. You'll be able to look on me as your son again." He knew the very mention of his Mama, her dearly departed sister would cause his aunt to ease up on him some, cut him a little slack.

His Aunt Lucy being a woman and all, he couldn't come right out and tell her the truth. What he would do is tell her what he thought she wanted to hear—her wayward nephew had done seen the error of his ways and was looking to do better. And once more and again, she would take him in. He was certain of that.

It would also give him a chance to court Flossie Mae—that pretty, but simple, little country gal up the road. He could see that she was real sweet on him, but a bit more innocent than he was accustomed to. She sure had a lot to learn. And this time, he would have more time to teach her.

There were plenty of country hard-heads around, but they had so much dirt underneath their fingernails, they could grow cotton. There was so much sweat in their eyes, they couldn't see all of those pretty, young things who were just right for the picking. That was all right too. Cause there was more than enough Augustus Atwater to go 'round. Last time, some of them were acting right forward, practically throwing themselves at him. And right on the church grounds too. No, he wasn't too busy to take up some of their time, but first things first. Miss Flossie Mae DuPont was on the top of his list.

CHAPTER SEVEN

When Flossie Mae heard the news of Augustus Atwater's return, she fluttered around like a butterfly. Her folks knew exactly what or rather who was behind her sudden change of moods.

"I just don't understand it, but That Boy got some sort of hold on our baby gal," Mrs. Bertha told her husband before he left out early that morning to attend the fields. "I didn't have to call her one time this morning."

"Wonder how she heard? He ain't showed his face over here, has he? Better not! That's all I got to say!" Mr. Frederick Douglass DuPont's feathers were ruffled worse than an angry rooster's. It was completely out of character for him to allow things or folks, one in particular, to get him all riled up. As much as he tried to be a reasonable man, he couldn't bring himself to like Mr. Augustus Atwater. It won't nothing in particular, it was everything about him.

"Morning, Mama. Morning, Papa. Me and Betty are taking the jellies and preserves down to the store first thing this morning, 'fore the heat of the day sets in. Miss Emily said that she has a few things for us to do today. We won't be long," Flossie Mae said.

"Is it gonna take both of y'all to take those few jars down there?   And since when did it take you and Betty both to do a day's work at Miss Emily's?" her Papa asked, his eyebrows raised.

"Papa, I—Betty and me figured," Flossie Mae stammered and stumbled in search of the truth. Biting her nails when the truth was far from her lips was a habit she had had from a very young girl. With Mrs. Bertha being Mrs. Bertha and wise to the ways of her gals, she said, "Flossie Mae, if you got a notion to sneak around, trying to see That Boy, you best think again. We done been through this. He ain't no good for you. We know you can't see it now, but the time may come when you will."

"That sun is bound to get mighty hot today. I got plenty of work to do. And I'll be needing yall's help with those taters. Ain't a thing changed 'round here. We still got to work so we can eat." With that, Mr. Frederick Douglass DuPont went out the back door and headed for the barn. Miss Bertha, Betty, and Flossie Mae knew that he expected them to soon follow.

For every day that Flossie Mae had to suffer the sun, the dirt underneath her fingernails, her back aching, and after all of that still being poor, was just another day she longed to be long gone. Today was no different. And even more so because it certainly won't no picnic walking behind her Papa or a mule all day long.

She had been hoping to catch at least a glimpse of Augustus Atwater as she and Betty just happened to stroll past Mrs. Lucy's house. That is, if they took the long way. Still, she did not want him to get it into his head that she loved or even liked him. She saw him in the same manner as before—her way out. He could choose to think and feel whatever he chose to think or feel and so could everyone else.

"Mae, are you gonna see him?" Betty asked. She always called her sister, "Mae." knowing how much she despised the name, Flossie.

"I don't know. Papa is watching over me like a hawk. But I got to see him before he gets away again," she said, careful to keep an eye on her folks.

"Mae, are you sure that he loves you? I mean, are you really sure?" Betty whispered as they bent over to pick up more potatoes.

"He says that he does. How can I really be sure? I can't see into his heart. Fine for him if he does," Flossie Mae whispered back.

"You never had a fellow courting you serious before. Do you love him?" Betty asked.

"What is love anyhow? I see it as a man and a woman who done decided that one got something that the other one needs. I doubt if many folk really got hitched because of love," Flossie Mae explained.

"Well, I believe that Mama and Papa really love each other. Look at them. They're side by side, even in all of this dirt," Betty pointed out.

"And for every mama and papa, there are two folk sitting 'round somewhere, grinning at one another, but love ain't nowhere about them," Flossie Mae said.

"Do you think that's gonna be you and Augustus Atwater? Are you planning on marrying up with him?" Betty asked.

"Child, I can't see into the unknown, but I got plans for Mr. Augustus Atwater," Flossie Mae snickered.

Betty did too.

Mr. Frederick Douglass DuPont called out to them for more work and less play. Mrs. Bertha gave both her gals a good, long look. She knew them. She knew that they were up to something. And she knew That Boy, Augustus Atwater was right in the midst of it. She would have a talk with her good friend, Lucy. They will have to keep a good eye on the two of them—a real good eye.

Flossie Mae didn't lay eyes on Augustus Atwater until the Sunday Morning Service. She was up in the choir box. He walked in behind his Aunt Lucy and sat on the back pew. From up there, she had a very good view. And so did he.

CHAPTER EIGHT

On his first Sunday back at his Aunt Lucy's house, Augustus Atwater had gone to church at his Aunt's insistence though he referred to it as, "nagging".

"Son, now you know there ain't no laying 'round in that bed this morning! This is the Lord's Day! You might as well git your lazy bones up from there!" she scolded.

"That old woman better leave me alone!" Augustus mumbled through his gritted teeth and tightly gripped jaw.

About half an hour later, she was standing at the door again. "Young'un, if you don't git yourself up, out of that bed! Don't make me come in yonder with my broomstick! In my house, we go to church on Sunday!" Mrs. Lucy fussed.

While on her way into the kitchen to finish her Sunday Dinner and to stir up a little something for breakfast, she couldn't help but wonder how such a young man could be so confounded trifling.

"Prying him from that bed is like trying to pry a rusty nail out of a board. He done gripped hold to trifling so tight, it will probably take breaking his fingers to loosen him, except, that'll be just one more excuse for why he can't work and do for his own self," she continued to fuss.

Augustus got up after getting a good whiff of the country ham his Aunt Lucy was frying. He licked his lips at the thought of hot biscuits, peach preserves, and fresh brewed coffee.

Augustus Atwater was certainly not a spiritual man. Except for the times he had spent at his Aunt Lucy's house, his feet hadn't even touched inside of a church, not counting the time he hid out in one. He reckoned that was the last place those Howard boys expected they would find him. And he doubted whether the Lord cared if he showed up at His house or not on Sundays or any other day, especially seeing and knowing that he didn't really want to be there.

His daddy didn't go to church. As far back as he could remember, whenever his Mama tried to drag him to church, his daddy would say, "Woman, leave that boy alone! For all the good it's doing you—you might as well sit down somewhere too."

Like his daddy, he tended to put his hope in a dollar. A fast and easy dollar which often times didn't work out in his favor, but once in a great while did.

Augustus walked into the church house behind his Aunt Lucy. He sat down on the back pew, watching, but mostly nodding. In church, he felt like a stranger, always had.

When he heard Flossie Mae singing, he sat straight up in his seat. He listened. And he watched. Folks started grinning from ear to ear. Some were standing. Some were clapping. He heard the tapping of feet on the hardwood floor, keeping time with the music. Some folk got happy in the Spirit. Like most of the folk in the Service, Flossie Mae's singing was touching something way down deep inside of him, but not necessarily the same something.

The little bit that Augustus Atwater did know about church told him that the girl truly had something, something real special. It was something that everybody who stood up in that choir box singing didn't have. Right then and there—right in the Lord's House—right in the midst of all of that praising, his old scheming nature churned its' filthy wheels.

He thought about a girl he used to know. She sang in a nightclub. Her name was, Rosie "Foxxie White" Whitehead. Foxxie sounded half as good as Flossie Mae. Still, she drew in a good crowd. In his eyes, there wasn't much difference between singing the blues and singing spirituals. Pain was pain. Folks just looked to different ways and means to relieve it.

He was sure if he took her to the city to see the right people (as if he knew or was privy to any of them) somebody would be more than willing to sign on Flossie Mae. He would be her manager. He had never done any managing before, but, how hard could it be? Of course, he would handle all of the money. With her voice, he was sure there would be plenty coming his, their way. All she had to do is sing her pretty, little heart out. He would take care of the rest.

However, there were a few obstacles which might hinder his plans. Two very big, almost insurmountable ones came in the forms of Mr. Frederick Douglass and Mrs. Bertha Mae DuPont. They would be tough. And of that, he was certain. Then he had to convince Flossie Mae that it was all for her good. And as her manager, the first thing on his list would be finding her a singing name, something catchy like, "Foxxie White". "What is a Flossie Mae anyhow? Sounds like somebody's great-grandma," he said, almost too loudly. A woman holding a baby, sitting in the pew in front of him, turned and gave him a stern look. It seemed the baby had peeped over his mama's shoulders and gave him the same look.

Through the remainder of the Service, Augustus' wheels continued to turn as if his plan was an already- done-deal. He couldn't have told a living soul what the Preacher had spoken about, even if they offered him good money to do it.

After Service, he made every effort to talk to Flossie Mae. He saw her standing beside her sister, Betty. They stood in the shade of the giant pecan trees. There were three fellows standing close by, but Flossie Mae was looking around as if she was expecting someone else to show up.

Augustus checked to see where her folks and his Aunt Lucy were. He didn't need any surprises, and neither did he need or want any more talks from his long-winded Aunt. Generally, he wouldn't be willing to put up with so much from one woman. From now and on, whenever he looked at Miss Flossie Mae DuPont, he was going to have his sights set way ahead onto the bigger picture—how much money that sweet, little country gal was going to make him. He eased up to Flossie Mae much like a cat upon an unsuspecting mouse. He touched her on the forearm.

"Hey, Flossie Mae. Did you get my letter?" he asked without waiting for her to speak, not entirely sure that she would considering how he had left the last time.

"I did," she answered coolly and intentionally.

"I missed you. And I would like to take up some of your time. Would that be all right with you?" he asked.

"If you want to court me, you have to see my Papa first," Flossie Mae answered as a matter of fact.

"Ain't there another way? I can't out run no buckshot!" Augustus said, half-jokingly. Flossie Mae smiled.

It was at this point in the scheme of things that Augustus Atwater reconsidered. Flossie Mae DuPont just might not be the catch he hoped her to be. There was no doubt in his mind how her folks felt about him. They wanted him nowhere near their daughter and as far away from Coley's Corner as possible. He also suspected that the only conversations Mr. DuPont wished to have with him were the short and one-sided kind. "Go away" and "Goodbye".

In December, he would be twenty-five years old. It had been a long time since he had to go to somebody's Papa to get permission to court their little girl. He had become accustomed to full-grown women, women who already had their own, women who weren't looking to him for no more than the time he spent with them.

Of course, Miss Pamela Statton Delmar had been the exception to the rule. She had hers' and access to her dear, old daddy's too. It was still hard for him to understand how she could have acted so unreasonably over a measly two-hundred dollars. If she had been willing to forgive him and forget his little slip-up, Flossie Mae DuPont wouldn't even be in the picture.

Augustus Atwater reasoned within himself that Mr. DuPont was a hard study. He was always watching and seldom spoke more than a few words at any given time. A man that quiet could fool you. Usually, he was pretty good at figuring people out—or so he thought—he had to be, but not that one.

Suddenly, he felt as if a rock had sunk to the pit of his stomach. He doubted if he was up to the task. Then he thought about the bigger picture again. His love of and need for money, lots of money won over his fear of some old man. However, Augustus always had a knack for talking himself into doing things that would cause the average man to reconsider.

"Augustus! Augustus Atwater!" Flossie Mae called. "Have you done drifted far away from here?"

"I was just thinking about how I'll ever get to see you short of coming over to your place and insisting that your old man allow me to court you," Augustus lied.

Flossie Mae shook her head and said, "I hope that's not the best and only plan you can come up with. Sounds to me like you fixing to ask my Papa to fill your hide full of buckshot."

"Girl, I'm going to figure this thing out. I got to see you. I'm thinking about you all day long. I'm dreaming about you at night. I'm in love with you, girl," he lied again.

In spite of herself, Flossie Mae started grinning, but soon regained her composure. Her Mama and Mrs. Lucy were coming out of the church house. Augustus Atwater did what Augustus

Atwater tended to do best. He fled.

Mrs. Bertha was relieved to see Betty and Flossie Mae standing underneath the pecan trees with Odell White, James Taylor, and Joseph Avery. She knew that Joseph was quite taken with Betty. Betty felt likewise about him. But she would have been happy for either one of the others to come, calling on her baby gal. They were good boys, unlike 'That Boy' lying up over yonder at Lucy's place.

Joseph walked Betty home. They held hands. Flossie Mae walked behind them at a decent distance. She noticed how Betty grinned almost every time Joseph Avery opened his mouth. They stared at one another a lot, too much according to her thinking. No doubt, he would be staying for Sunday Dinner again.

Flossie Mae could see it as plain as daylight—Joseph Avery was about to become son-in-law number six. Then everybody would be married except her which won't about to happen. She knew her folks would like nothing better than for her to hitch up with one of the fellows around Coley's Corner—with a 'good boy' as they so often put it.

Nonetheless, she had no interest in spending time with any of the knot-heads in Coley's Corner. Odell White and James Taylor were included regardless of how "good" her Mama took them to be. She didn't see them as being any better off than she was. All of them were stuck in the very same place she was—in the middle of nowhere, and as far as she could see, there was no way out except to grab hold onto somebody else's coattails and get pulled out. For her, that's where Augustus Atwater fit in.

Later that Sunday night, Augustus Atwater lay in bed, thinking about his plans for Flossie Mae. He had been unable to think about much else. He had plenty of time to think too. He hadn't gone to bed before ten o'clock since he was ten years old; and in his adulthood, it had been a very long while since he had gone to bed alone for more than a few nights at a time.

While lying there, all he could hear was country silence, crickets, and his Aunt Lucy's snoring. In all of his thinking, he realized that he didn't have a pot or a window to call his own. If he was going to ever make any ley way with Mr. Frederick Douglass and Mrs. Bertha Mae DuPont, he, at least needed a job or something. He needed to become a hardworking, respectable young man—for a little while—just a little while.

First thing Monday morning, Augustus Atwater woke up, rubbed the sleep out of his eyes, pried himself out of bed, readied himself, and prepared to go out looking for work, for honest labor. For him, that was an awful lot to accomplish in the span of an hour or two. His Aunt Lucy was certainly surprised to see him out and about so early. She hadn't had to call him one time. It was quite a surprise for him too. Howbeit, when it came down to getting what he wanted, he tended to amaze even himself.

"Aunt Lucy, I'll sweep the yard and fix the clothesline this evening," he promised.

"All right, son. I sure would appreciate it." She was convinced that the Sunday Morning Message, "A Slothful Man." must have really touched her nephew, causing him to see the error of his ways. Unbeknownst to her, Augustus Atwater hadn't heard more than two or three words of the Reverend's sermon.

"Son, your breakfast is on the stove," she added.

Augustus could tell by his Aunt Lucy's grin that she liked what she saw, and he wanted her to continue to do so.

After eating, he cleaned and straightened his place at the table and put his dishes and utensils in the dishpan. Then he put his boots on and took a good look at himself in the mirror.

"I'll be home later," he called out to his Aunt.

"All right, son. I hope everything works out for you," she called out, about to get happy in her own front room.

Walking along that long, dirt, country road toward town, Augustus thought seriously about his plans. Although he understood that it was going to take all that he was about to do and more. Still, it made little sense to him that he of all people would be going so far and doing so much just to get hold of some young, country gal.

Nevertheless, he still had to go through her folks as well as his Aunt Lucy. Therefore, he continued to put one foot in front of the other and kept on walking toward town, in hopes of finding a decent paying job.

That very day, on the spot, Augustus Atwater could have gotten a job as a grave digger. "You will also be expected to keep up the cemetery, mowing grass, removing dead flowers, trimming hedges, keeping an eye out on things, so forth and so on," the man in the small, cluttered, foul-smelling office had said.

Augustus didn't really want a job. Period. And if it meant working in a graveyard—well. Dead folks made him uneasy. He hadn't come right out and said, "No Thanks." but he knew the man would never see his face again unless it was by accident.

The foreman at Baldwin's Lumberyard told him to check again the following week. Determined, he tried every place that he could think of that might have even a remote interest in hiring Negroes for anything besides farm work. Everyone who had shaken their heads "no" or told him "to come back." didn't see or understand the urgency in his job search or his need to actually find a job.

He thought, the sooner he got his plans rolling, the sooner he could get himself out of this hick, country town with nothing to do and nowhere to go—back to civilization and fast money and easy living. Of course, all of this would be at the expense of Miss Flossie Mae DuPont. Everything he did was for something, but nothing he did was for nothing.

On his way back to his Aunt Lucy's, jobless, Augustus saw a sign in the window of a small diner. It read, DISHWASHER WANTED (INQUIRE IN THE BACK). Yes, he was willing to be a dishwasher if it meant having a chance with Flossie Mae, but she or no other woman he could think of was worth him becoming a grave digger. Besides, he had escaped death too many times to willingly put himself in a position to be keeping company with the dead.

The following day, when Augustus Atwater put his hands into that hot dishwater, he realized just how tender his hands were. He wasn't accustomed to manual labor. He considered himself to be a thinking man, always a man with a plan. Usually, he used his head to make his living. Sometimes, it worked out to his benefit. Many times, it eventually got him into trouble. But more often than not, it generally served him well even if it meant shifting and shuffling, but never shoveling. Different times called for different measures and methods. He had learned that from his daddy.

From his first pay day, as soon as he walked into the house, he handed over ten dollars to cover his room and board. Then he gave his Aunt Lucy five dollars to put up for safe keeping.

Before too long, she was doing just as he suspected. She was bragging to everyone within the sound of her voice about her *darling* nephew, Augustus. She began calling him, "Gussie" for short, the name of endearment, the name she had called him when he was a small child.

Never mind, she had told many of those same folks how trifling she thought her nephew was. She had also told them how he had stolen from her, and how he won't up to no good. Folks had heard and tended to remember even long after her opinion of him had seemingly changed. So no matter how many jobs

Augustus Atwater worked or how much money he brought home to his Aunt, they were still gonna watch him like a hawk.

Needless to say, the employment of Augustus Atwater did not impress Mr. Frederick Douglass DuPont in the least. He told Mrs. Bertha that it was past time that he got up off his narrow end. Nor did he believe "That Boy" was deserving of all those pats on his back from his Aunt. He was only doing what he should have been doing all along. He was just doing what a *man* is supposed to do. He was working for his own meat and bread and taters instead of trying to live off an old lady.

He would never say it to her face, but he believed that Lucy had had a hand in helping to ruin "That Boy". The fact that he was washing dishes proved that he won't use to hard work. And then to be working in Beal's Café, a place where a colored man couldn't even go in to get a drink of water, a cup of hot coffee, much less sit down to drink it. Beal didn't serve coloreds. Period. Not even at the back door. That helped prove to him that the boy didn't have much sense either. But at the same time, Mr. DuPont understood that sometimes, folks do what they got to do to get by.

Over the years, he had watched "That Boy" coming and going, but had never seen him attempt to lift a finger to help his Aunt Lucy out. He was always lying around, waiting on somebody to hand him something for nothing. And now, she's grinning all over herself just because he's making a few dimes. Mr. DuPont was still convinced that he had Augustus Atwater pegged right. He was still a snake in the grass, a weasel, a fox just awaiting his chance to get into the hen house.

He was still up to no good. And it would take more than a month full of Sundays to convince him of otherwise. So he didn't want his Flossie Mae or any other gal getting herself all tangled up with him. He wondered why it took some womenfolk so doggone long to see through the mess that those kinds of men be shoveling out to them.

He remembered his own sister, Odessa. She had went plum foolish over a fellow, Wilbert Heralds. The name came to him as plain as day. His folks had tried everything they could think of to steer her clear and see him for what and who he was, but nothing did any good. The more they talked, it seemed, the closer Odessa was drawn to him.

They even sent her to live with their Aunt Cora for a whole summer although she was needed to help out at home. As soon as she returned, she was right back, grinning like an old opossum in Wilbert Heralds' face again.

Won't too long afterwards, Odessa turned up in the family way. Old Wilbert Heralds came up missing. All of those promises he had made went right along with him too.

Mr. DuPont got that feeling in the pit of his stomach, the same feeling he always got whenever he remembered Odessa. His poor, foolish sister was shamed something awful. She even had to go up before the church and tell everybody how she was a sinner and all.

It took him a long time to get over that and the shame he felt behind his sister's shame. But she never did get over it or how Wilbert Heralds had done her. To this day, he believes that's why she turned out like she did. She never was any good to herself or that young'un of hers. She ended up drinking herself right out of this world.

He didn't want that to be Flossie Mae's fate. He was gonna have to find a way, some kind of way to keep his mouth shut about how he feels about "That Boy". For his baby gal's sake, he had to find a way to tolerate him for some time to come. He knew from experience that you got to watch a snake and then ease up on him if you want to get him. If you make a heap of fuss, he'll get away from you. And if you see him for anything other than what he is, he'll strike you.

CHAPTER NINE

With a few dollars of his pay, Augustus Atwater bought himself a second-hand record player and a few rhythm and blues recordings. He played them over and over again until he knew them by heart. His plan was to teach them to Flossie Mae.

"Oh, my baby done left me—left me sad and blue;

I said, 'my baby done left me—left me sad and blue';

Since he's been gone—I don't know what to do."

The recorded voice sang as Augustus Atwater sang along, snapping his fingers.

Another voice sang:

"Last night, I cried— I cried a river of tears;

Last night, I cried— I cried a river of tears;

Cause, I got a good man loving me—but I can't love him back.

He comes home every morning about half past five—

He comes home every morning about half past five;

He gives me all his money— and then he brings me breakfast in bed.

A man ain't loved me like that —since I don't know when."

"Now, this is music," Augustus said as he tried to imagine Flossie Mae up on the stage singing. He was sure that she could take any or all of those songs, add her special touch to them, and make an audience beg for more.

She was good, good sounding and good looking. However, it was going to take some molding to get the country out of her. The plans he had for that girl was going to take him far. And if she was lucky, she would get somewhere too.

He would have to keep an eye on her though. He had found it to be a dangerous thing to let a woman get too sure of herself, too confident. Once that happens, she'll start trying to make her own decisions, and get all independent on him, start looking at him differently —like she don't need him anymore. He couldn't let that happen again, not this time. Foxxie White came to mind.

Augustus Atwater had learned a valuable lesson. His success depended upon her success. In his plans for Flossie Mae, he couldn't get to where he was trying to get unless she got to where he was trying to take her.

He told himself, "I'm going to be whoever and whatever that little country gal needs me to be. If she's looking for a knight in shining armor, he would be that. If she needed somebody to tell her how pretty she is all day long and that she is the only woman he has ever loved, he would do that too."

Whenever he looked at the bigger picture, he saw himself gaining far more than he ever had or was ever willing to lose or give up for or to any woman. Sure, he could put her up on a pedestal, treat her like a queen—for a while, but only for a while—a very short while at that.

Once he was done, he was done. He always reserved the right to knock a woman off her pedestal every now and then. His daddy did it to his Mama. She didn't go anywhere. And no woman had ever left him either, not really.

Miss Pamela Staton Delmar may have slammed the door in his face, but he was the one who walked away. She was getting too possessive anyhow. No woman owned him and no woman ever would. If he had wanted to, he could have allowed her some time to cool off. Then he could have gone back like a puppy after his first bowl of warm milk. He was certain that she would have taken him back. He didn't have any more time to waste on Miss Uppity-Butt Delmar. She had served her purpose. It was her loss. There were plenty more fish in the same pond that she came from. He hoped.

He couldn't understand it or ever began to explain it. There was just something about him that women were drawn to, something they wanted. That is—until they got it. Augustus Atwater had become real good at convincing and/or lying to himself and others, especially women—almost as good as he had become at overlooking and/or denying the obvious.

He smiled at himself whom he considered to be smart beyond his years. Some would have said, "Too smart for his own good". His goal was to become rich in a short period of time and with as much ease as possible. He was not a man beneath taking the privilege of climbing up to his place of great expectation upon the back of any unsuspecting female he could find.

Mrs. Lucy was so impressed with her new-found nephew, 'Gussie' that she didn't say a word when she heard him playing and singing what she had before deemed, "the devil's music". Nor did she say anything about the plates, cups, and saucers that were beginning to fill up her cupboard, dishes that she was certain came from Beal's Café. She didn't fuss like she used to either. Unknowingly, that was a part of her nephew's plan too.

When he handed over the ten dollars for his room and board on Friday evenings, she grinned and said, "Thank you, son." as she tucked it in her bosom.

"And Aunt Lucy, this is to put up for me," he would always say as he handed her another five.

"If your mama, my dear sister could see you now, she would be so proud of you, but I'm proud enough for the both of us," she would say in return.

With his Aunt, things were going just the way Augustus had hoped. She didn't even bad-mouth his daddy anymore which was an unexpected bonus. Truth was, his daddy didn't like her any more than she liked him, probably a whole lot less if that's possible. One of the nicest things he had ever said about her was, 'Lucy, is a jealous, spiteful, old biddy who couldn't hang onto a man even if he was tied up to her.' Next to that, everything else was really bad.

He had heard his daddy saying that to his Mama after he had opened and read a letter that came addressed to her from her sister, Lucy. In the letter, she had advised his Mama to leave. "Bring the young'uns down South. You can stay with me. Give yourself some time to figure out what you want to do with yourself. Child, you can't stay there another day. You can't take many more of those beatings. That man is gonna wind up killing you. I always told you that he won't no good."

Afterwards, his daddy ranted and raved for hours—until his mama cried—until she said that she was sorry—until she promised that she wasn't going to allow anyone to bust up their family—until she said exactly what his daddy wanted to hear. Black eyes, busted lips or not—she was keeping the family together. He never allowed himself to think about how his Mama eventually paid the ultimate price for that decision. Just as her sister had said, 'That man is gonna wind up killing you.' And he did, but not really.

It was just as his Daddy had said, "It was her fault, son, all her fault. Women got a way of pushing you to do things that you never meant to do." Augustus wanted to and had chosen to believe his daddy. Over the years, he had convinced himself that it was true. It was his mama's fault. She fell just as his daddy had claimed. And since then, he had apparently been running from one truth after another.

He had never mentioned these things to his Aunt Lucy and probably never would. Nor had he bothered to mention that he had not seen his daddy in quite some time. For one reason or another, they couldn't bear to look one another in the eye anymore.

Though heavy drinking and hard living had practically withered his daddy up like a dried prune, he still possessed his sharp edge and tongue. His old lady was a pitiful sight to behold. At least his mama didn't have a taste for the hard stuff.

Nonetheless, he still loved his daddy. He saw him every time he looked into the mirror. He had learned a lot from him without even trying. His lack of respect for women was one of the lessons that he wasn't proud of. He had realized early on that real love was something that he would never get to experience if it meant giving up any part of himself to get it. Real love was a costly matter. Thus far, saying, "I love you" hadn't cost him much more than a few bus tickets.

However, the memories of his daddy along with the fear that he had instilled in him gave Augustus Atwater the courage he needed to go to Mr. Frederick Douglass DuPont to ask permission to court his daughter, Miss Flossie Mae DuPont. He surmised, if facing his daddy was like facing a lion, then facing Mr. DuPont could be no worse than facing a bear.

Much to his surprise and almost regret, Mr. DuPont listened to what he had to say without uttering a single word. Afterwards, he just nodded his head. Augustus decided to take whatever he could get. He supposed that it was just how things were done in the country.

Augustus never knew. No one did. Mr. DuPont had reasons that went far beyond Augustus Atwater's intentions, or claims of admiration and his feeble attempts at trying to sway him in his thinking. He wanted to keep a close eye on the snake trying to steal his little girl's heart. While at the same time, he was trying to do everything within his power not to push her any further into "That Boy's" path.

Mr. Frederick Douglass DuPont hadn't been forced to grip his jaw that tight in a long time. He had not since his mother quit trying to run her house and his too. It took her a long time to get the picture and keep her hands, nose, or her mouth out of he and Mrs. Bertha's home affairs, much too long in fact.

On her own, Victoria DuPont decided, the only way she could stay out of their business was to keep her distance. The threat of it, at first, made him sorrowful. However, his mother made the decision. He would find a way to live with it, especially, if keeping her distance meant keeping peace in his home.

Countless times, he had had to tell her in the most respectable way possible to please mind her own business. She didn't like it. And she didn't like it up to the day that she entered her eternal rest. She had claimed that he had taken another woman's side over hers. "After all." she had said, "I was the one who birthed you into this world, rubbed my knuckles raw on the washboard, got down on my hands and knees scrubbing floors, slaved over many a hot stove just so you could have food on the table and decent clothes to go on your back."

Trying to explain to his mother that Bertha wasn't just any other woman was like talking to that big oak tree in the backyard. "Mama, she is my wife, the mother of my children, the one who brings sunshine into my life. She is the one I want to grow old with. Mama, Bertha, is the one I love more than I love myself," he had told her.

Victoria DuPont didn't listen. She didn't want to hear it. She only wanted to be right. But she was not.

Mr. Frederick Douglass DuPont couldn't and wouldn't allow anyone, not even his mother to stir up trouble in his marriage. Life was already hard enough. His Bertha was one of the blessings the Good Lord had seen fit to give him. And he figured if his daughters could meet up with somebody who made them feel half as good about life and love as their mama made him feel, they would have themselves something precious for sure. His Bertha had helped him to see the light at the end of many dark tunnels.

She had been with him and stood by him through storm and rain, faults and failures. He had seen and heard enough to know that unions like theirs didn't come along every day. They should never be taken for granted. And they deserved to be protected from whatever and whomever they needed to be protected from, sometimes, even mamas.

It certainly was never his intention to hinder their happiness. But, just like in the Garden, a snake will try to entice you to do the wrong thing by speaking a heap of good sounding words to you. After everything is said and done, you done leaped yourself over, head first into something that you can't undo.

CHAPTER TEN

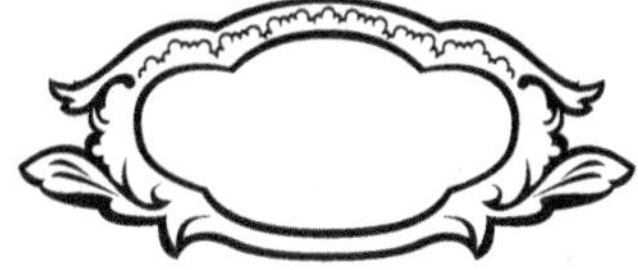

From the time they were little young'uns and thereafter, everything that she saw Flossie Mae and her sisters doing, Mrs. Lucy made it her business to mention it to their folks.

"I just thought y'all would like to know that I saw one of your gals doing such and such a thing," she would say.

"Bertha, I thought you ought to know that I saw your gals doing this, that, and the other," Mrs. Lucy reported.

Since Flossie Mae and Augustus had begun courting out in the open, she had been going over to Mrs. Lucy's every now and again to listen and to learn that "heathen music". With her own eyes, she had witnessed that gal up in the front room snapping her fingers and shaking her little bit of hips like she was in a juke joint or something. And that gal was up in her living room singing those devilish songs like she had been singing them all of her life.

She was certain that Bertha and Frederick would have a plum fit if they ever caught sight of that. She was quite certain of another thing too. If they didn't watch her, she was gonna git away from them. However, Mrs. Lucy didn't tell it.

There were quite a few things she had been keeping to herself lately, most especially, when they concerned Augustus Atwater. One evening, he came home with two, nice pieces of meat. She cooked them for their supper the next night, enjoying every bite right alongside him. She didn't bother with asking questions nor did he bother with volunteering answers though she was sure he hadn't bought them at the butcher's shop in town. She knew goodness well he didn't just happen to find them along the side of the road. And she would believe that she could take wings and fly 'fore she would believe that old man Beal just up and gave them to him out of the goodness of his heart. She was surprised that he was even paying Gussie steady, even if it was the bear minimum. No. They just ate, wiped their mouths, and threw the bones out to the dog.

From the outside looking in, it appeared that Flossie Mae DuPont and Augustus Atwater were getting closer to something that was bound to displease everyone, including them. Unbeknownst to either, both of them considered their own selfish schemes to be first and foremost. Their seemingly, growing relationship was being fertilized with deception, greed, and false hope. Those ingredients if left unchecked and unchanged were a sho'nuff guarantee for failure.

It seemed to be a natural thing—something as natural as a slow rain, to assume when Augustus Atwater began asking Flossie Mae to go away with him, he was also asking for her hand in marriage. She didn't love him in that way. She did like him as a friend though. Nevertheless, every time he mentioned that he loved her, in return, she would reply, "I love you too."

Flossie Mae continued to listen to and learn the songs that Augustus played on his record player. She liked them. She liked singing them. And she liked the attention and the fuss Augustus continually made over her whenever she sang.

Finally and without imagining too hard, he could see it. He could see her up on the stage. He could hear her singing. In his mind, he could see and hear the crowd as they begged for more. And in his mind, he was already counting up and spending up the money.

Normally, even for a gal like Flossie Mae, it would have taken more than a smooth talking fellow with some half-baked scheme to sway her. But, Flossie Mae herself made Augustus' plan much easier to work. He had two pluses on his side. First and foremost, she was more than ready to leave home and had been for a long time. Secondarily, she loved the attention she got when she sang. It would not be too much of an exaggeration to say that she thrived on it.

Maybe she had never given it too much thought on her own, but the more she thought about it, the more she believed. The more she believed, the more Augustus' dreams and schemes became a part of hers. For him, dreams and schemes went hand in hand. And one hand always washed the other.

However, when Augustus Atwater brought his intentions toward Flossie Mae to the attention of his Aunt Lucy, she was not happy. In fact, she was downright mad! As she put it, "Gussie, that gal done waltzed her fast self in here and turned your head. You are doing real good for yourself. She sees that you're a hardworking man. Now, she wants to come in here and take advantage of the situation. I been knowing that Flossie Mae all of her life. She always had the big head. Son, she ain't after a thing except your money! I done seen her up in that front room, shaking herself in front of you, grinning and going on. Mark my words! When your money is gone, she won't be far behind. Gussie, I done seen plenty of womens like that one!"

Augustus didn't have any idea why his Aunt Lucy was carrying on so. As far as he could see, he didn't have nothing when he came nor would he have much more than that when he left. Unless she was counting the best to his knowledge and remembrance, almost one hundred dollars he had been giving her to put up for him. Other than that, he still didn't have a pot or a window or a well to call his own.

Most men his age were already settled down with a wife and a few young'uns. Except for the good graces of his aunt, he wouldn't even have a place to lay his head. He suspected, more than anything else, her tantrum had more to do with the ten dollars a week she would be missing out on.

The very next day, Mrs. Lucy made it her business to pay her good friend, Bertha a little visit. All of a sudden, she felt that it was only right to mention to her how Flossie Mae had been carrying on. There was no need to just stand by and watch things get out of hand. And if they saw fit to keep that gal and her nephew apart, so be it. They would only be doing what was best.

From the moment Mrs. Lucy sat down and opened her mouth, Mrs. Bertha knew that there was much more on her friend's mind than the small talk she was making. Still, she listened while she talked about her tomatoes, the weather, the dollies she was crocheting—the neighbors up the road, before she got down to the real purpose for walking down the road in the heat of the day.

"Bertha, dear, you and Frederick Douglass knows that I think a whole heap of every one of your gals. And I say this here with nothing but the best of intentions—If y'all don't be mighty careful, that baby gal gonna git clean away from y'all. She done got her head filled up with a bunch of mess. Lord only knows where she's gitting it from. The other day, I heard her mentioning to Gussie something or another 'bout leaving 'way from 'round here. But we know how chirrens is. Don't we? Nothing may ever come of it, but then again, you can't chance it," she said.

"Lucy, I sure do appreciate you coming out of your way to tell me this. I'll be sure to look into it," Mrs. Bertha said. And that was all she said until Mrs. Lucy went back to talking about her tomatoes again.

Having to sit and listen to her friend Lucy made a cold chill run up and down her spine although it was good and hot inside and out. She had reminded her way too much of Mother Victoria with her meddling self—always telling somebody something for their own good, which was usually intended to serve her the most good.

Mrs. Bertha watched Mrs. Lucy fidget. She handled the tail of her apron, twisted it around her finger, and then straightened it over and over again. She never did look up for more than a minute or two at the time. Something had made her friend mighty uneasy. It made her wonder what was really behind her visit.

The news she brought about Flossie Mae didn't surprise Mrs. Bertha none. Ever since she knew there was somewhere else besides Coley's Corner, she had talked about leaving. But she wasn't in the habit of nor was she fixing to start talking about her gals before other folk—no matter how well intentioned they claimed to be. Yet, she had told herself that she would mention it to her husband.

Mr. Frederick Douglass DuPont had spent many a day out in the hot sun, plowing those long rows, praying almost every step of the way. He had prayed over and over again for the strength to do the right thing. He knew he needed help to step aside and allow his gals to live their own lives. If Augustus Atwater was the best that Flossie Mae could come up with—then so be it.

He hadn't spent all of his time praying just to waste it. After all, it had been almost a full year and "That Boy" hadn't gone anywhere. Except, he up and run him off—and he won't about to do that—it looked like he would be around for some time to come.

He had made up his mind. From now on, he won't gonna help or hinder whatever might be going on between them. It would never be said that he meddled in places where he was not wanted. However, if Flossie Mae was to seek out his opinion, he would be obliged to tell her the truth. He believed the boy to be a snake in the grass. Otherwise, he would have to keep on praying, grip his jaw, and bear it.

He would be the first to admit that all of his daughters had their own, separate, peculiar traits, but unlike his other daughters, Flossie Mae had always been so headstrong. Short of keeping her tied up, out back in the smokehouse, there won't a whole heap he could do. She was of age. And knowing her like he did, he knew that it was only a matter of time before she stepped out into the great, big world to try her hand at life.

Maybe some of those dreams of hers would come true. Who's to say? He just didn't want "That Boy" acting as if he was doing him and Bertha no favors.

⌐o⌐

CHAPTER ELEVEN

Around supper time, Mr. DuPont did what he had done for almost thirty years. He came in from the fields, stood on the back porch and pumped water into the pan, and washed up a taste. Then he went into the kitchen, gave his Bertha a great, big kiss on the lips, pulled out his chair, sat down and said Grace.

But today, he was feeling a little different, a mite frisky. He pulled Mrs. Bertha down onto his lap and held her real close, just to be holding her. She had always felt good in his arms. As usual, she giggled like a young schoolgirl. When he had a woman such as her to come home to, he didn't mind the hot sun and the long days so much. His Bertha had always made him feel like he was a rich man.

It took him a long time to let go of the guilt he felt for complaining about her not giving him any sons to carry on the family name and to help out around the farm. She had no say so over whether they were blessed with sons or daughters. He couldn't have asked for no better help than he had gotten from his daughters. There had been many days that they put in a hard day's work, work that would have put some men to shame.

They had done good, real good. It was a struggle, but he was able to get hold to a piece of ground to call his own. Last year, he put a new tin roof on the house. Someday, he hoped to give his Bertha running water and an indoor toilet. She certainly deserved everything he could give her and so much more. He was indeed a blessed man to know that kind of love.

"Gal, you better be glad it's still daylight," he teased, giving her a smack on her bottom, as she rose from his lap.

Again, Mrs. Bertha giggled. "Man, you better eat your supper before it gets cold. I'll keep 'til sundown," she replied.

Tired or no, he looked forward to that!

Their playful moment was interrupted by the opening of the kitchen door. Flossie Mae walked in. "Mama, Papa, I've been thinking about going away, going away with Augustus Atwater. We haven't made any for sure plans yet, nothing certain, but it's what I want to do," she said rather matter-of-fact as if it was already a done deal simply because she had spoken it. Victoria DuPont came to mind.

"Flossie Mae, honey, do you really love this boy?" her Mother asked.

"I do, Mama," she lied.

"Well, when is the wedding?" her Papa asked.

"Papa, we haven't really got that far yet," she answered.

"I see," was all her Papa said.

"Child, tell me, where will you live? What will you do? How will you eat?" her mother asked.

"Mama, I'm going to the City. I want to be a singer. I'll manage. One thing y'all taught me is, how to make due," she offered.

"Tell your young man to come and see me," her papa said.

"I'll tell him this evening, Papa," she said, smiling though the thought made her feel a bit queasy inside.

Then he looked up again and said, "If I'm gonna hand my young'un over, the least I should know is to what."

Flossie Mae walked out of the kitchen without eating supper. To her surprise, things had gone well, far more smoothly than she could have ever imagined. She thought they were almost too agreeable. It was as if they already knew and had already accepted her decision. But, what would Augustus Atwater do? And what would he say after she told him that her Papa wanted to see him? Whatever it was, she hoped it would not cause him to run off. At least, not run off without her.

It saddened Mr. DuPont to think that his baby girl would miss out on a chance to know what it is to have a good man alongside you, somebody who was there in the bad times as well as the good. She needed somebody she could count on in the heat of the day as well as the cool of the night.

He doubted if "That Boy" had the first idea about what it takes to be a good man. He doubted if he could count on his own self for too long much less having somebody else looking to him. If things proved out differently, he would be pleasantly surprised and would gladly be amongst the first to tell "That Boy" so. If not, Flossie Mae would always have a home to come back to.

"Let us do away with the small talk young man and get down to the business at hand," Mr. DuPont said as he shook Augustus Atwater's hand. Augustus nodded. He tried to look Mr. DuPont in the eye. He felt that he was being sized-up.

"Son, I am a man of few words. So, I ask you, after you marry my daughter, what then? Where are you looking to take her off to?

"Well—Well—Sir—," Augustus Atwater stammered.

He noticed how Mr. DuPont had sat up in his chair. "Sir, the truth of the matter—Sir, we haven't discussed that part yet, not yet, sir. "

"Now son, which part would that be? Y'all ain't discussed the part about where you planning on taking her to live or the part 'bout the marriage?" Mr. DuPont asked, looking Augustus Atwater square in the face.

Seeing that Mr. DuPont won't up to no foolishness, or side-stepping, or beating 'round the bush, Augustus tried to be as straight forward as possible. Of course, for him, honesty always involved throwing a lie or two in, here and there, every now and again.

"Sir, the part about where we'll live, and the marriage part, I was waiting to do things the proper way and ask your permission first," he lied.

"Since Flossie Mae declares to us that she loves you, we decided to go ahead and give y'all our blessings. The Preacher comes on the First and Third Sundays of every month. Y'all can talk to him then. Whenever y'all decide on something, me and the wife will put together whatever we can. Your Aunt Lucy can do whatever she got a mind to. A couple of her cakes sure would be right nice, but we'll leave all of that up to the womenfolk."

Things sure were moving along fast, too fast for Augustus Atwater. Who said anything about marriage? This thing was beginning to take on a life of its' own. None of this was a part of his plan! Where and who did he ever get an idea like that! He would have to think about marrying Flossie Mae though. And although Mr. DuPont hadn't come right out and said it, he had a feeling if he had anything to do with it, that was the only way she was ever going to leave with him—by way of marriage.

It occurred to him that these country Negroes were a whole lot smarter than he had given them credit for. He never could figure Mr. DuPont out. He still couldn't—calling him, "son" and all, shaking his hand—patting him on the back—talking about giving them his blessings—and parties. No, this was not the same man he had talked to when he came to ask permission to court Flossie Mae.

He wondered what was wrong with her? Why were they trying to get her off their hands? Why was her Papa so quick to push her off on him? If anything done happened, he won't the one! He had never went no further than a kiss. She wouldn't let him. They better be looking for themselves another fool. He won't the one!

His Aunt Lucy was right. That gal was out to get him. His daddy was right. 'A woman will make you do things that you never meant to do.' He had no intentions of marrying Flossie Mae DuPont or any other woman! He did not want to be tied down. And he wouldn't be tied down to any, one woman! What if something better was to come along? Well, he would just have to deal with that if and when it happened.

Augustus Atwater had a lot of questions, but no real answers. The only way he was going to get out of this mess was to do what he did best—disappear. Then again, what if that was what Mr. DuPont hoped for and wanted to happen? Well, he refused to give him the satisfaction! If the only way around this mess was marrying his country daughter, then so be it. This was one of those situations he would have to view as a good poker game, it was either a bluff, a call or a draw.

On the following evening, with aching hands and feet, along with a sore back, he walked over to the DuPont home with the intended and for the sole purpose of asking Flossie

Mae DuPont for her hand in marriage.

Needless to say, Flossie Mae said, "Yes" without hesitation. She said, "Yes" as if she had suspected and expected him to ask the question. She had said, "Yes" without the joy of a soon-to-be bride, without the joy of a woman in love with her man. So Augustus couldn't help but wonder why she had said, "Yes". Nevertheless, she had said, "Yes". Soon his dream would become a reality. Even better, she would be his wife. The way he saw it, she wouldn't be able to say, "No" to him again.

Unbeknownst to Augustus Atwater, Flossie Mae had said, "Yes" to marrying him, a man she didn't love because she knew there was a slim chance to none that her mama and papa would ever allow her to leave Coley's Corner on her own. But if Augustus Atwater thought he was the only one with good sense, he had another thought coming. He would soon began to wonder exactly who was taking advantage of who!

She was surprised to say the least at how quick her folks had agreed to her marrying up with the likes of him. It was almost scary how her Papa had treated Augustus. He was smiling and grinning. He was even patting him on his back, never mention calling him, "son". She supposed, maybe all of that was just their way of trying to scare him off.

———◦○◦———

CHAPTER TWELVE

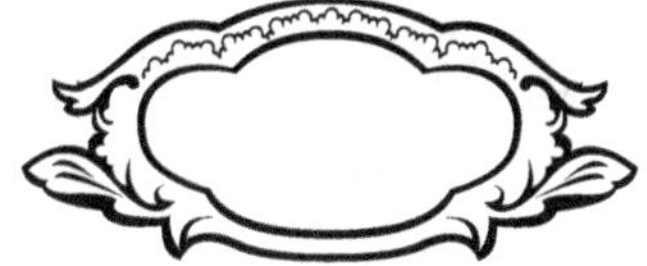

Flossie Mae was fluttering around worse than a butterfly in a field full of daisies. Mrs. Bertha couldn't help but notice how she was making a whole heap of fuss, except—it won't the usual fuss of a soon-to-be, young bride.

She also noticed how her daughter could've cared less about the dress she would wear. Whether she married in the Church or in the backyard or underneath the big oak tree or anything else about her wedding day in general. She only concerned herself with the business of getting it done as soon as possible. Mrs. Bertha knew her care-less-ness was because she planned to take off to Lord-Only-Knows-Where with "That Boy" soon after.

Over the years, she had witnessed a heap of changes in the lives of her seven daughters. The one thing that had not changed was their inability to pull the wool over her eyes. She could still spot a lie or the truth or whatever they cared to call any and everything that escaped from their lips. She could sense when they were speaking out of term. They practically told on themselves. And she knew her baby gal was up to something, regardless of how her words tried to make her believe otherwise.

Mrs. Bertha considered how she had already seen five of her gals smitten with their fellows. Eventually, they were smitten enough to say, "Yes" to becoming their wives. With every last one of them, she had seen that certain and special look in their eyes.

Recently, her knee-baby, Betty had become engaged to Joseph Avery. They had plans to be married the following summer. She believed him to be a fine, young man with a good, strong head on his shoulders. In a lot of ways, he was like her Frederick. She also believed Joseph Avery loved her daughter. In return, believed Betty loved him. Every chance Betty got, and to whomever was around to listen, she talked about nobody and nothing else. Therefore, she didn't feel the least bit uneasy about them.

However, all of that was lacking when she considered Flossie Mae and "That Boy." Augustus Atwater. She didn't see and hadn't seen nowhere about that gal nothing resembling love or anything kin to it. And "That Boy." he might be trying to say all of the right words to convince them of his intentions, but he won't fooling her. He didn't love Flossie Mae a bit more than a dog love ticks.

All of that considering lead her to ask herself, "Why?" Why in the world would Flossie Mae even fix her mouth to say, "Yes" to somebody she didn't have no real feelings for? Even more puzzling, why would "That Boy" bother 'bout asking her to marry him when he didn't have no special feelings toward her either?

Mrs. Bertha told herself that she might be getting older, but she won't nowhere close to being feeble-minded. And she might not have much schooling, but she won't nowhere close to being ignorant either. She was determined to get to the bottom of it all before her young'un jumped head-first into a pit full of serpents. She declared, "All the talking I done-done over the years, and that gal ain't learned nothing? Surely, all of our teaching should've taught her better than this here!"

While Mrs. Bertha was preparing supper, Flossie Mae fluttered into the kitchen with the pretense of wanting to help. Up 'til now, she hadn't shown no more interest in cooking than she had in lion taming.

After a while, she started up a conversation. "Mama, are you and Papa gonna talk to the Reverend?"

"Are we gonna talk to the Reverend? Talk to him 'bout what, honey?" Mrs. Bertha asked.

"You know. Talk to him 'bout me and Augustus Atwater marrying," Flossie Mae answered.

"No, we sure ain't! I figure, if the two of y'all done got old enough to be talking marriage, y'all old enough to talk to the Reverend for your own selves," Mrs. Bertha said, watching her daughter out of the corner of her eye.

"Mama, I just figured, you and Papa would be speaking to the Reverend on our behalf. I don't know what to do or what to say," Flossie Mae said, still wiping the same spot on the table.

"Ain't a whole lot to it, child. All you got to do is tell him of your intentions, ask him if he would do the honors of joining the two of y'all in marriage, and tell him when you would like for all of this to take place. He will take it from there and tell you whatever else you need to do," Mrs. Bertha instructed.

"But, I'll be too nervous to do all of that!" Flossie Mae cried out.

"Well, if you won't be too nervous to stand before God and make a whole heap of promises that you ain't got no heart to keep, you ought not be too nervous to talk to the Reverend," Mrs. Bertha assured her daughter.

"All right Mama, I'll do my own talking," Flossie Mae said as she turned to leave the kitchen.

Mrs. Bertha watched her. She thought, "That child is sho'nuff headstrong and sassy to boot!"

Flossie Mae was the only one of her young'uns who dared to talk to her in that manner. What it was, with her being the youngest, she had been spoiled rotten. She was used to getting her way in certain things, and getting by on some others. But, not this time.

Mrs. Bertha purposed in her heart and mind to have a long talk with Flossie Mae after supper. Then, her Frederick will be done with his supper and out slopping the hogs. Afterwards, he generally sat on the front porch, took his boots off and drew a few puffs on his pipe. That would give her plenty of time to say what she had to say.

Mrs. Bertha overheard Flossie Mae telling Betty that Augustus Atwater would be coming by.

Augustus Atwater had come in from his job at Beal's Café. As usual, his Aunt Lucy was waiting supper for him. She had been feeding him like a king. He figured, before she heard it from someone else, he best tell her about him and Flossie Mae. Tell her—right over all of that good eating.

"Aunt Lucy," he started, "I thought you ought to know, I—I done asked Flossie Mae DuPont to be my wife."

"WIFE!" Mrs. Lucy hollered. "Boy! What you go and do something like that for? I told you that fast-tale gal was after something! I told you, but you went ahead and done it anyhow! That old gal done got her fingers stuck in both of your eyes! And she got both of her hands stuck down in your pockets too!

Augustus eyed the clock. He was going to be late. Nine o'clock came mighty quick. He doubted if his Aunt cared about him being late. If she had her way, she would rather he never set foot inside the DuPont house again. And she told him as much.

By the time Augustus finished his supper and headed up the road to the DuPont house, Miss Lucy was madder than a heifer just lead into a pasture full of bulls. The news of her foolish, nose-wide-opened nephew's plans to marry up with that fast-tale Flossie Mae DuPont took her appetite plumb away.

All of that liver and onion gravy, rice, freshly picked snap beans, buttermilk biscuits, and sweet tea gone to waste. She won't able to eat another bite, but her nephew as usual sat there and ate just like it was his first, last, and only meal. There won't too much that he would let hinder him when it came to eating.

She knew he was considering doing something foolish. She never imagined he would go so far as to actually up and marry "That Gal". That was way past foolishness. She wondered how could and why would Bertha Mae and Frederick Douglass DuPont allow such a thing to take place? And especially, after she done suffered the heat of the day to go over yonder and have a talk with Bertha.

Mrs. Lucy tried with everything in her to convince herself that her anger stemmed from the notion that her nephew was being taken advantage of. She tried to pretend she only had Gussie's best interest at heart. She tried to deny that she was mad about something other than the threat of losing her weekly ten dollar stipend. But truth being told, that was it in a nutshell. She had gotten use to her stipend along with all of the other little things her nephew had begun to do for her.

There had been plenty of times when she wished she had her house all to herself again, like the times when old Claude Mann wanted to come over and take up a little bit of her time. He hadn't been over in a while except to bring her a bushel of peaches and a bushel or two of peas during the summer and some seasoning meat and collard greens for New Years. Other than that, he had just been nodding his head whenever he saw her and then going on 'bout his business. He did tell her once, "Lucy, I don't want to be in the way."

"Man, how will you be in the way when it's my house and my door and me doing the inviting?" She had asked. But Claude, if nothing else, he was sho'nuff set in his own ways.

So, on one hand, Augustus was in the way, but on the other hand, he was paying his own way. Surely, she could still use the money right on. The way she saw it, what "That Gal" needed to do was stay home and let her own mammy and pappy take care of her just like they'd been doing. And it wouldn't take too much more for her to tell her so!

Mrs. Bertha knew there wasn't much time so she got in a hurry. Her intentions weren't to sway her daughter in any particular direction. She just wanted to help her to at least see why she was doing what she was planning to do. She believed it was a shame to lie to other folks, but it was a greater shame and a pity to lie to your own self, then turn and walk around like you done started believing your own lie.

She called her daughter into the front room. Flossie Mae eyed the Bible lying on her Mama's lap. She thought she was being called in for devotions or something, but hoped not. Her Mama was always praying and reading that Bible of hers just like all of the stuff in it was written and meant for her. As far as she could see, it was written and meant for those other folk—the ones who had all of the privileges in this life, not them. They were the ones who had to scuffle and scrape, bearly getting by, but never quite making it.

"Honey, sit down. I want to talk to you 'bout a few things," Mrs. Bertha began.

Flossie Mae took a deep breath.

"From a young'un growing up in my folks' house, I always knew things won't quite right between them. Every time they had words, the subject of my Mama marrying my Papa just to get away from home would rear its' ugly head. To this day, I don't believe my Mama loved my Papa the way a man needs to be loved. And I don't believe my Papa's feelings were any different toward my Mama. From the outside looking in, life appeared to be pretty good, but for us on the inside, life told an altogether different story. Us chirren—we didn't know the half of it, and never will. Marrying takes a whole heap more than just a notion. I loved my Mama and my Papa. Still, I didn't want that for myself. What I saw and understood about their marriage seemed to measure out far more pain than it had love to measure. I didn't want somebody who was looking for his woman and his child to be rolled up into the same package. I didn't want somebody whose idea of a helpmeet meant expecting me to work alongside him like a mule from sunup 'til sundown without so much as a sigh. I didn't want somebody who wanted me to do whatever they said without question, somebody who whipped up on me if I didn't and even if I did. I didn't want it. And I never had it with your Papa. I wanted myself a man I could love, a man who could love me back. Your Papa has always been a good, hardworking man. He loves his family and he does all that he can to provide for us. Except, the way things are 'round here, I know he can't do but so much.

Flossie Mae shifted in the chair.

"I ain't trying to make out that we done had a perfect life. Lord knows, we haven't. We done had to suffer more than a few things. We had to put our hands to the plow and work on this thing. The Lord done seen us through a storm or two. He never left our side. Some things may have come along to destroy us, but instead, they only strengthened us. Through everything, your Papa and me had something to hold onto. We had our love for one another and our promise to stand with one another. Love helped to hold us in the hard times. When you don't even have love as your starting point, I can't see nothing much ahead for y'all except trouble. Baby, don't think I don't see you fluttering 'round here like a butterfly. You been talking 'bout everything except what a young woman in love talks about. I can't help but believe you're doing this thing for all of the wrong reason. I won't even ask you whether you love him or not. I don't want to force you to have to lie to me. And I don't want you lying to yourself either. But, if you're determined to go 'head, at least, step into this thing with your eyes wide open. Flossie Mae, rest assured, life ain't fixing to up and hand you all the good it got to give just cause you happen to want it. You steady talking like you looking to walk on a flowery bed of ease all the way to Lord-Only-Knows-Where, never bumping your head or stumping your toe along the way. Life ain't no fairy-tale where the story book always reads. 'And they lived happily forever after'."

"Mama, I was never looking for no fairy tale kind of life. The only thing I'm looking for is somebody who'll treat me decent. I want somebody to appreciate me just for being me. I want somebody who will stay put in the bad times as well as the good. I ain't looking for nobody to give me a whole heap of fancy either. Regular is all I'm asking, Mama, just regular. Augustus Atwater may not be you and Papa's pick for me, but he's who I pick for myself. Why can't y'all be happy for me? Why, Mama? That's all I'm asking!"

"Honey, I'm your Mama. If I don't tell you the truth, who will? Your Papa and me, we never tried to pick nobody for none of y'all. We just don't want you to walk into something blind, looking so hard, you can't see. For some folks, it appears, everything falls into place for them. Sometimes, it appears, that things fall right into place for them, without them ever having to put much effort behind it. For you and me as well as for plenty more, it looks like we have to fight our way through more times than not. We have to push harder to get half as far. Our hills seem steeper. And our storms seem to linger longer. There's no right or wrong to it. It's just the way things appear to be. It's called life. Please hear me, honey. Though you believe life has gone and treated you unjustly, life happens to every one of us in some shape, form or fashion. Every which a way you try to run, life will be at the door, waiting for you to come in. And in this life, we have to fight hard enough. I don't see no sense in making up no extra battles or fighting no unnecessary wars if I can escape them. Don't get rattled just because life won't let you live it on your own terms. This boy, he ain't no stranger to us. We done seen how he's been carrying himself over the years. Here lately, his own Aunt who knows him a sight better than we do, just started having something good to say about him. Chances are, you done seen something in him that the rest of us done missed seeing. Then again, we could have seen something that you don't want to see."

"All right, Mama! If you must know—I don't love him! But I'm fixing to marry him anyhow. Maybe I will learn to love him—in time. For now, I just see him. Augustus Atwater is gonna take me to the City. After that, he can go on 'bout his business if he got a mind to. I don't care. Mama, I will make something out of myself. I'm not gonna marry up with any of these nappy-headed, farm boys 'round here, and end living my life as just another farm hand. Just like you wanted a life different from your folks, I want mine to be different too. I don't want to stay stuck in the middle of nowhere forever. Mama, if you must know, all I want from and expect out of Augustus Atwater is for him to take me away from here!"

Mrs. Bertha began carefully. Tears were in her eyes. Pain was gripping her heart. And her emotions seemed to have gathered in her throat. "That's what I said all right. 'I wanted something more or different for myself than what my folks had'. But, unlike you, child, I didn't go 'round looking down my nose at them because they didn't live the kind of life I thought or wished they should live. If anything, I learned how precious family is. Flossie Mae, they won't be with you always. Before you knows it, time done slipped by and your family done slipped away. But you are of age. I reckon, you got to choose your own way. And if you feel like you got to go 'way from here to find your place in the world, so be it. I would rather, you didn't, but it's not my decision to make. Lord knows, I don't want you to stay 'round here, living a life of misery. If you carry this thing out, it's certain to bring about pain. And if you stay, it's certain to bring about pain. No, I don't want you to stay for my sake."

There was a knock on the door. Betty answered. Mrs. Bertha and Flossie Mae heard the voices of Joseph Avery and Augustus Atwater.

Mrs. Bertha said, "Child, I reckon you better get yourself in there to greet your young man. I got more to say, but it will keep."

As Flossie Mae left the front room, she didn't flutter. She walked like a young woman who just had her deepest, darkest secret brought to light. However, in the few seconds it took for her to stand face to face with Augustus Atwater, she had gained her composure. Or at best, she had hold of the self she always presented before him.

She thought, contrary to her folks' belief, Augustus Atwater had a whole heap more to concern himself with than she did. For now, he might see her as just another young, country gal. Well, he could go right on believing that he done swayed her with his lying, city-slick ways. But, he would soon see.

Mrs. Bertha slipped into her and Mr. DuPont's bedroom. She cried for her daughter and the decision she was set on making. She prayed to the Lord to be with Flossie Mae. She had always prayed to the One whose arms stretched much wider than hers and whose eyes could see much further. She relied on the One who knows all and is able to do all things. And she would continue to do so for as long as she had breathe.

—◦—

CHAPTER THIRTEEN

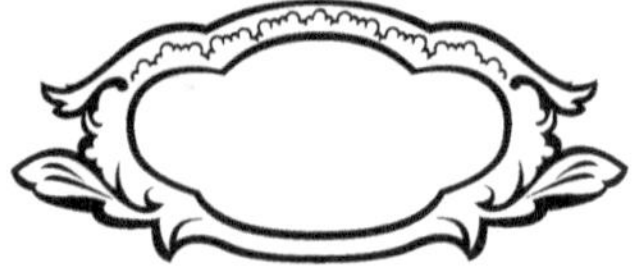

On a breezy, but hot July afternoon, Augustus Atwater and Flossie Mae DuPont stood before God, the Reverend and every one within the sound of their voices and repeated their marriage vows to one another.

They repeated their vows word for word just like any and every other couple would. They stood repeating the sacred and solemn commitment to love and honor one another through sickness and in health, in the good times and in the bad, for better or for worse—until death do them part. They both stood, boldly repeating a vow that neither intended to live up to.

During the brief ceremony, Mrs. Bertha cried. Mr. Frederick Douglass gripped his jaw. And Mrs. Lucy huffed and puffed. Later that day, the heavens must have been saddened too because a terrible thunderstorm arose, cutting short the tiny outdoor reception of fried chicken, potato salad, cake and punch.

In all of the planning or lack thereof, through all of the scheming(s) going on in the heads of Flossie Mae and Augustus Atwater, neither had thought much about where they, Mr. and Mrs. Atwater would live. Nor had anyone else thought to inquire about the couple's future living arrangements.

After the storm ceased, everyone was sitting around in the DuPont's house, finishing up the food. It was then the subject came up. Flossie Mae had made no plans to live with Augustus, not immediately any way. And Augustus had assumed, took for granted, and considered without bothering to ask, naturally thought, they would stay with his Aunt Lucy.

Eyebrows began to raise, especially his Aunt Lucy's. "What? Ain't nobody asked me nothing 'bout y'all staying with me! If you man enough to git yourself a wife, you best be man enough to put a roof over her head too!" she said disgustedly, not caring who heard it.

Augustus asked permission to step into the back room with his Aunt for the purpose of having a little, private talk. It seemed he was always asking permission in that house to do one thing or another. There was no way he was going to stay there. He doubted if the DuPonts would allow them to anyhow.

"Aunt Lucy, like it or not, I got myself a wife now. We need a place to stay for a little while. For as long as we stay, I'm willing to add another five dollars to go 'long with the ten I'm paying now. I know that Flossie Mae's folks ain't about to turn her out. She will have a place to stay as long as they got one, but she's my wife now. I don't want it to be said that I ain't man enough to keep her up."

"Well—Gussie, I'll do it this time since, as usual, you seem to have yourself in a bind. But don't think I won't tell you, 'I told you so'. Always got yourself a whole heap of big ideas with no place to put them. You're always digging a hole for yourself that ends up caving in on you. This time, it appears, I done got stuck in the hole with you. I ain't never seen nothing like it! Then again, I have—your Pappy! Just so you knows, I want my money first thing on pay day. I don't want to hear no excuses, no poor-mouthing, or no nothing! I just want my fifteen dollars! Or else, y'all will have to find yourselves somewhere else to play house!"

"Aunt Lucy, don't I always give you your money? I haven't missed a week yet. And I don't intend to start now," Augustus reminded her.

"Yea, but things bound to change. Womenfolk be needing things. Some of them be expecting a whole heap more than they'll ever get or can ever use up. That gal is one of them kind. You got what you wanted though. And from now on, if you can keep a penny to your name, I'll be mighty surprised," she told him.

Augustus didn't and had never said what he wanted to say to his Aunt. His day would come. Before too long, he would make her eat all of those words. He won't digging no holes. He was digging his way out of one. But as long as she allowed him and his wife to stay with her, she could say whatever she liked. At the same time, he made a mental note not to keep silent if she started poking that nose of hers into their affairs. He wasn't about to pay her fifteen dollars and tolerate her meddling too.

One thing he did know about Flossie Mae, Aunt or no Aunt and room or no room, she was not going to stand for too many of his Aunt's tantrums. He was too close to getting what he had worked so hard toward. He couldn't allow nothing or no one to come between him and it now.

On the first night, Augustus and Flossie Mae Atwater consummated their marriage. It had taken the long road to get there. He had gotten what he wanted though it had almost taken a dog fight to get there. The important thing was, he got there. He had had more than a few doubts, doubts that he would ever see this night. But there had also been times in his life when he doubted if he would see another night.

Flossie Mae was a virgin. Sex—another thing she had not given much consideration. Augustus Atwater had been all over her like butter on bread, breathing hard and sweating even harder. He sort of reminded her of a dirty, sour dishrag. She had shut her eyes as tight as she could get them, gritted her teeth, and gripped the bed linens until it was over.

Afterward, Augustus seemed to be real pleased with himself. As far as she was concerned—she was any and everything but pleased. She vowed to herself, "This will not be happening too often".

Flossie Mae was up first thing the next morning. She felt the need to clean herself up again. She needed to scrub herself, her clothes, and the bed linens. Then, she would go home to gather a few more of her things. Although she knew married folks were supposed to have those kinds of relations, she felt not only ashamed, but she also felt dirty.

Augustus Atwater woke up with a big grin on his face as if he had just won the grand prize at the State Fair. Flossie Mae turned away. He understood. After all, it was not his first encounter with a young, virgin gal. He was sure that she would come around before too long. There were two things Augustus was not short on, lies and ego. He considered himself to be among the best. He doubted if there were any who could hold a candle to him, especially a bunch of countrified Negroes.

Much to his surprise, Flossie Mae did come around, but it was much sooner than he had expected. She became what every other man could only dream of. She was more than willing. It soon became apparent that she was only interested in using him for her own selfish pleasure. Augustus, being a man who had for quite some time, burned his candle on both ends, sometimes, failed short in pleasing his wife.

The deeper he got into his scheme, the more he became concerned that things might not work out as he had planned. They hadn't so far. Nevertheless, he expected things to turn around soon and start working in his favor.

Once again, something came up that hadn't been pondered over or given too much consideration. Flossie Mae's ability or inability to cook or her lack of interest in cooking, period–had never come up.

Mrs. Lucy had intentionally spent the day away from home. She stayed well past supper preparing time. She reckoned, then Flossie Mae would have no choice. She would for the first time, be forced to cook a meal for her husband.

When Augustus came home, he didn't smell the usual, mouth-watering aromas coming from the kitchen, aromas that generally met and beckoned to him from the back porch. Instead, he smelled something, but had no idea what it was he was smelling. After he had washed up a little, he sat down to the supper table. His wife sat before him a plate of unrecognizable food. He didn't want to, but he didn't know what else to do except try to eat it. He honestly tried. It tasted even worse than it looked. He loved to eat. Up 'til that day, he hadn't turned down too many meals. Surely, she didn't really expect him to eat whatever it was that sat before him. He was certain, even the hogs would have a hard time trying to eat it.

"Baby, I'm not that hungry. I ate a sandwich at the café. Mr. Beal insisted on making me one of his specialties," Augustus lied. "I swear, if I had known you were going to cook, I wouldn't have touched it with a stick."

"Oh, that's all right. I don't mind," Flossie Mae assured him. And she didn't. In fact, it suited her just fine. Now, she wouldn't have to worry about him asking her to cook. She was not her Mama or his. She didn't plan to be slaving over no hot stove for nobody. Her plans didn't include none of that! She was already doing about as much as she intended to do.

During most days, Flossie Mae spent much of her time, that is, when she wasn't at her folks', in the back room, away from Mrs. Lucy. She played those records faithfully, learning every one of them. She learned quickly and soon had them down to a tee. She often held her hairbrush up to her mouth and practiced just like she was getting paid good money to do it.

Mrs. Lucy had begun to spend far too much of her time going from house to house, baring gossip. She didn't bother 'bout visiting her friend, Bertha much anymore, being most of the news she toted concerned that gal of hers. And she knew Bertha wouldn't stand for her bringing her nothing contrary, supposedly friend or no.

How do you tell a Mama that she done raised herself a lazy, no cooking, blues singing, nephew stealing, good for much of nothing young'un anyhow? She hadn't found no right way to go about it. So, she just decided to stay clear of the DuPont house altogether. However, as often as she mentioned it to other folks, she apparently had no problem making her feelings toward Flossie Mae known. Whenever she did see Bertha at church, she had a very few words to say to her.

She had considered Bertha to be a friend for the better part of twenty years. Flossie Mae had managed to mess that up too. She remembered how that grand mammy of hers, Victoria DuPont used to say, 'That gal won't bring y'all nothing but trouble'. She hadn't cared much for old lady Victoria, but it appeared, she was right about that fast-tale grand young'un of hers.

At this point, Mrs. Lucy was more than willing to blame Flossie Mae for every ill wind along with any and every other thing that went wrong. The evening before, Augustus had told her, he would be needing the money she had put up for him. He had also mentioned to her that from now on, his wife would be holding onto his money. He mentioned how he believed it was the right thing to do. Right! To her knowledge, "Right" and Augustus had never even met one another. That gal would soon come to realize it too. But, then again, she wouldn't recognize "Right" if it sat down in her lap. They were pitiful, just plain pitiful.

That boy had kept up with every red cent of his money. Mrs. Lucy hadn't. Somehow or another, some of it must have gotten mixed up with her money and she had spent it. She had been so turned around lately, ever since this marriage mess took place, she didn't hardly know her knees from her elbows. Augustus had said she was holding onto one hundred and thirty dollars of his money.

She could only account for ninety five dollars of it. She didn't have no idea where it had gotten to unless that wife of his spotted her hiding place and took it for her own use. How in the world was she gonna come up with thirty five dollars. For more than half of the day, Mrs. Lucy fretted over the missing money.

While making biscuits that evening, it came to her where the missing money went to. Augustus had asked for it to buy a ring for Flossie Mae. If he didn't have any recollection of it, she would just point at those well rested fingers on his wife's well rested hand and show him.

A week before Thanksgiving Day, Augustus drove up in a nineteen forty five Studebaker. He said that he had bought it from a man who did business with his boss. Mrs. Lucy wondered, but couldn't understand how a man could spend one hundred hard-earned dollars on a car when he didn't even have a place to call his own.

It was hard for her to understand how a car could be on the top of his list when he needed to hurry up and get that gal out of her house. She had come along and ruined everything. Still, it came as quite a shock to Mrs. Lucy when she found out her nephew was preparing to do just that. Around the first of the year, he planned to go back to the city to look for work and find a place for him and Flossie Mae.

She was told, while he was gone, Flossie Mae would be staying over at her folk's. After he got set up, he would come for her. Augustus thanked his Aunt for everything. Most of it, he was sure she would not have done without money being involved, but he didn't say it.

Mrs. Lucy said how glad she was to do it. How she had enjoyed his company. And she mentioned how she was gonna hate to see him go. She never made any mention of Flossie Mae.

As planned, Augustus Atwater went to the city. Flossie Mae went to stay with her folks. Mrs. Lucy got her house back. She doubted if her nephew would show his face 'round there ever again. Mrs. Bertha and Mr. Frederick Douglass DuPont waited along with their daughter. They waited and just hoped for the best.

Flossie Mae had been married for six months. It was much longer than they would have given. Nonetheless, they still didn't trust "That Boy". However, their daughter appeared to have found peace with the choice she had made.

Not one time, while he was there or since he had been gone did her folks utter a contrary word to their daughter concerning her husband. Nor did Mr. DuPont ever let on to his daughter that he knew about the talk she and her mother had. He knew it wouldn't solve nothing anyhow. It seemed that his baby girl was bent on having her own way, no matter what or where it might take her or how much it might cost her.

At least, Flossie Mae had plenty to do while she waited for Augustus to return. Betty and Joseph were getting married. Betty being Betty, she wanted a fancy wedding. She wanted it to take place in the church house. She had been getting a whole heap of fancy ideas out of the catalog. Since there was no money falling out of trees, once again, they would have to make due.

Flossie Mae couldn't cook worth nothing. And she could never clean to suit her Mama or her older sisters. Besides singing, she was a very good seamstress. She could study a dress in a catalog one week and be wearing it the next week. She had figured out a long time ago, since she liked nice things, if she couldn't afford to buy them, she best learn how to make them. And so she did.

With so many dresses to make, her sewing knowledge and skill came in handy. Betty wanted all of her sisters to take part in her wedding. Fanny and Ruby were with child, again. If Ruby didn't deliver in time, it would take a tent to cover her. Flossie Mae had told her sister there had to be more than one cake in the oven. Ruby hoped not. "There appears to be at least two, maybe even three," they had teased.

Nonetheless, Flossie Mae was enjoying the change of pace and scenery. For now, she was glad she had other things to keep her company. Though she still intended to leave, she had missed home more than she cared to admit. She had also missed the way her and Betty often carried on like two school-aged girls.

She and Mrs. Lucy seldom exchanged more than a few words. If she won't watching her like a hawk, she was somewhere clucking like a sitting hen and blaming her for every little thing. When had she become so attached to "Gussie"? If she never set foot in that house again, it would be too soon!

Hopefully, Augustus was almost done. Waiting was hard work.

After checking the mailbox every day except Sunday as if she could will a letter to come, Flossie Mae finally received a letter from Augustus.

It read:

"Baby,

> *I miss you so much. My arms are lonely for you. My lips are too. Girl, I hope you been missing me half as much as I have been missing you. Things are taking a little longer than I expected. But I'm going to do what I promised. Don't let nobody tell you nothing different. You will be here, in the city, with me before the Easter lilies start blooming. Tell your folks I said thanks for looking out for my wife, and will you tell Aunt Lucy that I asked about her too?*
>
> *Augustus,*
> *Your loving husband*

However, Augustus Atwater neglected to tell his wife, his bride the real reasons behind his delay. Once more and again, his past messes were catching up with him. The Howard Brothers heard that he was back in town. They had paid him a little visit and had very strongly insisted that he pay them their money or else. Being a little short on cash, Augustus attempted to satisfy some of his debt by turning his car over to them.

Then a certain female he knew from 'way-back-when' had seen him out and about. They had spent a little time together, one thing had led to another. It hadn't meant anything to him. When he woke up, the woman was gone and so was his wallet. So he had been stuck in the city with no job, no money, no car, and no prospects. On one hand, it wasn't much to write home about, but on the other hand, the truth was far too much to write home about, especially to your wife.

Augustus believed everyone expected him to fail, including Flossie Mae. But he was determined to keep his word—some kind of way. Sooner or later, life had to give him a break. But, he would rather it be sooner than later.

Maybe he did fix up the truth a little. Maybe he didn't tell everything. "Who in their right mind would?" he asked himself. It was so hard trying to do the right thing. It seemed, if he didn't run into trouble, trouble hunted him down and ran over him. Either way, they usually ended up meeting somehow and some way.

—◦—

CHAPTER FOURTEEN

The Easter lilies along with Mrs. Bertha's Iris and azalea blooms had come and gone before Augustus lucked up (as he had put it) on a job. He had heard from the cousin of the owner of a bar about a block from the boarding house that they were looking for a singer and a bartender at La'Rue's Place. He hadn't done any real bartending, but he had certainly sat at a lot of bars, and had seen how it was done a plenty. Augustus had no doubt, once they heard Flossie Mae sing, they would hire her on the spot.

However, he still had a few problems. He had no way to get her to the city. His car was gone and so was his money. If the Howard Brothers hadn't been willing to give him another chance and let him hold a little something, he would have been out for sure—out of luck, out the door, out of time—just plain out.

La'Rue's Place was on the corner of East and 10th Streets. The door was opened, so he stepped inside. He gave the place a look-over. "Not bad, not bad at all," he said to himself.

"May I help you?" a voice called out. "We're not open for business yet."

"Yes, I'm here to see about the job," Augustus called back. Still, not seeing the person he was talking to.

"Which job are you seeking? The singing job? The bartending job? Or the cleaning job?" the voice called out again.

"The singing and the bartending job, but I'll take cleaning or anything I can get," he called out again, beginning to feel a bit uneasy and slightly annoyed . He never liked being in situations where he couldn't see who he was dealing with.

"Young man, can you sing? Do you know how to tend bar?" the voice asked.

"Well, to be honest—no, but my wife can. I—I never did no bartending, but I know that I can do it," Augustus tried to explain.

"So—Then, you are here about the cleaning job," the voice said with a bit of humor attached.

Before he could answer, a woman entered through a narrow doorway opposite the bar. "Son, are you sure you want to work? I don't have time for no one-nighters, no-shows, convicts, trouble-makers, wife-beaters, drunks, thieves, and the like. And if you are one of those who are expecting a whole lot of something for a little bit of nothing, may I Shuggest that you look somewhere else. I run a clean business. And as you can see, I'm not much bigger than a minute, but I pack a mean punch. I don't have time to take no mess from no jive-time Negroes. I'm not your mama, your nurse, your baby-sitter, your shrink, or your banker. So, don't bring me none of your woes. You work. I pay you. And now, I ask you again, 'Do you really want to work?'" the small framed woman asked.

"Yes ma'am. I do," Augustus answered.

"My name is Mrs. La'Rue Baker. You may call me Mrs. La'Rue or Mrs. Baker. Now, what may I call you?" she asked.

"My name is Augustus Atwater," he said, reaching out to shake Mrs. Baker's hand.

"Like I said, Mr. Atwater, I run a clean business. I don't like dirt! Period! My place closes late. That means, you'll be working late. Is your wife going to go along with that?" she asked.

"Yes ma'am. No. She won't mind," he answered.

"Well, Mr. Atwater, looks like you have found yourself a job. My place opens in two weeks, but I need you to start sooner than that, bright and early Monday morning to be exact. If I were you, I wouldn't hang out too late. I'm not about to tolerate my people coming up in here with no hangovers. I believe we understand one another. Don't you?" she said, about to turn away, but stopped. "Mr. Atwater, please write your name and address down on the piece of paper on the bar."

Augustus figured, it was now or maybe never. "Mrs. Baker, my wife really can sing. I heard you was looking for somebody. If you could just hear her, I believe you will want to hire her."

"I like a man with confidence. Tell you what, I don't know if this little songbird of yours is as good as you say, but if you bring her in about six this evening, I'll listen," she promised.

"Mrs. Baker, truth is, my wife isn't in the city right now. She's at her folks' place, waiting for me to send for her," he said.

"I guess you better get to sending then. Whenever she gets here, I'll listen as I promised. I believe you have figured out by now, I don't believe in beating around the bush. I don't have time to waste on stroking egos. So don't bring nobody in here who sounds like they're clinging tin cans together. If you do, don't expect me to graciously tell them, "No thank you". When people can't sing, they need to know they can't sing. It may sting a little at first, but it will help them in the long run. Understood?" Mrs. Baker asked.

"Thank you, Mrs. Baker. Thank you for everything," Augustus said.

"Honey, don't thank me yet," she said. "I'll see you first thing Monday morning."

Augustus Atwater walked down 10th Street like a man walking on clouds. Things were finally going according to his plans. He was beginning to think that he might have to ditch the whole thing, Flossie Mae included.

Thoughts of Flossie Mae brought him back down to earth. He couldn't go get her. So, he needed to send for her, but he didn't even have the money for a bus ticket. Augustus decided to take his ring to THE HOCK SHOP to see if he could get at least ten dollars on it. He didn't know, but it was worth a try. Together, he and Flossie Mae's rings hadn't cost him more than thirty dollars. He had bought them at a second-hand store in Coley' Corner.

It took a lot of talking, but the man in THE HOCK SHOP finally agreed to pay him twelve dollars and fifty cents, but only if he also threw in the ring on his other finger. That ring had been the only thing he had managed to hold onto. It was the same ring he had taken from his Aunt Lucy a few years back.

Next, Augustus walked to the Bus Station. The ticket cost him eleven dollars and ninety three cents. He was left with only fifty seven cents to his name.

He went to his room at the Boarding House. At least, he still had a place to stay, a place to bring Flossie Mae to. With the money from the Howard Brothers, he had had the good sense to pay his rent in advance. He was good for another month or so.

Augustus sat down at the little table in the corner to write Flossie Mae a letter.

Well Babe,
It may not be as soon as I had planned, but I got a job. I told my boss about you and how you can sing like a songbird. She wants to hear you real bad. I'm sure she will be begging you to sing for her as soon as you open your mouth. Mrs. Baker's Place opens up in two weeks. I need you to come as soon as possible. Here is the bus ticket. I know I promised to come back to get you, but things didn't work out with the car. You got the number at the place I'm staying. Call me and let me know when you plan to leave so I can meet you at the Bus Station. I miss you. I can hardly wait to see you.
 Signed with love,
 your husband, Augustus

Augustus walked down the street to the Post Office. The postage stamp cost him three cents. He counted his change. Fifty four cents was all the money he had in the world, not a penny, a pot, or a window nor a well more. But his luck was about to change. He promised himself.

Flossie Mae received the letter on a Saturday. She read it several times before she mentioned it to anyone. She put the ticket up for safe keeping. Finally! Finally! Finally! Her insides seemed to scream. Finally! Augustus Atwater was coming through on at least one of his old, watered down promises. Finally! She was going to bid Coley's Corner good-bye and not a minute too soon. Finally! Some of her dreams were gonna come true. Finally! Finally! Finally!

Mrs. Bertha had seen Flossie Mae skipping from the mailbox earlier like a young school girl. Her actions could only mean that she had gotten another letter from "That Boy".

"Lord, how mercy!   She hangs onto those empty promises of his like they gold. He's been gone almost four months. With every letter, seems like she sinks deeper and deeper into the mire. I ain't never seen nothing like it in my life! The more you talk, the more she clings to him," she said aloud.

As she looked out of her kitchen window and toward the heavens, Mrs. Bertha asked, "Lord, can I try just one more time? After that, I'll wash my hands of it. I done just about done and said all I know to say and do. But I need to try one more time. Then, if she still wants to follow after "That Boy," I got no other choice except to let it be."

Ophelia, the oldest had come by on this particular Saturday morning to help her Mama with the cakes and pies for the Church's Homecoming on Sunday. She was Flossie Mae's second Mama, so to speak.

"Gal, lately, you been dragging 'round here worse than an old, broke down car. This morning, you skipping and humming like you use to do. Child, who done come along and lifted your storm clouds away?" she asked.

"Who? Who else?" Flossie Mae answered. Then she blurted out without meaning to, "He done sent for me! I got my ticket in the mail this morning. I'll be leaving as soon as I can gather my things together. Shortly, I'll be joining my husband in the city!"

It disgusted Ophelia to the pit of her stomach to see how foolish her sister had become. And all for what? To run behind a man whose promises up 'til now, hadn't amounted to a hill of beans?

"Shugar, you sure that's what you really want to do? You know, Mama and Papa's home is still your home too. All of us make mistakes. You've been walking with your head up in the clouds long enough. It's time for you to come on back down here with the rest of us."

"I know what all y'all think! Y'all act like there's something wrong with me having dreams! Well, it ain't! I'm leaving just as soon as I can gather my things." Flossie Mae said, looking her older sister right in the eye.

"Are you gonna miss Betty's wedding? You fixing run off just like that? What about the dresses? Aren't you supposed to be singing?" Ophelia asked, hoping to buy a little more time.

"Betty will understand, but this ain't about Betty or you or Mama and Papa. It's about me! Am I supposed to push my dreams aside and just sit and watch while everybody else's come true? I know y'all don't like it. And I know y'all think I'm just being foolish, but I'm going. Like it or not!" Flossie Mae said, switching off like she had all of a sudden got up and turned grown.

She had become even more headstrong during her wait for Augustus. She wasn't listening to anything sounding as if it had a hint of good sense to it or was contrary to what she wanted. All she wanted was what she wanted. Period.

Her patience had grown real short. Augustus Atwater didn't know it yet, but she planned to make him pay for making her wait so long.

Flossie Mae had already started burning bridges, bridges she hadn't yet crossed. She sounded real sure of herself, but deep down inside, she wasn't that sure. She knew Augustus Atwater had a way of stretching the truth 'til it suited him, 'til it was no longer the truth at all.

She didn't know for sure if things would be exactly as he had written. She didn't know for sure if there was even a possibility of her getting a singing job. She didn't know for sure what kind of place he expected to put her up in. She didn't even know for sure if he really had a job. What she could be sure of was the realness of the bus ticket she had held in her hand. She finally had the ticket that would take her out of Coley's Corner to—somewhere, anywhere else.

Ophelia didn't waste any time making her way to the kitchen to tell Mrs. Bertha about what had just went on between her and Flossie Mae. "Mama, I declare, that young'un of yours gets so bent out of shape whenever you try to talk some sense into her. I don't know what you gonna do with her. I just wish she was a little bit younger. I would get me a hickory switch and sting those legs of hers a few good times. And she's about to be a sassy somebody too!" she complained.

Mrs. Bertha let Ophelia go on and on. She kept silent. There wasn't much time. She knew her youngest when she was after something. She knew just as sure as she had the ticket, she would get on the bus. There won't a whole heap more they could say or do to sway her.

Flossie Mae was more like her grandmother, Victoria DuPont than Mrs. Bertha ever cared to admit. The woman would poke her lips out, fold those arms of hers, and not move a lick, much like a little spoiled, pouting child. What she said didn't have to be right. She just wanted to be right. And she wanted others to act accordingly. It had made her no never mind if they didn't like it.

She ended up being a mean, old woman who spent most of her last days alone because she had convinced herself that everyone had wronged her, especially her son. With that in mind, whether she agreed or not, whether she liked it or not, Mrs. Bertha was determined to do things in the right way.

Every one of her chirren had left home through a door that swung on open hinges. And it was her intention to see

Flossie Mae leave in the very same manner, knowing that she always had a home to come back to.

Ever since he had been back in the city, Augustus Atwater had stayed at a Boarding House ran and owned by Miss Francine Black. She was a big woman who wore her head tied up in a rag most of the time. She had left the country for a life in the city more than twenty years before, but the country had never quite left her.

Although his rent was paid up until the middle of the following month, he felt it was only right to inform Miss Black that his wife would be coming soon.

"Wife! Oh no! My rule is, one person to a room. That's what you paying for! And that's all you paying for! Boy, don't none of this here come as no surprise to you! I told you 'fore you ever put a nickel in my hand!" Miss Francine fussed.

"Miss Francine, can't you just cut me a little slack—just this—just one time?" Augustus pleaded.

"No! Boy, I can't afford to cut you no slack. If I do it for one, the next thing I know, everybody will be expecting it! That man Downtown don't be cutting me no slack! Only thing he wants to hear is, the sound of me counting out his money," she continued to fuss.

"You see, Miss Francine, my wife is practically on the way. I got to have a decent place to put her up in when she gets here," he pleaded some more.

"You young fools make me sick!" Miss Francine began, pointing at Augustus as if she wanted him to have no doubt she was talking about him. "Y'all drag these young gals 'way from home, knowing you ain't got a pot or a window to your name. Tell you what, since your rent is already paid up until the middle of next month, that's how long I'll let you stay. You best get to looking for something so you can have a decent roof to put over that gal's head!"

"Thank you, Miss Francine. I really do appreciate this," Augustus said, flashing her one of his boyish grins.

"Honey, don't get it wrong! Knucklehead, I ain't doing you no favors! I'm doing it for some Mama's little gal who you done fooled up by promising her the whole world when you ain't got so much as a scoop of its' dirt for your own self. And I mean it! You got to find another place! Cause I told you up front, 'Singles only'. First comes the wife. Then, 'fore I know anything, up pops a bunch of crumb snatchers, running all over the place, making a lot of racket and breaking up my stuff. Oh NO! I ain't having it! Y'all got to go!"

Augustus walked away with his head down. It seemed as if every time he took one step forward, life pulled him back two. He thought, where was he going to find another better than decent place he could afford? He thought again, and then spoke out loud, "A place THEY could afford?" He had spoken it more to himself than anyone else, but Miss Francine obliged him with an answer.

"Well, you wanted to be a man and have yourself a wife and all. There's a whole heap more to this thing besides wearing the pants—ain't it Shugar? But, I ain't worried. You'll figure it out," she added.

Around the same time Augustus was in his room, beating his head against an invisible brick wall, Mrs. Bertha was set to have another talk with Flossie Mae. But, she had no intentions of talking just to hear herself talk. If she couldn't change her mind, she was gone at least give her something to take with her.

She called out to her daughter from the kitchen. Flossie Mae entered looking confused, impatient, and tired.

"Gal, I want you to sit down with me so I can talk to you 'bout a few things," Mrs. Bertha said, wiping her hands in her apron, before pulling a chair out for herself.

"Mama, I" Flossie Mae started.

"I know. You ain't done with your packing and all. Well, I ain't trying to change your mind no more Flossie Mae. I done come to terms with your leaving, but I still want you to hear me out. First, let me ask you one thing. Do you really plan on going all the way to the city just so you can sing in somebody's juke joint? Seem to me, if "That Boy" cared anything about you, he wouldn't want that kind of life for you," Mrs. Bertha began.

"Mama, it ain't no juke joint. Augustus cares about me and my dreams. All he's looking to do is get me a singing job. He said, 'When the right people hear me, I ain't got no choice except to strike it big, make records and everything. Then, I promise you Mama, I'm gonna send you and Papa money real regular. Maybe I'll even be able to buy you something much better than this, something with an inside toilet and running water. Mama, one day, maybe I can buy you one of those fanny washing machines I saw in the catalogues. You see Mama, I done included y'all in these dreams of mine too," Flossie Mae promised.

"Honey, you got a beautiful voice and a beautiful face to go 'long with it. That's your husband. I ain't trying to bad-mouth nobody. Regardless of the circumstances, he's the one you choose for yourself. But don't you think you looking to "That Boy" to offer you a whole heap of something for nothing in return? Child, mock my words, it ain't fixing to happen just like he say. There's something else attached to all of these promises of his, something he done neglected to tell you. One way or another, he done seen a whole heap of something in it for him. It's got to be more behind this here than the eye can see, the heart can feel, or the mind can think on. How can I believe any different when the two of you were willing to marry without having any real, true feelings for one another? You may not see it now, but you already got more working in your favor than many of us. The Lord, He done gifted you with your voice. He's using you to do His work. Child, can't you see how much your singing be moving folks?" Mrs. Bertha asked, attempting to move the conversation in the direction she wanted to go instead of the road her feelings were trying to take her on.

"Mama, I don't mean to be blaspheming. I feel like I'm being used all right. Sunday after Sunday, I stand up there in that choir box and sing. For what? Is it just so folks can stand and clap, pat their feet and shout? Am I up there singing just so they can have a little bit of joy, for a minute or two? Then, as soon as they step back through the church house doors, they step right back into their misery. Mama, many of those folk at the church house are just like me, no better off for it. Some are even worse off cause they don't even believe for their own selves what they standing and singing and shouting about. No sooner than the Service is over, they back to poor-mouthing again. Well, I want a heap more for myself than that!" Flossie Mae said.

"Gal, you ain't thinking straight right now. I know why you done started talking such foolish talk. "That Boy" done filled your head full of sweet talk and foolishness. In your eyes, have we done got too simple-minded to even know what we believe? Have you done started looking down your nose at us and the life you been living like we something worse than yesterday's trash? What is better than to be used by God? You were picked out to sing His songs. Now, you want to take the voice He gave you for His glory to go sing for the devil! Honey, I don't know of no other way to put it. Like it or not, folks in these parts done had it hard, real hard for a long time. For some, hard is the only way they have ever had it. Don't you think we would appreciate some of the easy times too? Just like the next man, don't you think we want to enjoy a little sunshine every now and then too? If we didn't have our faith to hold onto, we would be mighty pitiful for sure. I know how I done got this far. It won't nobody but the Lord! Flossie Mae, you got to learn some patience. Maybe it'll take you bumping your head and stumping your toes a few times 'fore you get any. You always want and expect things to happen right now. When they don't, you get yourself in a big hurry and run ahead of God and even yourself. That ain't no way to git to where you trying to git to. You been acting like everybody fighting against you, but ain't a soul fighting you right now but you. If it was in my power, I would give you everything you want for yourself. I can't. None of us are on our own time. God ain't on our time either. We are on His time. So sometimes, we just got to wait and trust him to make a way," Mrs. Bertha explained.

"Wait? Wait for what, Mama? It looks to me, folks 'round here done already wasted up way too much time waiting! Some are just waiting to be waiting. I doubt if they expecting anything to really come of it. They're just waiting because they ain't got no other choice. Well, they can keep waiting if they like, but I'm sick of waiting. I'm fixing to make something out of myself. I plan on being more than a cotton picker and a tater digger. I want more, Mama," Flossie Mae cried.

"Child, let me tell you one thing, we done the best we could. If this life ain't good enough for you and it appears it ain't—you'll just have to go on out and find your own way. Say what you will about us, but we ain't never lied, cheated, or stole from nobody to make it. Every crumb of bread that went into your mouth, every piece of clothes that covered your back and every dime we ever gave you to spend, we come by it honest. No matter how folks done us, we were able to sleep at night because we didn't wrong them in return. I know you sees things different. Howbeit, I don't see none of my waiting was ever in vain. And neither do I see my life as having been a waste. I birthed seven fine daughters into this world. I have loved every one of y'all as much as is possible for anybody to love. I view y'all as my treasures from God, treasures in the midst of a world heaping with misery. I never had a plenty to give y'all in the way of money and fancy things. Nonetheless, I tried to give y'all as much of myself as I could muster. And if it had taken everything in me, I would have gladly given that too. I gave y'all what little I had in the way of knowledge. I gave y'all what was in my heart to give. I tried to teach y'all the things mothers are supposed to teach their young'uns about life. I cradled y'all when you were sick. I cradled y'all when you were well. If y'all failed to get anything else from me, I always hoped you knew how much I loved you. Most of all, I tried to bring y'all up in the way of the Lord. I always knew, in spite of my best intentions, still, I was bound to fall short in some way or another. Lord knows, I ain't never been perfect, but I tried to do my best. I knew whatever came or went, the Lord was gonna always be with you. And I ain't got and I ain't never had nothing no better to offer to you than Him. Flossie Mae, it appears, all you done got from me is how much you don't want the kind of life I had to give you. Still, can't none of that stop me from loving you. You see, my love ain't based on a thing except love. You got to decide for your own self though. Whatever you decide to do and wherever you go, I pray the Lord be with you and guide you along the way. He loves you too. No matter what you might be thinking, child, the Lord loves you," Mrs. Bertha said.

"Mama, all I ever hear from you is, The Good Lord this and The Good Lord that! The Good Lord and how much He loves me! You know what I say to that? Seems like to me, He's good and gone 'way from here! Even He don't want to have nothing to do with this here place! And I can see that He loves me all right! Do He love to see me living in this misery too? You keep telling me to wait. How long am I supposed to wait on Somebody Who done forgot all about me? Look how long you been waiting and praying. Have things ever changed for you?" Flossie Mae dared to ask.

"That's more than enough Flossie Mae! I ain't fixing to sit here and listen to you talk about my Lord that a way. He might not be good enough for you no more, but mock my words, there's gone come a day when you will need the Lord. Can't none of us do nothing on our own and expect it to last or any good to ever come of it. For now, in your eyes, it may seem that the liar, the cheater, and the thief prospers more than the righteous. They don't. None of their gain will be for keeps, none of it . You can't hold onto nothing that you done did wickedness to get. Oh, they may live high and walk around with their chest puffed out and their noses turned up in the air for a while. By and by, one way or another, sooner or later, all of that is bound to change. Child, you can't climb high and stay there by looking down. I understand how you want something different for yourself and all. I ain't saying you wrong for it. All I'm asking you to do is to git it in your own head what it is you wanting 'fore you run out yonder into this mean, cold world, trying grab hold to it. If you don't know what you looking to find, how is anybody else supposed to know for you? And you'll find some out there who'll just be acting like they know better than you. Child, let me tell you one thing, there's folks out there who will trick you something terrible. They will say that they got your best interest at heart, but they won't. They will be out only for their own selves. They will grin at you and be as sweet as honey— today. If you ain't mighty careful—all of that sweetness will turn to bitterness—tomorrow. And they will willingly say to you whatever they think you wanting and needing to hear. Truth is, I had intended to try just one more time to see which a way your head is leaning. I see a lot clearer now. I see that me and your Papa got to let you go on. There ain't no other way," Mrs. Bertha acknowledged.

In spite of what Flossie Mae thought, her Mama was not putting her blessing upon her departure. Sure, she would be praying for her. However, she knew if her young'un had gone so far as to turn away from the Good Lord, the only one who could turn her back was Him.

She knew, sometimes, it takes a few hard knocks as well as a few bumps on our hard heads to make us realize, we can't make it by our own selves. We can't see far enough. We don't know enough. We can't overcome every snare or straighten no crooked places. And without the Lord, if we run into anything, we can rest assured that it met up with us for a reason. But sometimes, it takes time and trouble to make us come to ourselves.

There won't nothing more to do except to let her go on out there so she could find out things for her own self. Maybe everything will go just like she hoped they would. Then again, maybe they wouldn't. She wanted to leave an opening for her to come back through if things turned sour. She didn't have no confidence in "That Boy" or Flossie Mae's decision making, but she trusted in the Lord.

"Baby, there ain't a thing wrong with having dreams. As old as I am, I still got some dreams of my own. There's gonna come a day when your Papa and me can take it easy. He won't have to push and sweat all day long for a little bit of nothing. It appears to be a ways off, but I know it can come to past. One day, not too long ago, I dreamed about what it would be like to hold my first grandbaby in my arms. Now, I got me more grands than one lap can hold. I also had a few dreams that never came to light, but I never stopped hoping. I dreamed about your Grandma Victoria finally having something decent to say to me. Even after she had got old and feeble, she still went on something terrible just like I went and stole your Papa right out of his cradle. She never did accept our marriage nor did she ever attempt to. She could never bring herself to treat me like a daughter or anything close to one. In her eyes, I had no right to love your Papa and have him love me back. The biggest part of her dislike stemmed from me being a few shades darker than your Papa. I had no part in the hue of my skin. Child, looking down on folks can sure enough cause a heap of unnecessary misery. She did everything in her power to break your Papa and me apart. I never once said or done nothing out of the way to her in return. I treated her with nothing but kindness. Your Papa went to her more times than I got fingers and toes to count on. It never did a lick of good. That woman was more stubborn than that mule out there in the barn. It was never my intention to come between her and her son. She made things hard because she was only willing to have things go her way. I asked your Papa to leave things be, but he wouldn't hear of it. I figured she would come around in time. I'm glad I didn't sit 'round, holding my breath for it to happen. She chose the way she wanted to go and she stuck to it to her dying day. Mother Victoria had closed out everybody and acted as if she didn't need anybody. That old stubborn pride got in her way something awful. Her own son had to go through other folk just to help her. Though I knew that it won't none of my doing, I couldn't help but feel bad for her and your Papa. You see, your Grandma had rather give up her son than her stubbornness. If my way is the only way I'm willing to see to the extent that it might cause me one of my young'uns, then, that's a price I ain't willing to pay. Honey, believe me, I ain't trying to stand between you and "That—I mean your husband, go to him if that's what's in your heart. I hope every last one of your dreams come true. Mind you, if I had my way, I would keep you right here with me. If a baby bird is gonna ever learn how to fly, its got to git out yonder, away from the nest, and test its' wings. I love you, child. Now, go on back to your packing," Mrs. Bertha said, reaching out her arms to her daughter.

"I love you too, Mama," Flossie Mae said, holding onto her Mama as if she was afraid to let go. "I love you too."

Mrs. Bertha thought about how sad it is when folks chose to listen to outsiders, believing them before they listen to or believe family. Between Flossie Mae's dreams and "That Boy." her head was so full of mess, her ears couldn't hear nothing right now. Before long she would. Yes, she would.

But, until that day, she planned to stay on bended knee, her eyes lifted toward Heaven, with a prayer on her lips. Her child was no different. She needed the Lord too. She would see. One day, she would see. And it wouldn't take a month full of Sundays or forever either.

Lately, Augustus Atwater had been working harder than he had ever worked in his life. Mrs. Baker sure expected a lot out of him for the dollar and twenty-five cents an hour she was paying. He won't about to complain too much though. His pay was double the minimum hourly wage.

There was a lot of work to do to make the Club ready for business in two weeks. If she had told him up front that he would have to work like a mule, he doubted if he would have been there, lifting all of those heavy boxes.

"Mr. Atwater, bring those over here. No, you better put them over there on the bar. Be careful, those are glasses in there," Mrs. Baker said.

"Yes, ma'am," he said, straining under the weight. He knew full well what he was carrying. He had heard the clinking sound when he stumbled coming in from the back.

"How many more do we have out there to move?" She asked.

"There's three more large boxes and two small ones," he answered. However, he asked himself where the 'we' was coming from? She hadn't moved any boxes. But then again, he didn't really expect her to. She was the boss.

"I'm expecting a delivery this afternoon. When they get here, I need you to help them to put it in the kitchen. I believe this floor can come cleaner than this, don't you? We'll go over it again tomorrow. And the painters left some of their mess up in my office. That's got to go too," she commanded.

"Yes ma'am" was about all Augustus had the strength to say.

Ever since he started working for Mrs. Baker, after he returned to the Boarding House all he wanted to do was wash up and go to sleep. As good as he loved to eat, he had been almost too tired to chew. But he won't about to give up. At least, not before Mrs. Baker got a chance to hear Flossie Mae sing.

On his first payday, he began to see the bigger picture again. Mrs. Baker had paid him in cash.

She counted out seventy-five dollars to him. She threw in an extra five dollar tip just for him working so hard. That night, it seemed, he got energy out of nowhere. It sure felt good to have some money in his pockets again.

Flossie Mae didn't see any point in dragging out her days. She had a sinking feeling, if one more person came to her, she might not be strong enough to get on that bus. Every one of her sisters had tried to "talk some sense into her" as they had put it. In so many words, she had gotten the go ahead from her Mama and Papa. Yet, she knew that they would like nothing better than for her to change her mind, but she couldn't. She had heard everyone out. There won't nothing left to do except get on the bus and go.

She had sat on the front porch with her Papa for a while on Sunday evening. By him being a man of few words, she hadn't found it peculiar that the two of them were just sitting and watching. Then he asked, "Baby Girl, will you sing a little portion of the song you sang this morning?"

> *"He is the Rock of my salvation, the strength of my joy. He is the One I can call on morning, noon, or night. Jesus is the Comfort for my sorrows, a Shelter from the storm.*
> *And He is, Oh, He is the Lover of my soul. Oh—Jesus, Jesus! He is my Everything."*

Flossie Mae sang while her Papa patted his foot and shook his head in agreement.

"You know, every last one of those words is nothing

but the truth. No matter which a way you go, you can never go so far that He can't see you or hear you when you call out to Him. I done spent many a day out in the fields, plowing and thinking and praying. I ain't never been short of things to pray on. I told Him 'bout the big things. I told Him 'bout the little things too. Yeah, the Lord and me, we done had plenty of talks. Every day ain't been Sunday in my life. I done been blessed with plenty of them though, more than I ever deserved. I couldn't have asked for no better wife than the one He gave me. Then He turned 'round and gave me seven beautiful daughters. Child, I tell you, He overflowed my cup. When I look back over my life, I see His goodness. It has been through Him that I been able to make it through thus far. During those times when life tried to weigh me down, I looked to the Master. I know it was Him Who carried the heavy loads that I couldn't bear. And can't nobody ever tell me nothing no different either."

Mr. Frederick Douglass DuPont turned his head and started looking out toward the pasture. It was a sign to Flossie Mae that her Papa was done with his talking. Unlike her Mama, her Papa didn't and wouldn't tolerate her sassy mouth, not even for a minute. She knew it. So, she went back to just sitting and watching again too.

———⌗———

CHAPTER FIFTEEN

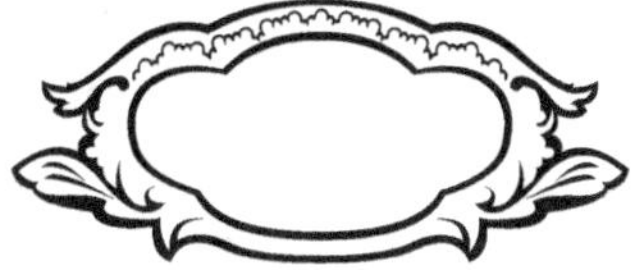

On Tuesday, Flossie Mae walked down to the General Store so she could call Augustus to tell him she would be leaving on Wednesday morning.

"He's not here," the woman on the other end said.

"Can I leave a message, please?" Flossie Mae asked, putting forth her best manners while trying to mask her irritation.

"Sure can," the woman answered.

"Will you please tell Augustus my bus leaves first thing in the morning?" Flossie Mae asked.

"And would you please tell him that I should get there 'fore dark, 'round six o'clock in the evening.

"You must be Flossie Mae, the wife he's been talking 'bout?" The woman asked, her disposition changing to a more pleasant sounding one.

"Yes ma'am, I am," she answered.

"Well, honey, I'm Miss Francine. I'll be sure to give him your message just as soon as he comes in the door," she promised.

"I sure do thank you, ma'am," Flossie Mae said.

"Shugar, just call me Francine. We'll have to get all of that straight when you get here," she said.

"Good-bye and I thank you again for your kindness," Flossie Mae said.

"Baby, you are quite welcome. I'm looking forward to meeting you," Miss Francine assured her.

After placing the telephone back on its cradle, Miss

Francine thought out loud, "She sounds like she's a sweet somebody, but that gal got to be 'bout as blind as that old alley cat out yonder. Or she is just another foolish, little, country gal who don't mind suffering underneath the weight of a mess of empty promises. What she sees in that nappy-headed, so-called husband of hers—I'll never know!"

Augustus reminded her of the worst mishap of her life which came in the long, tall and bow-legged form of the one and only Charles "Hucklebuck" Black. He had wrangled his way into her heart and fooled her 'way from home with a bunch of empty promises too. After he got her in a place where, besides him, she didn't have a soul to depend upon, he turned on her faster than a lizard can change colors.

She had learned early on, if she ever intended to have anything, she would have to be the one to get out yonder and work for it. All that Negro thought he was supposed to do was drink liquor and beat her upside the head.

She was a young, skinny thing way back then. She had no doubt, if she hadn't become tough, sooner or later, she would have seen her last day on this here earth. Every now and again, she had nightmares about taking one of Hucklebuck's beatings. She wanted to forget, but it seemed some nights were set on forcing her to remember. And remembering was why she didn't take no trash from no man! She had taken way too much already.

She made plans to keep an eye on Flossie Mae, at least, while they were staying at her place, and she had better not see no funny stuff either. She wouldn't want to have to snatch a knot in him that even the doctor wouldn't be able to git out.

First thing Wednesday morning, well before the cock

even crowed, Mrs. Bertha was up. She had done enough tossing and turning to last her. There won't nothing left to do except make sure her baby gal got sent off with a full belly and a piece of change in her pocket.

She had packed up a few other things for her to take too. Along with a Bible, she had gathered some preserves, a few jars of soup, the fancy laced hanky she kept wrapped up in the top drawer of her bureau, the hanky she had intended on giving Betty on her wedding day. But she still had time to work another one before their big day came. She had also scratched out a note and placed it next to the Twenty-Third Psalm:

Baby,
The Good Lord will never leave you nor will He ever forsake
you.
Love, Mama.

There was not much else left to say that hadn't already been said.

Mrs. Bertha had been lying in the bed wide awake for quite some time. She didn't see any use in ringing her hands or getting herself all tied up in knots. She didn't want to keep laying there and take a chance on disturbing her husband out of his sleep. Like always, he had a full day waiting on him. He needed every lick of rest he could manage.

Truth is, Mr. DuPont hadn't slept much either. He had laid awake, thinking and praying for quite a while—long before his Bertha got up. He had wanted to take her in his arms, hold her real tight, and assure her that this thing with their baby gal would turn all right. But he hadn't.

Sitting on the porch, Sunday evening, it had taken

everything he could muster not to get choked up in front of Flossie Mae. Except the Good Lord do it, he had no idea how he was gonna get through her leaving. It certainly would be one of the hardest things he ever had to do. It would be even harder than staying down there in the fields on the day she was born while his Bertha was up in the house having such a hard time. But much like that day, he knew it would also be even harder for his Bertha.

Flossie Mae and Betty hadn't slept much either. They had talked well over into the night. One thing was clear, both of their lives were soon to change. For the better—they hoped for entirely different reasons.

"Sis, from tomorrow and on, things will never ever be the same," Betty had declared.

"Tomorrow, when I get on that bus—there won't be no looking back!" Flossie Mae exclaimed, unaware of how her words deeply pained her sister.

"You better look back! I'm gonna stand there and wave at you 'til that old bus gets clean out of sight!" Betty said, pulling the bedcovers up over her head. "Good night, Sis. You better git some sleep."

"Good night, Sis," Flossie Mae said.

She had laid awake thinking. It occurred to her—she may not be running toward nothing better, maybe it was just something and somewhere different. In her rush to get away, she had almost lost sight of the love she had at home. Still, her heart or something way down on the inside of her belly was telling her to go.

There won't much talk at the breakfast table. With every word Mrs. Bertha tried to speak, she felt herself choking up.

She told herself that she would rather hush up than to give in to the hollering fit trying its best to ruin Flossie Mae's send off. She knew her Frederick won't having it much better. She could see it in his eyes.

Betty was beside herself, but she was trying hard not to be. She would not only be saying, "Good-bye" to her sister, but also her best friend. She knew that she would soon be moving into a new life of her own. Yet, even that wouldn't stop her from missing Flossie Mae something terrible.

Mr. DuPont put his daughter's bags in the back of his old truck. He had to drive her to the General Store which also served as a part-time Bus Depot, but he sure won't in no hurry to do it.

Mrs. Bertha sat by the door, looking out at her husband, and waiting for her daughters to come out of the back room. While she sat twisting the corner of her apron, praying for the strength to get through this day, her Frederick was standing by the truck, looking out 'cross the field, praying.

When Flossie Mae and Betty came out of the back room, Mrs. Bertha stood. Betty continued.

She slowly walked out of the door, down the front steps and stood next to her Papa, waiting. She took hold of his hand and leaned her head upon his shoulder, but neither spoke.

"Baby," Mrs. Bertha said, pressing a piece of money into Flossie Mae's hand, "you are a woman now. You got your own mind. Always have—I suspect, you always will. When you was just a little thing learning to walk, you would lose your grip sometimes. Your Papa or me or one of your sisters was always there to catch you or pick you up when you would fall. And Somebody still is. Your Papa and me love you enough to let you go. We'll just have to pray for you a little harder now. You'll be out of our reach, but none of us can ever go so far as to be out of His reach. There'll be things that we can't see no more. There will be some things that you won't see either, but He'll be seeing and hearing everything. So, we'll be careful to put you in His hands and ask Him to guide you along your way. Baby, we seldom get a notice when trouble is soon to be knocking on our door. You may meet some wolves and foxes out yonder, some things you ain't never come up against before. I pray that the Lord have mercy on you. And if out yonder gits too much for you, I pray that He leads you back home, home to where you belong."

Mrs. Bertha took a deep breath and asked, "Child, you got everything you need?"

"Yes, ma'am Mama, I got everything," Flossie Mae answered.

"Well, your Papa and Betty fixing to drive you to the station. I'm gonna say my good-byes right here. So, come and give your Mama a hug. Don't forget to write us. And Flossie Mae, if you ever need anything, don't be afraid to ask. Like always, if we got it, you got it. God be with you, Baby."

Mrs. Bertha patted her child on the back, let go, and walked toward the door. Flossie Mae walked out of the door, onto the porch, and down the front steps. She had her hand on the door handle of the truck before she dared herself to take another look at her Mama. The grief-stricken looks upon everyone's faces were similar to the faces of those at a funeral service.

As a mother, Mrs. Bertha doubted that her heart had ever been so wrenched. She stood in the door watching the truck drive up the road. She wept. She wept for herself, for Flossie Mae and the road ahead of her. She wept for her husband and the task ahead of him. And she wept for her daughters, especially Betty who was closest to Flossie Mae. This was indeed one of the saddest days of her life. Somehow, they had to get through it. They would get through it—with the help of the Lord.

As promised, Betty waved until the bus got out of sight. Mr. DuPont watched. His jaw was gripped tightly. He blinked steadily. He gripped onto the steering wheel until the veins in his hands bulged. As much as it pained him to see that bus drive away—he had to let his baby gal go.

CHAPTER SIXTEEN

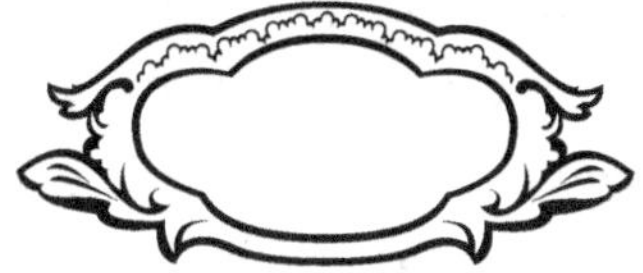

Flossie Mae had finally arrived in the City, Philadelphia, Pennsylvania. Up 'til now, the city had not been a place she could visualize. It was certainly bigger, busier, more crowded, and so very different from Coley's Corner.

She was tired. In spite of three previous stops, her legs were stiff. Her belly was empty. Yet, she was too nervous to eat. As she looked around and about, she saw folks moving along as if they were cattle being driven to pasture. But Augustus Atwater was nowhere in sight. She had already waited an hour or more. "Trifling" kept replaying over and over again in her mind. Where was he? The thought crossed her mind more than once that maybe he wasn't going to show up at all. And she wondered what she was supposed to do if he didn't?

She believed, some folks would like nothing better than for her to come right back home with no more to show for her troubles than the stub from a used up bus ticket. Mrs. Lucy was at the top of that list. She hadn't bothered about parting her lips, not even for a simple 'hello' since her nephew left.

She had already told herself, "If I have to make it on my own—so be it!" She didn't know how, but she was determined that she won't gonna be outdone by Augustus Atwater.

Augustus woke up around half past six. He scrambled to get his shoes on. He splashed cold water on his face. Then he hurried down the stairs. He was late. He hoped

Flossie Mae hadn't been waiting too long. If she had, he hoped that she would understand. Regardless, he had better be prepared. You could never figure a woman. If necessary, he would have his jaws packed full of humble pie.

"If need be, I'll eat the whole pie. For now, Flossie Mae is holding the winning hand—but only for now," he said aloud.

He had planned to just lay down for a minute or two, for a little nap. He had no intention of over sleeping. Lately, he had been working his tail off. La'Rue's Place was taking an awful lot out of him.

Howbeit, he was about to get some of that back. If he wasn't trying to stay in good with Mrs. Baker, there was no way and for no other reason would he be working like a slave.

Once in the station and after searching her out, Augustus ran over to Flossie Mae, grinning from ear to ear. He grinned as if it wiped out his lateness and her irritation.

"Hey, Baby," he said as he reached out to her.

Flossie Mae turned aside.

He could clearly see that she was about as mad as a hemmed up wasp. And he could feel the chill coming from her cold shoulder.

In spite of her disposition, he leaned forward in an attempt to kiss her.

She turned her head. His lips bearly had the opportunity to brush her cheek.

"As usual, I had to wait a long time," were the only words she uttered.

For several blocks, Flossie Mae walked alongside Augustus. He talked on and on like a man with something to hide. She kept silent. Being content, she gripped her jaw tightly, almost as tightly as she gripped the handles on her second-hand satchel containing her most personals.

"Baby, what you got in here? Rocks?" Augustus asked, sitting the suitcases down on the sidewalk.

Flossie Mae kept on walking though she had no idea how to get to the Boarding House or anywhere else in the city. She didn't even know how to get back to the bus station.

After receiving no answer, Augustus resorted to a survival skill he learned in his childhood, having conversations with himself, within himself. "I thought about hiring a taxi, but I lost most of my pay in the card game Saturday night. I can't even afford to buy a good laugh. I can really use one though; and before the laugh was over, I would probably run up a tab that I couldn't afford to pay. With my luck, the Howard Brothers would be the ones doing all the laughing. That is, if they ever laughed. They're better at making you cry, or play duck and run, beg for mercy, and promise whatever you believe will save your hide."

He looked up to see his wife several paces in front of him. He thought, "There's nothing like the strut of a mad woman." Then he laughed. "Look at her, switching up there just like she got a handle on things, including me. And the girl don't even know where she's going."

Augustus stopped in front of a large blue and white house. "Whew!" he said, glad for more reasons than one that they had finally arrived at their destination. "Shugar, we're home!" he called out to her. Flossie Mae turned and followed him up the walkway.

BLACK'S
BOARDING
HOUSE

Augustus sat the bags down on the front stoop and opened the door. He stepped aside and allowed her to go in first. He followed. She looked around. Suddenly, Augustus' words rang in her ears, "Shugar, we're home!"

They had not lived together as husband and wife for four months, actually never. For the few months they did, the knowledge that she could always go back home was ever present. Up 'til now, they had merely been playing house. They had never been alone. She had never been so far away from home. And she never had to follow after a man before, much less one as trifling as Augustus Atwater had proven himself to be. Nonetheless, he had gotten her out.

They were halfway between the front door and the staircase when Miss Francine came out of the kitchen. "How are you doing, Honey? My name is Francine Black. I'm sure your husband has not told you all about me," she said, half-jokingly.

Flossie Mae reached out her hand and introduced herself. "I'm pleased to meet you, ma'am. I'm Flossie Mae DuPont—I mean Atwater," she said.

"Shugar, I know you must be hot and tired. You done been on that devilish bus for what must've seemed like forever."

Flossie Mae smiled shyly and shook her head, "Yes."

"This here is your first trip 'way from home too, ain't it, honey?" Miss Francine asked.

Augustus inched closer to the stairs. He didn't want Miss Francine to talk Flossie Mae to death on her first night. And he certainly didn't want her to mention that they had to find somewhere else to live.

"After you get yourself together, come on back down. I got some sweet, iced tea. If you like it hot, I got that kind too. And if you ain't scared of ruining that figure of yours, I'll cut you a big, old hunk of homemade pound cake," Miss Francine said.

Augustus was halfway up the stairs. He wondered what Miss Francine was up to? Not one time had she been that nice to him.

Flossie Mae thanked Miss Francine for her kindness and followed Augustus. But, once up the stairs and in the room, she remained silent and kept her distance as much as possible in a thirteen by thirteen foot room.

She stood by the window, looking out onto the streets. There seemed to be more of everything in the City. There were more folks, more lights, more cars on the streets, streets instead of dirt roads, and more noise along with more places for Augustus to run off to whenever he took a notion.

But for a time, she wanted to keep her distance from Augustus though there was little chance of that. And it looked as if he insisted on talking to her whether she talked to him or not.

"Babe, I'm going to take you over to the Club to see Mrs. Baker tomorrow. She's real anxious to hear you sing."

No response.

"Honey, do you like the room? Miss Francine got a real nice place, doesn't she?" he asked.

Still, not a word. Instead, she folded her arms and walked over to the window on the other side of the room.

"How's your folks doing? How's Aunt Lucy?" he asked, hoping she would at least nod or grunt, or something.

"She had nothing to say. When she did—she would say it. But would he want to hear it? She doubted that!" she thought as she continued to stare out of the window.

"Gal, your ears stopped up with wax or something?" rested on the tip of Augustus' tongue. He dared not say it. Instead, he walked out of the room and to the end of the hallway. 'You young fools make me sick!' He remembered Miss Francine saying. He was not going to give her the satisfaction of an "I told you so" or anything close to it. So He turned and went back into the room with Flossie Mae in it, the room that seemed to be getting smaller and colder with each and every passing minute.

"Flossie Mae, Baby, I'm sorry! I'm sorry for everything! Is that what you want to hear? How long do you plan to act this way? We ain't laid eyes on one another for the better part of four months. When we do, you act just like I done turned to poison or something!"

"Oh, now, you sorry! You're sorry about everything!" she began, repeating Augustus words back to him. Exactly what is it that you're sorry about? Are you sorry that you done lied to me? Again! Sorry, you kept me waiting for four months? Are you sorry about me sitting in that bus station waiting on you? You knew, besides you, I don't know another living soul in this place! I can't even git from here to yonder without getting lost! Yet, you didn't concern yourself 'bout none of that! Tell me, are you sorry that I depended on you to be there like you said you would? Or are you just sorry just for the sake of being sorry? Do you think that's all its gonna take to smooth things over with me? Well, it ain't! I done had four long months 'way from you! If you really missed me as much as you claim, the least you could have done was meet me at the bus station on time. You came in there grinning like I had just stepped off the bus. I reckon you were expecting me to run and jump into your arms like some love sick, little puppy! But I won't and I didn't! And you best not be expecting that tonight or no time soon. Because of you, I done had to do a whole heap of growing up. So there ain't no need in wasting your time or mine trying to treat me like a young'un. If you sorry, that's well and good! Just don't expect you being sorry to get you no favors," she fussed.

Augustus was sorry. Only now, he was sorry he had sent Flossie Mae that bus ticket. He was sorry that he had took on a wife. He was sorry that he was shut up in the room with her and her mouth. And he was also sorry that he needed her to stay. Oh yeah, he was one good and sorry young man.

With Flossie Mae upstairs and Miss Francine downstairs, he felt worse than someone caught between a rock and a hard place. He felt as if the rock was sitting on top of him. But for a night, he would just have to bear it.

If Augustus or Flossie Mae had slept any closer to the edge of the bed, both would have hit the floor for sure.

"Here I am, lying in bed with a woman dressed in a flannel nightgown in the summer time. I might add, a woman who don't want no parts of me and won't even talk to me except to nag," he mumbled to himself.

"Here I am, in the city—just where I wanted to be. Here I am, laying in this bed with a fool! I'm living in the midst of strangers. And I already miss home," Flossie Mae thought.

"I'm taking this woman over to see Mrs. Baker. If she don't like her singing, I'm going to send her back home on the first bus going that way. What happened to the sweet, little country gal I left behind? Who is this sassy-mouthed woman? I've never seen her before!" Augustus grunted loudly.

"I ain't talking to him today, tomorrow or next week! He's fixing to pay! And he's gonna pay big! If he thinks I'm 'bout to up and leave, then he's got another think coming! I came to the city to stay and that's what I'm gonna do!" Flossie Mae moved even closer to the edge of the bed.

It reminded her of her childhood and the many stormy nights that occurred. Fearing the lightning bolts, the thunder clashes, the fierce winds, and the hard-driving rain that pounded upon their tin roof, she and her sisters would run to Ophelia's room and climb into bed. They would snuggle up to their eldest sister as if she were their ark of safety. Sometimes, in life, all you got is an edge to hang on to. And this appeared to be one of those times.

Somewhere in the midst of all of that thinking, night passed and morning came. Augustus got up earlier than usual to go to work. Flossie Mae continued to lie in bed, pretending to be asleep.

"I'll be back later on today to take you over to the Club," Augustus said, leaving without waiting for a reply. He knew she wasn't asleep. The girl had tossed and turned for half the night and then snored like a freight train for the other half.

Flossie Mae turned over. She took in her surroundings. She then pulled the bedcovers over her head and cried. This time, she didn't cry for Augustus making her wait. Instead, she cried for herself and the dreams she didn't want to give up on.

Miss Francine waited to hear Flossie Mae stirring around, but she never did. She could hardly wait to talk with her while Mr. Knucklehead was gone.

Flossie Mae lay in bed well past ten o'clock. In Mrs. Bertha's house, no such thing would ever take place unless you were sick. She took a deep breath and looked around the room again. This time, she was in a different frame of mind. "This is home? It's certainly not what I imagined," she said aloud, but quickly added, " Well, I reckon, it could've been much worse."

Bam! Bam! Bam! She was startled out of her daydreams by the loud knocks on the door. Then a voice she recognized spoke up. "Shugar, you all right in there? Are you all right?" Miss Francine asked.

Flossie Mae jumped to her feet, smoothed out her night clothes, and pulled up the bedcovers.

"Yes'am, I'm fine," she answered through the closed door.

"I was worried 'bout you, Honey. I hadn't heard you stirring 'round none this morning. I heard what you said. Nevertheless, I'll feel much better if I can see for my own self," Miss Francine said.

Flossie Mae cracked the door just enough for Miss Francine to peep at her. "I'm just fine, but I do thank you for asking," she said in an attempt to appease her landlady's concerns.

"Shugar, I don't mean to pry, but as you might not know, the walls in this old house is practically paper thin. I know that you and your fellow got into it last night. I just wanted to make sure nothing else passed between y'all except a few heated words. I know for myself, it don't take but a little bit of something for an already crazy fool to turn into an even bigger fool and go to whopping up on somebody."

"Ma'am, like I said before, I'm just fine. You needn't concern yourself with Augustus Atwater laying a hand on me, in that way. My Papa didn't whip up on me, and I ain't fixing to take nothing off him or no other man either!"

Flossie Mae said, trying to assure Miss Francine even further.

Miss Francine liked the girl's spirit. She knew Flossie Mae meant every word she had spoken. She reminded her of herself many years ago. Time and experience had taught her, at times, the hard way that your big dreams and ideas don't serve well on a platter full of smoke streams.

You can't trust or follow after somebody who ain't got nothing except puffs of smoke to offer to you. How in the world can they offer you any better when that's 'bout all they got for themselves? And her vision won't clouded one bit by that knuckleheaded boy's smoke. He was full of smooth talk, but he was too shifty-eyed for her liking. She didn't trust him no further than she could pick up the house and chunk It. She wondered if he had even bothered to mention to her that they had to find another place to stay? She doubted it. But she wouldn't mention it either. Not now.

"Child, if you ever need Miss Francine, be sure to call me. You hear? We womens don't have to be taking all kinds of mess offen these old mens. If that—if your man done brought you way up here, he best do right by you! And he will as long as I got anything to do with it," Miss Francine assured her.

Flossie Mae didn't bother with telling Miss Francine that she really didn't have nothing to do with what went on between her and Augustus last night, tomorrow, or next week. She just thanked her again for her concern. Then she made an excuse about having to get ready to meet her husband which was really the truth.

After she had closed the door, she laid back across the bed. She laughed at the notion of Augustus being her husband. At the time, she didn't see or feel like treating him as such. And she had no idea when those feelings would change.

Augustus came for Flossie Mae around four o'clock. She walked down the stairway behind him. In spite of it being close to ninety degrees outside, he felt a cold chill. It could have very well been a cold dagger. His wife's eyes seemed to pierce his flesh every time he caught her staring at him. He knew the chill he felt was due to the huge block of ice she carried on her shoulder.

He was all too aware of her game. However, it was beginning to interfere with his pleasure. If she expected him to come home every night, she had better award him for the favor. Forgive him or forget, he was not going to put up with her holding things over his head forever. As he use to hear his daddy telling his Mama, "Woman, you got two choices. You can forget about that or I can make you wish you had." And he was his daddy's son.

They were at the bottom of the stairwell when Miss Francine appeared. Since Flossie Mae's arrival, it had become her custom. "Where in the world y'all off to in all of this here heat? Honey, as hot as it is out yonder, don't let this knucklehead be dragging you all over creation," she said.

"Flossie Mae, we got to go. I'm supposed to have you there by five o'clock," Augustus said, choosing not to address Miss Francine at all.

"I declare, when they was giving out brains, looks to me some peoples must've been too late and had to leave with a head full of leftovers," Miss Francine said, not bothering to address anyone in particular. But they knew all too well who she was referring to.

Flossie Mae snickered.

Augustus rolled his eyes.

'If I was you, I would be mighty careful 'bout whose company I placed my wife in. She's mighty pretty. Boy, don't you think you the only one with a set of eyes and a mouthful of sweet talk and promises," Miss Francine warned.

Augustus took Flossie Mae by the arm.

She nudged him in his ribs.

Miss Francine couldn't help but notice. "I reckon I better let you two lovebirds go on 'bout y'all's business," she said, shaking her head.

⬥

CHAPTER SEVENTEEN

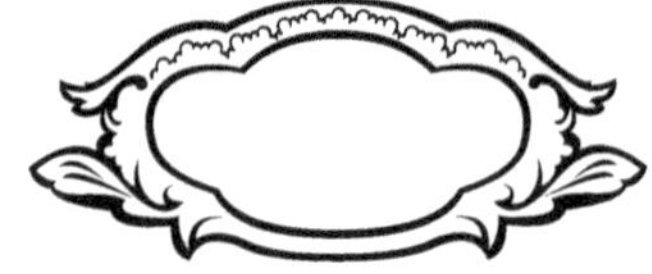

La'Rue's Place was about five blocks over. They walked in silence. Augustus kept a steady pace. Flossie Mae kept up.

The Club was not as Flossie Mae had imagined it and neither was Mrs. Baker. When she entered through the side door, she was holding a lite cigarette in one hand and a bottle of pop in the other. If she stood on her tip-toes, she would have probably been about the height of Ophelia's daughter, Emma, and that won't very tall at all.

"You must be Flossie Mae," Mrs. Baker said in a voice deeper than she had ever heard—coming from a woman.

"Yes ma'am," she replied.

"Well, Miss Flossie Mae, your husband has been telling me that you can sing. And I hope he's right, but like I told him, 'my time is too precious to waste. So, if you can't sing, I will let you know.' And if I don't think your kind of singing is right for my club, I'll let you know that too," Mrs. Baker said.

"Yes ma'am," was all Flossie Mae said. She saw no need to go into a song and dance about how well she could sing.

Augustus stood behind her, doing something with his bottom lip—chewing or biting it as if he was nervous or unsure about the outcome.

"Honey, you can go on up and stand on the stage. Have you ever sung before a crowd? You sure are quiet. You aren't the shy kind are you?" Mrs. Baker asked, glancing in Augustus' direction.

Flossie Mae climbed the few steps leading up to the

stage. She walked across the stage until she was about midway.

Mrs. Baker sat down at one of the front tables, crossed her legs, and took a long drag off her cigarette.

Augustus stood. His knees buckled as though they were going to let him down.

Flossie Mae opened her mouth. To all of them, it seemed as if time had stopped.

> *I cried—I cried. I cried a river of tears,*
> *I said, I cried—I cried. I cried a river of tears.*
> *Since my man been gone, I've been so sad and blue.*
>
> *He left me on a Monday, about half past ten.*
> *I said, he left me on a Monday, about half past ten.*
> *He came back on Wednesday.*
> *And now, He's gone again.*
>
> *I cried—I cried. I cried a river of tears.*
> *I said, I cried—I cried. I cried a river of tears.*
> *Since my man been gone, I've been so sad and blue.*
>
> *He told me that he won't—he won't be back no more.*
> *I said, he told me that he won't—he won't be back no more.*
> *Then he picked up his bags and walked out the door—*
> *I cried—I cried. I cried a river of tears.*
> *Oh—I cried—I cried. I cried a river of tears,*
> *Since that man been gone, I've been so sad and blue—*

Mrs. Baker put down her cigarette.

Augustus clapped.

Flossie Mae had sung like it was her last chance to sing. She had felt that thing all the way down to her toes. She could see it. They had felt it too.

Augustus came forward. "Mrs. Baker, I told you that my wife is a songbird, a natural-born songbird!"

Flossie Mae looked down at him. He was grinning like an opossum. Before, he was uneasy, acted as if he was full of doubt. But she never doubted herself. She was certain of one thing, she could sing.

"Singing like that, I would be a fool not to hire you!" Mrs. Baker exclaimed. "But Honey, this is a Supper Club. We dress a little different than what you got on there. What's that your Sunday-Go-To-Meeting dress?" Mrs. Baker asked, pointing to the soft pink and white, flowered print dress that Flossie Mae had made especially for this day.

"Ma'am, I was going to take my wife out, and buy her a few things this week, things more suited to the city," Augustus butted in, lying.

That was news to Flossie Mae. She was going to hold him to it though. But she wondered, "What kind of things?"

"You still do that, but I'll pick up a few pieces myself, a little extra bonus to you," Mrs. Baker said, winking her eye at Flossie Mae.

The truth of the matter was, LaRue Baker knew that she was going to make her money back ten times over and then some. Her act of kindness was nothing more than business, plain and simple. Country or no, this little gal sure could sing. Sort of reminded her of herself a while back. She wished.

"Shugar, you got the job. Opening night is next Wednesday. You can come in around six tomorrow evening to get acquainted with the band. You all can get together and feel your way around a few songs 'til you find yourselves a nice spot to land on. They are going to love you, Shugar. In the meantime, get yourself good and rested.

Opening night is going to be a long one."

In spite of the heat, Flossie Mae enjoyed the five block walk back to the Boarding House. After all, she was floating on clouds. The sun had dimmed its' light. The city's lights began to burn bright. She took in the view. In the darkness, the city appeared to be a place lite up by shining stars.

Augustus could not hide what he felt inside. All of his time had not been wasted. Finally, something good was going to come out of his plans. Soon, he would be living on easy street, living the kind of life he's always wanted for himself. Thanks to Flossie Mae and that voice of hers!

When they entered the Boarding House, Augustus hoped Miss Francine would show herself. He wanted to rub her nose in his good fortune. Much to his dismay, she didn't.

Miss Francine had promised herself that she was going to leave well enough alone before she had to swat that boy upside his nappy head a time or two. There was something about him, something that troubled her, something other than who he reminded her of. But she couldn't seem to put her finger on it; not yet.

Later that night while the City was anything but tired, Flossie Mae and Augustus went to bed. They started out in their usual way. She laid on the very edge of the right side of the bed. He unwillingly assumed the same position on the left side.

He accidently or coincidentally brushed his wife's leg. She didn't flinch this time as if she had just been touched by a red, hot coal. One thing lead to another. Shortly thereafter, Flossie Mae was being the woman he remembered her to be. Once again, she was a woman who found pleasure in his affections, a woman he thought to be quite selfish in seeking out her own pleasures.

Life sure seemed to be on the turn-around for the Atwaters. Flossie Mae was seeing her dreams come true right before her eyes. It was like somebody was handing them to her just for the asking. She was far from Coley's Corner. She was living in Philadelphia, the City. Before now, it had only been a dream with no name or face stamped upon it. Until now, it had just been somewhere other than Coley's Corner. And now, she had herself a singing job.

Augustus couldn't have been prouder of himself if you had paid him. He was taking full credit for everything that had happened thus far (at least all of the good). He had no intention of letting Flossie Mae forget that he was the one who got her the job. And if she continued to act as grateful as she had lately, he would be reminding her often.

Regardless of what Augustus thought, he had not gotten his wife anything. In fact, it was her singing, her looks, her figure and to a small extent, her country manner. Mrs. Baker being the kind of business woman that she was, was in the business of making money. And she recognized money when she saw it. And she saw money, lots of money when she heard that little country bumpkin sing.

Flossie Mae arrived at the Club a good twenty minutes early. Mrs. Baker entered from one of the side doors. She grinned one of her grins reserved for the people she really liked or the ones she felt could do something for her. Augustus had never gotten one of those grins, not even after Mrs. Baker heard Flossie Mae sing. She had several bags in her hand.

"Honey, I want you to come in the back. Usually, I'm a good judge of these things, but if something doesn't fit quite right, we'll get it adjusted," she said.

Augustus raised up from his seat. He wanted to see too.

"Hon, will you put those things up in my office for me?" She said, pointing at him, the packages, and then in the direction of her office."

"Boss or no boss, she is starting to get on my nerves!" Augustus told himself through gritted teeth. But for now, he had to look at her as part of the bigger picture. After all, she had the Club, the jobs, and the money. Soon he would have what he wanted too, his pockets full of m-o-n-e-y.

Mrs. Baker took the things from the bags and spread them out on the table in the back room. Flossie Mae's eyes began to shine like a child with a pocket full of quarters, turned loose in a dime store. She had never seen such lovely, store-bought things before.

Everything was brand-spanking new! Dresses with shiny things on them, undergarments, a couple of fancy hair clips, earbobs and necklaces, everything. Mrs. Baker hadn't forgotten anything!

"Shugar, I'm going to give you the address of the lady who does my hair. I told her that you would be coming. She's good. We need to show off that pretty hair. I'm going to step out for a minute. Try this little blue number on first," Mrs. Baker said, holding up a sequined dress. It was as blue as the sea. The bright, overhead light reflected against the sequins, causing them to twinkle like stars.

Flossie Mae put the dress on. There was no buttons or nothing like that to mess with. The dress wrapped around her hips sort of tight and tied on the side. It sure came down a whole heap lower than what she was use to wearing. For a moment, she imagined how her Mama would have fussed with it 'til it looked decent. She felt a twinge of homesickness, but shook it off as quickly as she could by focusing on the dress again. As Flossie Mae viewed herself in the mirror, she said to the imagine peering back at her, "This sho' is a pretty dress, but its' lacking something."

Mrs. Baker knocked. When she came into the room, one glance, and she felt disgusted on the inside, but she kept on grinning in hopes that it would not show on her face. "Honey, you got to put this on first," she said, holding an undergarment in her hand. "You probably have never seen a brassiere like this, have you?"

That fancy looking undergarment did things to Flossie Mae's bosoms that had never been done before. It not only lifted them, it also caused them to stand out further than they had ever stood. When she put the dress on again, it was more than filled out. There was nothing lacking, not one thing.

Flossie Mae walked out of the back room. She was trying to imagine herself walking on clouds. That was easier said than done in spike-heel shoes. Her bosoms were not the only things lifted up—so were her heels. They had never been lifted that high off the ground before. "There certainly was a heap of things to get use to in the City," she concluded.

Augustus' jaw dropped! When he laid eyes on Flossie Mae, he almost dropped the box he was carrying. A big whistle escaped from his lips. She looked good! He knew it. Mrs. Baker knew it. And he could tell that Flossie Mae knew it too.

While Flossie Mae was in the back room changing, she heard unfamiliar voices, unfamiliar men's voices. Suspecting that it might be the Band, she hurried. From the side door, she saw several men gathered on the stage. One sat at the piano. One was on the drums. One sat, rubbing his trumpet with a cloth. And the other man stood, holding up a contrabass. All of them looked her way, apparently waiting for her.

Mrs. Baker took Flossie Mae's hand and led her up on stage. "Fellows, I want you to meet our singer. This is Mrs. Flossie Mae Atwater." They bowed their heads politely. She smiled and then bowed her head, trying not to look too closely. She sometimes got shame-faced around strange menfolk. But she saw enough to see them looking in her direction as if they doubted her singing ability. She made up her mind that she would just have to prove them wrong.

Mrs. Baker took a seat at one of the front tables.

Augustus leaned against the bar.

Flossie Mae walked across the stage and took her place in front of the microphone. Everything was so new to her. And all of it seemed to be happening so fast. She could hardly wait to write Betty and tell her all about it.

"Okay Honey, show these old Doubting Thomases what you can do," Mrs. Baker said, fanning away the smoke from her cigarette.

"Miss Lady, you go ahead. We'll pick up and follow you, if we can," the piano player said.

Flossie Mae didn't feel moved to answer. She just stepped up to the microphone and sang.

"Oh, I found someone who loves me. I found someone who really cares—
"Oh, I found someone who loves me. I found someone who really cares—
And he makes my sun shine brighter with each passing day—

I tell you, my man, he really loves me. My man, he really cares—
I said, my man, he loves me.
My man, he really cares—
He keeps on loving me 'til my gray skies turn blue"

Then she began to sing softly and seductively, snapping her fingers.

> *"When my man comes home at night I wrap my arms around him*
> *and squeeze him real tight—*
> *Then, I turn down the lights—*
>
> *No matter what comes or goes—his love makes it right*
> *Cause he loves me with all of his might*
> *And, one thing I know, my man really loves me—*
> *And I really love him back—"*

The Band kept on playing. Flossie Mae swayed back and forth. She began to make sounds which to her, felt as if they were coming up from her heart, to her throat, and out of her mouth. They seemed to take on a life of their own. She had never done or felt anything like it before. She became lost in the music. She had stepped into a place far beyond herself, a place that understood her. She was in a place that belonged to her and she to it.

"Baby, do that number you did for me the other day. I liked that," Mrs. Baker said.
After doing, "A River of Tears." Flossie Mae and the Band rehearsed a few more songs. She could have stayed there all night—singing.

On one hand, she was a fast-maturing, confident young woman. On the other hand, Flossie Mae was still as vulnerable as an innocent, insecure child.

"Miss Lady, you sure surprised me. That's some voice you got there," the piano player said.

"It's sweeter than a hummingbird with a mouthful of honeysuckle blossoms," the bass player said.

Flossie Mae smiled. She never grew tired of folks complimenting her on her singing. She never grew tired at all.

Augustus walked up in time to hear part of the bass player's comment. He felt a twinge of something strange, something akin to jealousy. But it was also something that he could not and would not allow to get in his way.

He thought about the song she had sung, 'My Man Really Loves Me. And I Love Him Back.' "Touching." he mumbled. But since he was still himself, he still didn't love Flossie Mae in a way that a man is supposed to love his wife. He found it to be an unreasonable burden for jealousy to suddenly enter into the picture.

Furthermore, he viewed her more as an object in his possession rather than the object of his affections. She most definitely was not! No woman was. His one and only true love was and would always be m-o-n-e-y.

Mrs. Baker drove them as far as the corner of Eighth Street. They walked the remaining two blocks to the Boarding House. During the walk, Flossie Mae began to hum, "My Man Loves Me". As she thought about the words of the song, she realized that she and Augustus never had and probably never would have that kind of love. It was the kind of love that her Mama and Papa had. Theirs' was a kind of love that gave you joy on the inside even when the sun was scorching your head. Theirs' was a kind of love that still held up and held on when dirt was underneath your fingernails, when your hands had callouses, and when you are tired and your back ached. It was the kind of love that gave away more than it took.

For her and Augustus, their relationship was one step away from being a business deal rather than a real marriage. It was more like one hand washing the other. It was also a sad and empty life, a life consummated for the purpose of taking. But, for now, it was a life that would have to do. It was a life where she sang in a night club, wore fashionable, expensive, sparkling garments. Life had allowed her to step inside of her own dream. And she loved it. Yes, she was in love with her dream.

CHAPTER EIGHTEEN

As hoped, La'Rue's Place was jumping! Flossie Mae sang with the Band three nights a week. Folks came in to good music, the best pork chop and chicken sandwiches in town, strong drinks, and lots of attention from Mrs. Baker.

Mr. Walter Saunders was a regular patron of the Club. But he was much more than that. He was also part owner of La'Rue's Place. Whenever he came in, which was often, everyone seemed to take notice of him. He dressed sharper than any Negro Flossie Mae had ever laid eyes upon. More than once, she had told herself, "He struts in here just like he's the only rooster in a chicken coop full of hens". From the first time she saw him, she figured him to be, above all else, a man full of himself.

Mrs. Baker always gave him her personal attention. He always got one of those special grins of hers. It was the type of grin which generally meant that she really liked him or there was something she wanted or was already getting from him.

Mr. Saunders had his own special table. Mrs. Baker knew what he liked to drink, what he liked to hear, and seemed to oblige him at every turn. "Mr. Saunders, could I get you anything special?" Flossie Mae had overheard Mrs. Baker asking on more than one occasion.

She didn't want to go 'round prying, nevertheless, she wondered. One thing was plain as day—whoever he was— Mrs. Baker went out of her way to please him.

One evening, Mrs. Baker came into the back room that had been set aside for Flossie Mae's dressing room. "Honey, I know it's late and you have already sung your sets for tonight, but Mr. Saunders would like for you to sing that little number you sing about loving your man. I sure would appreciate it. I promise to make it worth your while," Mrs. Baker asked with a wink and a smile.

The same things that seemed to work in Flossie Mae's favor also seemed to work against her. Thereby, her singing ability, her good looks, as well as her love of attention began to be put to the test.

Mr. Saunders began to make a habit of requesting songs and then asking Flossie Mae to join him at his table after her set was over. Mrs. Baker had made it clear that she aimed to please him. And that also applied to everyone who worked for her.

Strangely, Augustus Atwater appeared to be overly pleased with all of the attention Mr. Saunders was paying to his wife. For him, nothing came before money. Absolutely nothing! No thing and no body! Not even a wife!

He had looked into some things. He had heard that Mr. Saunders had lots of money. Some, he came by the hard way. Some, he came by easy. The easy money was what impressed Augustus the most. He didn't need anyone else telling him or trying to show him how to work his fingers to the bones for nickels and dimes.

He was interested in green backs! Dead presidents! Big money! Lots of dollar bills! He didn't need nothing jingling in his pockets, keeping a bunch of fuss. He had keys for that. He wanted the kind of money that cushioned your backside, made you sit up higher and stand taller. And if Flossie Mae could get it out of Mr. Saunders, so be it.

Thereon, the more attention Mr. Saunders paid to Flossie Mae, the more Mrs. Baker and Augustus Atwater grinned though each of them had their own separate, in Augustus' case, desperate reasons for doing so.

Regardless of the reason, it only proved to stir up the anger in Flossie Mae. She saw, in spite of what Mrs. Baker might say out of the hearing of Mr. Saunders, she really didn't care about her. She only did what she did to make herself look good before him, to satisfy the source of her bread and butter.

If the truth be told, but unfortunately, it seldom was, La'Rue Baker did what she did, the way she did it, trying to save her own butt. Mr. Walter Saunders held the Deed to her Club. He had put in the "up front" money. He had pulled her out of the hog pen of despair and helped her to feel like somebody again. In short, she felt that she owed him big time though he hadn't, up 'til now, made any effort to collect on the imagined debt!

For over a decade, her name was one of the biggest names around. She had the ability to hit notes that others only dreamed about hitting. Back then, she was known as, "Sweet La'Rue Baker". And she lived the life to prove it, the kind of life she knew Flossie Mae yearned for.

Her old man, Teddy was her piano player. She had married Theodore Baker when she was nineteen years old and still fresh behind the ears. He was twenty-six and already wise to the ways of the world.

Teddy was quiet. At times, he was too quiet. He smiled a lot. And seemingly went along with everything that being in the life involved. They traveled to some of nearby cities, singing and playing the blues, having a good time along the way or so she thought.

Then it happened, the incident that she'd spent years trying to forget. One rainy night, they had just come home from an engagement. They had bearly gotten their feet in the door when Teddy broke! He snapped! He almost choked the life out of her. If it had not been for one of the neighbors, he would have.

One act—one night— one instance, destroyed years of hope, promise, and hard work. Her vocal cords were permanently damaged. She hadn't sung a decent note since. And couldn't. She was left with no explanation and a deep, raspy voice. La'Rue Baker hadn't seen hide or hair of Teddy since.

A few years back, Saunders came to see her. He started helping her to get back on her feet. She was more than ready and willing to try. She had known him way back when. There had never been anything between them except friendship, mostly he and Teddy's.

Though she never had an inkling of evidence to support it, in the back of her mind, she sometimes hoped even believed that Teddy was behind it all. Somehow, she and Teddy were a team again. But just as often, she told herself that she was being foolish. After all, Teddy was the one who had choked her, caused permanent injury to her voice, and changed her life forever.

Over time, La'Rue found that even being alone can become a mighty crowded place. She couldn't drink enough liquor to drown her kinds of sorrows. Besides, liquor didn't agree with her. It made her sick for days.

After he had done it, Teddy offered no explanation nor did she have time to ask for one. She had really loved that man. She had not loved like that since, and probably, never would again. So why had he gone nuts on her? She never understood. And wondering why had haunted her to no end.

Her life had become a vicious cycle. She sought answers. The answers didn't come. She hid. She drank. The more she sought, the more she drank, but neither was ever enough. Eventually, she had gotten sick and tired of being sick and tried. Then one day, Saunders knocked on her door. And the cycle shifted, offering her a new beginning. She gladly accepted and had been trying to stay out of the gutter ever since.

Though he never said, even in the dimness of the Club's lights, if she had to guess, there wasn't much difference in Mr. Saunders' and her Papa's age. Yet, they were as different as a mix-matched pair of shoes. Whenever she looked into his big, brown eyes or listened to him or saw him smile, she got warm all over, but put it on her nerves. But he still made her uneasy.

He talked to her about things that Flossie Mae had never heard of before. He described places that she couldn't even imagine ever seeing. To her, those places sounded as if they were a world and a lifetime away. He had certainly been around. Outside of her Papa, he was the most interesting man she had ever met.

Boosted by anger along with the hope of taking vengeance out on Augustus Atwater, Flossie Mae started receiving and returning Mr. Saunders' attention. Whenever he brushed her hand, she didn't move it away as she had done in the past. On those all too frequent occasions when his leg would accidently brush up against hers, she would pretend not to notice. Except, Augustus never showed the slightest sign of jealousy. His only reaction was one of jubilation which only served as fuel for Flossie Mae's anger.

Apparently, her husband suffered from a severe case of money-itis. Its' symptoms were bad vision (the inability to see past a dollar bill). He had a love of money like she had never seen, but was also misguided and lacking in knowledge, unskillful. When it came to money, he seemed to lose the few good senses he had. She soon saw that Augustus wrongfully placed his affections for and his loyalty to money and was willing to go to any lengths to obtain it. Above all else, he was prideful and foolish to boot. His claims of putting it to good use proved to be just another lie on a long list of lies.

However, Walter Saunders was not one to be knowingly used unless he saw some kind of benefit in it for him. He had seen how "Miss Bettye Devine" tended to cozy up to him whenever that husband of hers was around. He smelled something. And it wasn't just that cheap perfume she wore.

Frequently, Augustus left the Club early. He returned later to help close up and to walk Flossie Mae home. However, Mrs. Baker was keenly aware of his comings and goings. In fact, she encouraged it. Besides, he saw his time as too valuable to waste it hanging around, babysitting a wife he didn't really want. Howbeit, need and want was two entirely different things.

Augustus was gambling away their money like money was about to go out of style, like he had found the tree that it grew on. He didn't appear concerned in the least that he was losing their money faster than you can send water through a sifter. Along with his gambling habit, Augustus Atwater had not lost his appetite for the ladies. There just happened to be a pretty, bright-eyed gal who lived around the corner. He had grown real fond of her. She had that certain appeal that Flossie Mae had when he first laid eyes on her, an appeal that she no longer possessed.

For him, young gals or trouble seemed to meet him at every corner, sometimes, they came wrapped up in the same package. That was one thing he and Saunders had in common, they both had a pension for young, sweet, and tender gals.

Between his job at the Club, gambling and being stupid, Augustus didn't have time for much else, including Flossie Mae. Still, he had the part of her that he cherished the most, her money. But never let it be said that he didn't have a tender spot for her. Her singing money had brought her more than one piece of chocolate, more than one soda pop, and to the best of his recollection, a chicken sandwich or two. So what if the money didn't actually come out of his pocket.

Whenever guilt tried to attack the little bit of conscience he had left, he told himself that it was never about anything except money. Besides, Flossie Mae had gotten what she wanted. She had left home, escaped from the boondocks. She's singing. And she's getting plenty of attention. He considered his job to be done!

Of course, he wasn't about to leave her though, not yet anyway. If Saunders could keep her occupied, it would leave more time for him to spend doing what he wanted to do. It would also leave more time for him to focus on the part of her that he really desired—her money.

Flossie Mae and Augustus' time had run out at the Boarding House. Miss Francine, against her better judgment had extended their staying privileges more than a few times.

"I'm doing it for this gal's sake," she had told them.

With the things they had accumulated, their room was getting crowded anyhow. Augustus had searched for and found them a small apartment a couple of blocks over. It was decent enough, but nothing extra, nothing too fancy. Nonetheless, he was leaving because he was tired of Miss Francine poking her nose into his business.

She was one of the few women in his life who could see through his mess. She boldly and unapologetically told him so right to his face. "You ain't meaning that gal no good! Why don't you let her go on back home to her folks where she belongs? You ain't had a bit of business fooling her here! You ain't got a thing to offer her except a heap of hard-knocks and empty promises!"

Sometimes, Miss Francine talked to Augustus like she did because a small piece of her hoped that he would get mad enough to try something so she could knock him down and sit on him. But the most he ever did was roll those old, lying eyes of his and mumble underneath his breath.

For the first time since leaving home, Flossie Mae felt like she had a home. She made curtains for the windows. She cleaned. But she still didn't cook unless she just had to. And Augustus still didn't eat her cooking unless there was no way around it. The girl could even make water taste bad.

Though small, the apartment was a refuge from the Club and the world in general. She was often there alone, but she wasn't making no complaints about it.

However, before long, her refuge began to feel like a cage.

Flossie Mae was finished at the Club. Augustus was more than an hour late. Mr. Saunders was grinning at her. Again. She grinned back. She felt safe in flirting just a little. "Nothing will ever come of it anyhow," she told herself. At the end of the night, he always went his way and she went hers, except on this particular night.

Mrs. Baker was about to lock up. Augustus still hadn't shown up. Mr. Saunders offered her a ride home. She accepted. She wasn't about to walk home alone that late at night. Mrs. Baker lived on the opposite side of town. Sometimes, she would take them as far as Eighth Street.

He parked the car in front of the apartment building, immediately got out, went around to the passenger side and opened her door. "A gentleman always sees a lady in," he said.

Flossie Mae didn't think nothing of it. She was feeling a little woozy in the head. Tonight, her seltzer water had tasted differently. As best as she could recall, she had drank three or four.

He waited while she unlocked the door to her and Augustus' first floor apartment. "Before I go, let's make sure that old boggy man isn't hiding in there," Mr. Saunders said, teasingly.

"I'll be fine. And thanks for the ride," Flossie Mae said, swaying slightly.

"Any time, Shugar–it was my pleasure. If that man of yours don't appreciate you enough to see you home safely, there's plenty of men who will," he said, taking hold of her arm and putting his arm around her waist, in a supposedly attempt to steady her.

"Good night" was all Flossie Mae had to say to that.

As she turned to say it, Mr. Saunders took her in both of his arms and kissed her. Hard. She tried to catch her breath. She tried to move out of his reach, get away, go inside and lock the door behind her, but she couldn't. He kissed her again. This time, without meaning to, she kissed him back. To say that it had been a long time since she had been kissed like that wouldn't have even touched on the truth. Never would have been a more honest and accurate statement. All she was certain of was that her knees were wobbly and she couldn't think.

With one hand resting on the back of her head, his lips still pressed against hers, he opened the door with the other hand. Still kissing her, he slowly maneuvered her inside of the apartment. In her head, she heard herself saying, "No". Either her body was sending out another message or Mr. Saunders wasn't listening. He kissed her lips, her eyes, her earlobes, her neck. She tilted her head.

Flossie Mae became like putty in his hands. And now, he had his hands all over her. She had never known any man, except Augustus, her husband. Knowing that it wasn't right, she wanted to put a stop to it. She didn't love Augustus, but she never had any intentions of being unfaithful to him. She wished that it was him kissing her that way, but it wasn't.

She heard herself moaning. She felt herself responding to a man who had no rights to her. She felt herself giving herself to him. Afterwards, Mr. Saunders left. He had said something. What? She wasn't sure. Overcome by guilt and shame, she cried. She laid there, trying not to think about what had happened. However, the more she tried not to think, the more she thought.

She wondered. How could she bring herself to face Augustus? What if he had come home? How can she ever face Mrs. Baker or Walter Saunders again? How could she face herself? What kind of woman will they take her to be after this?

Flossie Mae got up, picked her clothes off the floor, clothes that were shorn from the tiny living room to the bedroom belonging to her and Augustus. And then she ran her a hot bath.

She eased down into the bathtub filled with steaming water. She scrubbed hard. She scrubbed as if by doing so would wash away what had taken place less than an hour before. She scrubbed as though she was punishing her skin for betraying her. She scrubbed, vowing that it would never, ever happen again.

Exactly when Augustus came home—she had no idea. She did know that it was well after five o'clock a.m. It had taken her that long to fall asleep.

The next evening, she walked into her dressing room at the Club to find flowers on the table.

"Thanks for allowing me to drive you home last night. Maybe, I can take you home again. Soon. I hope."

The card was not signed. Flossie Mae crumpled it and shoved it into her coat pocket. She just wanted to forget that last night ever happened. She hoped that Mr. Saunders would do the same. There would be no more rides home. There would be no more sitting at his table, grinning. There would be no more brushing of the hands or the legs against hers. As much as possible and whenever possible, she would stay her distance. What she had allowed to happen was wrong! It would never happen again!

She had bearly gotten the thought out of her mind when she heard someone say, "Shug, did you get my note? Do you like the flowers?" She turned to see Walter Saunders standing in the doorway, grinning while looking at her as if she was as naked as a jaybird. She wanted to run and hide. Flossie Mae didn't utter one word. She didn't even acknowledge his presence. She was ashamed of herself. And with him appearing to be so shameless—shamed her even the more.

"Well, honey, I understand. I just wanted you to know that the flowers are only the beginning. If you want something, anything—all you got to do is think of it and you got it," he said.

She still didn't respond. She dared herself to.

"I meant it when I said, 'Any time you need a ride, I will be more than glad to take you home'. See you later, Shugar," he said, finally leaving, closing the door behind him.

According to Flossie Mae's thinking, Mr. Saunders was being way too familiar with her. He had no business calling her, "Shugar" or "Honey". He had no business inviting himself into her dressing room. He had no business sending her flowers; and he certainly didn't have any business pushing his way into her life.

While another man persistently and purposely and skillfully inched his way into his wife's life, Augustus Atwater was far too busy being himself to notice or to really care. Things had gone a whole lot further than he knew or would have ever imagined. Sure, he knew that Mr. Saunders had offered to buy drinks for Flossie Mae or Miss Bettye Devine, but her drinks were no more than soda water. And that was not enough to make a gnat tipsy. He also knew that he had been eyeballing her worse than a child eyeballing a table full of cakes and pies. And he knew that Saunders had been tipping his wife pretty good for singing the songs he requested. Beyond that, he considered things to have been fairly innocent.

Perhaps, maybe, possibly, if he had slowed down long enough to even consider, things would not have progressed that quickly or gone so far. Augustus Atwater himself would have never gone so far out of his way to impress unless he was after something.

He figured, Flossie Mae was her Mama's daughter. She would be at home, waiting on him no matter what he did. If he had said it once, he'd said it a hundred times, "That's what those 'country gals' are raised up to do".

As time went on, Augustus Atwater showed up less. Mr. Saunders took Flossie Mae home more often. And she was falling for him though she knew she shouldn't. She wasn't sure whether it was love, but she knew that it was something. She knew that he was forbidden fruit, yet, she did not heed her up-bringing or her own warnings or anything that her senses told her. She just wanted to be held and to be told that she was beautiful and to be taken care of and treated like a woman. She just wanted to be loved.

In the beginning, Augustus had made her feel like a schoolgirl. Mr. Saunders made her feel like a woman. He was teaching her things about a man and a woman that she never imagined. Except, she wasn't his woman and he had no rights to the love they were stealing.

"Baby, with all that we have shared, don't you think it's about time to stop calling me, 'Mr. Saunders'?" he asked.

"Walter—Walter Saunders," she said. His name escaped her lips with a mixture of her homegrown, country and recently adopted, city accents mingling together like salt and sugar.

Flossie Mae began seeing more and more of Walter Saunders, but saw less and less of Augustus though they shared a marriage relationship, a tiny apartment, a job location, and a plan.

Unbeknownst to Flossie Mae, Augustus Atwater or Walter

Saunders, there was another crook about to be added to an already crooked stick.

The closer Flossie Mae got to Walter Saunders, the more attention he paid her. The more he grinned at her and called her, "Shugar" and "Honey," the more La'Rue Baker's heart sank. She had come to the realization that she was in love with him.

Until recently, she hadn't understood why she didn't like seeing him with other women. Perhaps, she thought if his attention was on other things, her gravy train would soon dry up. But, that wasn't it. She was on her feet now and doing well. She was sure of herself again. She believed that she could make it, that she was going to make it.

Some things come by habit. Some things come by chance. Some things come by force. Some things come only by truth. Some things come by invitation. Some things come by lessons learned and lessons taught. Some things come by love, peace, and joy. Some things come through trial and error.

Some things come by knocks, bumps and bruises. Some things come by choice. Some things just come. And some things come by circumstance. But some things will eventually turn and go in the opposite direction.

Maybe, it began many years ago in that tiny apartment on Mason Street. He used to hold her head in his hands and tell her things about herself that she never appreciated or had allowed herself to forget. He told her things that made her get up and at least try. He told her things that seemed to speak of someone else's life.

Depending on who you might ask, Flossie Mae grew up more in those few years, in the City than she had grown in almost two decades, living in Coley's Corner. Supposedly. Surely, she had seen and heard, learned and experienced many different kinds of things. But in some instances, more is less.

Some things come by habit. Some things come by chance. Some things come by force. Some things come only by truth. Some things come by invitation. Some things come by lessons learned and lessons taught. Some things come by love, peace, and joy. Some things come through trial and error. Some things come by knocks, bumps and bruises. Some things come by choice. Some things just come. And some things come by circumstance. But some things will eventually turn and go in the opposite direction, such as the likes of an Augustus Atwater and a Walter Saunders, regardless.

—◦◦◦—

CHAPTER NINETEEN

"Rue, Teddy, he told me that he was sorry about everything," Walter Saunders said.

"Sorry!" she retorted.

La'Rue Baker jerked as if she had been stung by Walter Saunders' words.

"He told me that he never meant to hurt you," he continued.

"Did he tell you why he did it? For the life of me, I have never been able to understand how he could have done that—to me—me of all people—me!" La'Rue Baker said, her voice breaking, yet, rising at the same time much like the singing voice she had been left with. Her pitch was now unsteady, raspy, and off key.

"I'd rather not say," he answered. Walter Saunders took in a deep breath. Then he wished that he had lied and said, "No".

"But I want to know! Don't you think that I have a right to know? After all, he ruined my life!" she persisted.

"Listen Rue, I don't want to hurt you," he said.

"Walter, I'm not leaving here until you tell me everything you know about that night!" she said, sitting down on the sofa and folding her arms in defiance.

He offered her a cigarette. She shook her head in refusal.

"Mind if I do?" he asked, his hands trembling as he attempted to lite up the cigarette.

She waited without answering. She could tell that he was in no hurry. And neither was she. She had waited years for an answer. Two or three more minutes wasn't going to make a whole lot of difference.

"Look La'Rue, let's just forget that tonight ever happened. Go home. Fix yourself a drink. Get a good night's rest. And try to forget about Teddy," Walter Saunders said, doubting that she would take him up on the Shuggestion.

She waited.

He sat on a stool at the bar, turned toward her and began, "Teddy had been complaining for months that you were treating him like your 'fetch and carry'. Sure, he was your piano player, but he was your husband first."

"But, I never meant to," La'Rue Baker began, but stopped in mid-sentence.

"As Teddy tried to explain, that wasn't what made him act the way he did," Walter Saunders said, searching for the words to help soften what Teddy had told him about that night.

"What then? I don't understand," she pleaded. "Rue, are you really sure that you want to hear this?" he asked.

"Man, I said, 'I did'! Now, quit stalling and tell me!" she demanded.

"That night, Teddy had seen Roman Clark hanging all over you in one of the back rooms. He said that he knew you were willing to do almost anything for a record contract, but you, standing there, allowing Roman to handle you like you were some two-dollar-a-night-street-walker was more than he could take.

La'Rue's reacted to Walters Saunders' account of that dreadful evening as if each word stung her to the very core of her being.

"He said that he had asked you on the way home whether you had seen Roman Clark that night? He said that you looked him right in the eye and lied to his face. He said that there was no excuse for what he had done, but something he couldn't understand or explain took over him. It was more than jealousy, more than ordinary anger, and more than his dislike for Roman Clark. La'Rue, Teddy loved you. He went along with what you wanted because of that love. He would have rather been at home, raising babies, and cozying up with you in front of a warm fire or the two of sparking a little fire of your own. He knew that Roman Clark was a no-good rascal who would say any and everything it took to get next to a pretty woman," Walter Saunders paused, took a long drag off his cigarette.

"But Teddy knew that I did everything I did for us! He knew that I loved him! I would have never— Wait a minute! He is not going to lay this at my feet!" La'Rue said, standing. "He is to blame for this! Every bit of it!" she exclaimed as she clutched the scarf around her neck.

"I don't know what really happened that night. But I do know it's time to move on. It's time to forget about Teddy. Rue, you are doing well now. You're back on your feet. The Club is doing well. You can't go anywhere on the Southside where the people don't know who you are. Isn't that what you've always wanted?" he asked. He was tired. And it was late.

La'Rue Baker was angry. She was hurt. She was also confused. She had come to Walter Saunders to confess her love for him. Instead, he had in so many words told her that he wanted no parts of it. She wanted to run, but then again, she wasn't a woman who took "no" that easily. She tried again. The second time, she used a different approach. She walked around the sofa and over to the bar. She rested her hand on Walter Saunders' thigh and slowly moved upward. He stopped her by holding onto her hand.

"Look La'Rue, why don't we just call it a night? I believe both of us have had enough. We don't want to do or say anything that we will regret in the morning," he said, sliding off the bar stool, still holding onto her hand.

"But why not give us a chance, Walt? We will be good for each other," she said, trying to look into his eyes.

He looked away.

"Girl, didn't you hear anything I said? Let's not make this any harder than it already is. I couldn't. I just couldn't. Besides, we have a fine business partnership. Let's not mess that up too," he said, leading her to the door.

"You black—!" she said, lifting her other hand in an attempt to slap him. "You no-good, stiff-necked, sorry excuse of a Negro!" What has she got that I don't have? Why would you rather have a girl when you could have a woman?" she ranted.

"It's time for you to go, Rue," he said, opening the door wide. La'Rue Baker left, but not without further insistence. And not before he felt like picking her up and sitting her out on the front stoop. Due process had worn itself out and overstayed its' welcome. He made a mental note to tell Flossie Mae to watch her back. Then he rethought the notion. Better yet, he would tell La'Rue Baker, in no uncertain terms, "If she bothered her in any way, she would have to deal with him."

Things had become strained around the Club. Walter Saunders continued to come in. He still sat at his favorite table. He was still served the best that the house had to offer. And he still made requests for Flossie Mae to sing his favorite songs. But, La'Rue Baker no longer treated him like the king he never was. Though she was cordial enough, still, she gave him what came mighty close to being the cold shoulder. And he wasn't the only one who had noticed.

Flossie Mae had noticed, but asked no questions. At first, she thought it may have just been her imagination. Nonetheless, the way La'Rue Baker had begun to treat her had nothing to do with business. She had gone so far as to tell her that Walter Saunders wasn't the only customer in the Club.

Apparently, Augustus Atwater was running short on money. He was unable to get his hands on Flossie Mae's money as easily as before. Therefore, he started spending more time than usual at the apartment. When he was there, he laid around like a bump on a log, sleeping and drinking and running that mouth of his. He acted as if she ought to be happy that he had decided to grace her with his presence.

Flossie Mae was fully aware that she wasn't entirely in the right or without fault and surely not without failures. Nevertheless, by this time, she wanted nothing more to do with him. She didn't love him. She didn't trust him. And she never would. But she had also had enough upbringing to know that the way she was living—was no way to live.

She couldn't rightly love one man while being married to another. Every time she looked at Augustus, she wished that he would just go on about his business. Despite her wishes and her expectations, he had no intentions of making things that easy or convenient for her. Besides, she was his business. Including her in the business of making him money was the sole purpose of him bringing her to

Philadelphia. And he intended to help her keep up her end of the bargain.

One Monday night, the Club was closed as usual. Augustus decided or as he had phrased it, "Woman, it's high time that you perform your wifely duties". He had been drinking all evening. And even if Flossie Mae had been inclined to fulfill his needs, the smell alone was enough to persuade her to do otherwise. He had been wallowing in his drunkenness all day like a blind, filthy skunk. His appearance alone spoke of a man who didn't care about himself, any one, or anything else.

Any and all of those things were more than enough to nudge her further into the opposite direction. She was willing to wash and iron his clothes, clean up behind him, cook when there was no way around it, make her own way, and share a dollar or two with him, mainly to keep him from stealing from her, but cuddling up to him—no.

"Come here, gal," he commanded in a drunken slur. "Come to Papa," he said as he reached out his trembling hand to her.

"Augustus, why don't you go to sleep? I don't feel like your mess tonight!" she shouted.

"Gal, you better get over here! You haven't gotten too good to give me a little Shugar, have you?" he questioned.

"I ain't fixing to give your drunk-self nothing!" she replied with a gone-all-the-way-back to the country attitude.

"I bet if I was Walter Saunders, you would rush right over here to give me anything I wanted. Wouldn't you?" he said, trying to stand up.

"Man, you need to stay put before you hit the floor," she said, trying to ignore what he had said.

"Yeah, I saw you. Don't think I haven't. I don't blame

you though. I done had my fun too. I got me a fine, little gal. I don't have to beg her for nothing. She don't have her nose stuck up in the air like she think she's better than me either," he confessed.

"Good for you! Why don't you go to her then? She sure can have you right along with all of your lies and broken promises," Flossie Mae yelled.

"I'm not going anywhere! If you want to leave— leave!" he yelled. Though his words were slurred, Flossie Mae had heard them loud and clear. They were probably the first words she'd heard come out of Augustus Atwater's mouth that could really be taken to heart.

"If you want to leave— leave!" echoed in her ear.

Augustus began to sway and wobble back and forth. He fell backwards, onto the sofa. In no time at all, he was snoring loudly. She stood, watching him for a moment. His chin rested on his chest. Drool spilled from his mouth like a toothless babe. If past times were any indication, he wouldn't wake up before morning.

Flossie Mae went into the bedroom, pulled out her suitcase, and forced as many of her clothes into it as she could. She then called a taxi to take her to the Boarding House. She couldn't spend another night with Augustus, but she did not want to go running into the arms of Walter Saunders either.

She walked slowly up the walkway. She dreaded what Miss Francine would say, but she kept walking anyway. She knocked on the door. The door-knocker seemed twice as loud as before.

She could hear Miss Francine as she made her way to the door. "Who in the world got the nerve to be knocking this time of night? Ain't a thing out this late except for hoot owls!"

She peeped out. Then she hurriedly opened the door. "Gal, what in the world? Git yourself on in here! Baby, what's the matter? Where's that old knuckle-headed boy?" Miss Francine asked without bothering to wait on a reply.

When Flossie Mae did open her mouth, no words came forth. Instead, tears began to pour as if they had been damned up and waiting for this moment for a very long time. Miss Francine held her until she had cried herself out.

"Baby, I got just the room for you," she said in a soft voice. It didn't sound like the voice Flossie Mae had grown accustomed to. "Shug, it's 'way from everybody. You can have some peace and quiet in yonder. Come on. I got your things. I keeps this room for my special folk," she said, opening the door. "Let me turn down this bed for you. Then I'm fixing to go on and git out the way so you can git your rest."

"Miss Francine, let me pay you for everything. Just tell me how much I owe you for the room," Flossie Mae said. With or without her husband, Flossie Mae wanted Miss Francine to know that she intended as well as insisted on paying her own way.

"Honey, there'll be plenty of time for that lessin' you fixing to skip out on me 'fore day," she said, patting Flossie Mae on the shoulder.

"No, ma'am," Flossie Mae answered slowly.

"Well then, let's take care of that later," she said, placed her hand on the door knob, and paused long enough to give Flossie Mae a good, head to toe glance. Then added, "Child, I best git myself out of here so you can git some rest."

Flossie Mae had lain across the bed, but then got up and changed into her sleeping clothes. After snuggling underneath the warm covers, she fell asleep sooner and more easily than she had expected to.

Miss Francine was up earlier than usual. She hadn't gotten much sleep. Still, she didn't see any sense in lying in a bed that had begun to feel like it had been stuffed full of rocks instead of duck's feathers.

During breakfast, her tenants got to enjoy an extra good meal. She had to busy her hands doing something. But what she really wanted to do was go out and find that sorry scoundrel and ring his doggone neck. Then, after Flossie Mae was well rested, she wanted to give her a good whipping.

"Don't make no kind of sense how these gals can't see no further than the end of their noses, following these rascals all over creation on a hope and a promise! Well, she done seed how far love done got her! Nowhere!" Miss Francine fussed as she mopped the kitchen floor. "It don't take but a little bit of sense to see, if a man ain't got nowhere to lay his own head, he ain't got nowhere for you to lay yours either. I could tell just by looking at that rascal that he won't worth the dusk that it took to make him. Fooling that gal 'way from home like he done. It wouldn't take much for me to…"

"Miss Francine, I got to step out for a little while. I'll be back before lunch," Flossie Mae interrupted.

"Gal, you fixing to leave 'way from here this morning 'fore you eat breakfast?" Miss Francine asked. "I put some aside for you."

"I'm not hungry," Flossie Mae answered.

"Let me tell you one thing," Miss Francine said, pointing her finger in Flossie Mae's direction, "on top of everything else, don't you mess 'round here and ruin your health over no sorry Negro. Child, I'm here to tell you that he ain't worth it."

"Yes ma'am, I'll try to eat when I get back," Flossie Mae said in hopes of appeasing Miss Francine.

"Child, don't think that you'll be doing me no favors. All I'm trying to do is help you. You can eat or not eat. One way or the other, it ain't fixing to put one bit of meat on these bones of mine. Cause, as you can see, I got more than a plenty. But, from what I can see, it don't look like you can afford to be losing none of yours," Miss Francine scolded.

"Miss Francine, I promise. I WILL eat when I come back," Flossie Mae said, reaching for the door knob.

She laughed as she walked down the stoop and onto the sidewalk. Miss Francine reminded her of her sister, Ophelia. She sure didn't believe in hedging 'round no bushes either. Like she had overheard Walter Saunders tell Mrs. La'Rue Baker while they were discussing business, "Shugar, I take my whiskey straight. I don't need nothing to chase it down. I'm man enough to take it. If I don't like something, I don't mind telling you. And I expect you to do the same."

With Miss Francine, it didn't seem to matter to her much whether somebody liked what she had to say or not. On the outside, she appeared to be a woman put together with long nails and sharp tacks. However, Flossie Mae had caught a glimpse of her other side. And it was as soft as a mother's bosoms.

CHAPTER TWENTY

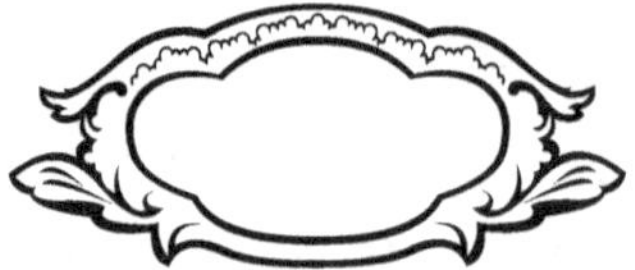

Flossie Mae unlocked the apartment door. Augustus Atwater was nowhere to be seen. She walked into the bedroom and began to gather her things and placed them neatly into the boxes she had gotten from the corner market.

She cried. Why? She didn't understand. She was leaving Augustus. The truth of the matter was, they had been apart forever. Yet, she was not leaving him for Walter. She was leaving for herself. She had allowed him to drag her down into the ditch with him. "What kind of man is he? He doesn't even care if his wife spends time with another man!" she heard herself asking out loud.

"He's the kind of man who is willing to do anything in order to make a dollar. That's all he ever cared about anyway," she heard herself answer.

"Well, he won't have to worry about spending mine no more!" she exclaimed, kicking the box much harder than she had intended. She sat on the bed and rubbed her toe. It throbbed. She looked around the room. From the curtains and throw pillows that she had stitched together with her own hands to the pictures on the wall, everything she had done trying to make the place feel like home. She had failed. They had failed.

"Truthfully, how can folks make a home when there ain't and never was any love in it?" she asked herself.

"From what I hear, they got places to put folks who go 'round talking to themselves," Augustus said. Flossie Mae jumped. She hadn't heard Augustus Atwater come in.

"What?" she asked, more than a little startled.

"I said, 'They got places to put folks who talk to themselves,' he repeated, grinning.

"You best go on and put your fool self in one then," she said, rolling her eyes at him.

"Gal, you are so sassy. I use to like that about you. As a matter of fact, it was one of the first things that caught my eye. But, it wasn't the only thing," Augustus said, walking toward Flossie Mae. She moved toward the door.

"Girl, why you gonna be like that? Why you don't want no parts of me? What have I done to you?" he asked, steadily and slowly moving closer, closing in on her like a cat upon its' prey.

Every step he made toward her wasn't just a feeble attempt at humor or flirtatiousness, but rather a calculated effort to taunt Flossie Mae to the fullest extent of his ability…

"If you don't know, I ain't fixing to waste my time telling you!" she answered, stepping backwards.

"All I ever tried to do is help you. Look at all I've done for you. Is this how you repay me? Do you plan to just run off on me to be with some other man?" he asked accusingly.

"Think whatever you like, but this has nothing to do with nobody except you and me. Augustus, you don't love me and you never did. But that's okay. I don't love you either. And I never will. You have done nothing but use me since I came here. You stole my money from me. You don't come home 'less you want something. You made me a heap of promises, but I don't see them coming to nothing. Sure, you bought me a bus ticket to the City. Yes, you're the one who told Mrs. Baker about me. Still, I had to do the rest. If I hadn't opened my mouth and sang worth something, she wouldn't have hired me, regardless of how many times you called me a, "Songbird." You know I'm telling the truth. So don't keep telling me about all the things you think you've done for me. Man, do you think I'm supposed to be beholden to you for the rest of my life?"

Augustus reached out and grabbed Flossie Mae's arm. He held onto it, squeezing hard. "You ain't going nowhere 'less I say so! You womenfolk are all alike! You think a man is supposed to see after your needs while you neglect his! My head was bad last night, but I'm able to stand on my own two feet today. Girl, you ain't about to get away from me that easy. You are my wife! And until I say different, you gonna keep right on being my wife. And I plan on getting all of my fringe benefits too."

Augustus began laughing like a lunatic.

Flossie Mae struggled to get away from his grip. He held her even tighter. She tried everything she knew, trying to loose herself. He was as strong as a raging bull. She could not get herself free.

"You might leave, but I'm gonna get what I want even if I got to take it!" he threatened, dragging her into the bedroom. He pushed her hard against the still made bed. He then pressed his body hard against hers.

"Augustus, please don't do this!" she cried, still trying with all her might to break free. His strength, his intentions, his control stifled her every effort. She felt imprisoned and increasingly enraged.

She did not know and neither did he, but he was well past the point of no return. He was not himself. How many times had he heard his own mother crying in the next room? How many times had he heard his daddy say that sometimes you got to show a woman who's the boss.

His daddy had told him more times than he was able to count, "Son, you can't let no woman run over you. If you do, you will regret it for the rest of your life. A man can do whatever he wants to do. A woman can do whatever her man tells her to do. If she gives you any lip, put her in her place."

Up 'til now, the women he had dealt with had had too much say so about how things were going to be. He aimed to put a stop to that—one way or another. For the time being, Flossie Mae was his meal ticket. And that's how he intended things to be until he said differently. He sure couldn't count on that job to meet his needs.

"After I finish my business, you're going to unpack those boxes and forget about going anywhere," he said as though saying it made it so.

Flossie Mae had no intentions of ever being with Augustus Atwater again. Her left hand became free. She pushed! She clawed! She hit! She did whatever was necessary, but none of it deterred him.

He pinned her down again.

She cried out the more.

He seemed to be getting some kind of sick pleasure out of her pleading. But no matter how much she pleaded, he had all intentions of being with her.

"All right, Augustus, you win. You don't have to take anything from me. I'm willing to give it to you. I'm still your wife. You got every right. But please, not like this," Flossie Mae relented as if she had become as prey in the lion's mouth, focused on its release.

"Girl, I knew you would start to see things my way," he said, pressing his thick lips over hers.

"But— let me make myself decent for you," she pleaded.

Flossie Mae went into the bathroom. Her only thought being, how in the world was she gonna git away from Augustus?

"Gal, how long is it going to take for you to shed those clothes?" he asked, trying to turn the door knob.

She glanced at the closed door. "I'll be out in a minute," she promised.

She checked the bathroom window. There was no way for her to squeeze herself through it. She had no way of escape except to go out the same way she had come in. But first, she would have to go through Augustus.

There was no doubt about it, she was frightened. She had seen something in his eyes that let her know that he meant business. One way or another, for whatever reason, he intended on being with her. And just as sure as she came out, he planned on doing just that.

When Flossie Mae came out of the bathroom, she was still fully dressed. The sight of her seemed to aggravate Augustus the more. "Are you trying to fool around with me, gal?" he asked. In comparison, his anger was as thick as her fear.

She didn't say anything.

Augustus moved toward her.

She saw that he had turned back the bedcovers.

He stood between her and the doorway.

She stood motionless, hoping once she quit fighting him, he would change his mind.

He grabbed her and pulled her close.

Flossie Mae trembled.

Augustus kissed her.

She did not, could not kiss him back.

Without warning, he picked her up and tossed her onto the bed like a sack of potatoes.

She no longer had any intention of fighting him, but she intended to leave just as soon as the nightmare ended.

She knew that anything she endured had nothing to do with desire, romance, or even lust. It was nothing less than a willful act of disrespect. It was nothing more than a man trying to prove to himself that he had power over a woman. Augustus was trying to put her in her place. And she would soon put him in his place too.

Augustus Atwater 'finished his business' with Flossie Mae.

He smirked.

She wanted to cry, to claw like an alley cat, but she was too numb to do either.

He began to talk to her worse than someone he had just picked up off the street. "On second thought, you can leave anytime you get ready. I don't have no more use for you," he said.

Flossie Mae said nothing. She could feel the rage building up in her. It seemed to be screaming. Nonetheless, she was speechless.

"Old man, Walter Saunders can have you now! I don't want you!" he continued.

She heard something or someone rearing up in her, urging or daring her to stand up and defend herself. Upon hearing Walter Saunders' name, guilt opened its door, trying to convince her that somehow this was all her fault. She covered herself with the bedlinens and hid her face in her hands and cried.

"You're not even worth the time it's going to take for me to teach you a lesson like you need to be taught," he said.

She didn't know what it was. She just picked up the first thing she could get her hands on and threw it with all her might, aiming straight for Augustus' head.

It hit its' target.

Blood gushed.

Augustus looked stunned, shocked.

Flossie Mae was frightened.

He became preoccupied with trying looking out for himself to bother her any further. The beer bottle he had left on the bedside table had been used as a weapon against him. The wound was not as bad as it appeared to be. For once, Augustus' hard head had served him well.

Flossie Mae gathered herself. Then she gathered her things. She moved as quickly as possible. She didn't know whether Augustus would be coming back. If he did, she had no intentions of waiting on him.

She was a mess. Her comb and hairbrush were at the Boarding House. She changed her dress and ran her fingers through her hair as best she could.

Flossie Mae couldn't take everything she wanted. She mostly took what she needed. She pushed the boxes outside. She thought it to be a shame that the time she had spent in the City thus far could be summed up in two boxes.

CHAPTER TWENTY ONE

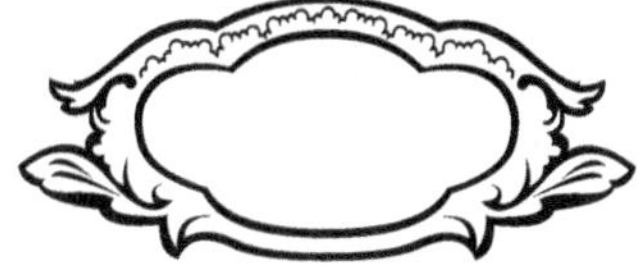

The taxi driver took the boxes out of the trunk and sat them on the sidewalk.

"Thank you," Flossie Mae said, wincing in pain as she reached to pay the driver.

"Thank you. Take care of yourself, Missy," he said, looking at her as if she were his long-lost daughter.

When she entered the Boarding House, Flossie Mae had hoped to get past Miss Francine, but no such thing happened.

"Lord, ha' mercy! Child, what done happened to you? You looking like something or other that the cats done drug home!" Miss Francine exclaimed. Flossie Mae's eyes began to fill with tears. Her lips trembled. She shook her head. She did not speak.

"Gal, tell me that you didn't go back over yonder by yourself! Did that crazy fool do this to you?" Miss Francine asked.

"I'm fine" was far from the truth, but it was all Flossie Mae managed to get out. She just wanted to go scrub herself until she forgot all about Augustus Atwater and every other man.

"Well, I can see with my own two good eyes that you ain't fine! You will be though! I got half a mind to go find that little piece of so-called man and show him a thing or two. I bet he'll think twice 'fore he even think about lifting his mangy hands to hurt another woman again!"

Flossie Mae could tell that Miss Francine was just picking up steam. She won't nowhere near the finish line.

"Miss Francine, I'll be all right. I just need to get these boxes in the room. I'm fine," she said, trying to manage a smile.

Gal, if you say, 'I'm fine' one more time, I might be forced to give you whipping. You can say it until the cows come home if you got a mind to. Honey, even if I had a sharp stick poked in one eye and a log poked in the other, I could still see that you are a long ways from being, 'fine'. And you won't be fine until some things get turned around for you," she said.

Miss Francine sat one of the boxes on the floor at the foot of the bed.

Flossie Mae wrestled with herself. She wanted to keep everything a secret. At the same time, she wanted to tell somebody. She looked out of the window. The folks walking down below looked so happy, so at peace, so free while she was all tied up in knots.

She believed that she was in love with Walter Saunders, yet, hated Augustus Atwater. She was living the life she had always wanted and miserable nonetheless. She wanted to run and hide. However, she also wanted to face up to what Augustus Atwater had done to her, what she had done to herself.

By the time the last box was in the room, Flossie Mae had mustered up enough nerve to talk to Miss Francine. She told her everything even those things that she had not been able to and could never write home and tell Betty about. She spoke of her love for Walter Saunders, the loss of her money, and Augustus' attack on her.

Miss Francine listened. She was silent, but she knew that she could not keep silent.

After Flossie Mae had run out of words and confessions, she sat with her head hung down. Miss Francine reached out and took her by the hand. It was now her turn to speak. Her words would not come easy. They would awaken painful memories which were only reminders of how quickly a life can go wrong.

"Shug, there are some things in life that can't be helped. And then, there are some things in this life that can't help themselves. Now, you take a tree, it can't do one thing when a dog takes a notion to hoist up its' leg to pee on it or use it as a scratching post. The dog don't mean the tree no harm. He just being a dog. The worms can't do one thing if a bird decides to swoop down and snap it up for supper. The worms do what they do. The birds do what they do. But, if that bird ain't mighty careful, its sure to end up in some cat's mouth as just another tasty meal. That's just the way those kinds of things go. Then, there's us. Now, there's a whole heap of things that we can't help neither. We can't help who bore us into this world. We can't help the color of our skin, not that I would want to. And we can't help it if we grows up to be four foot three or six feet eleven. What we can help is, allowing other folks to make a horse's hind parts out of us. Sure, they might try, but we ain't got to let or help them. If somebody takes it upon themselves to make a floor mat out of you, you ain't fixing to just lay there so they can walk on top of you. Are you? I didn't think so." Miss Francine answered, without bothering to wait on an answer from Flossie Mae. Nor was she really expecting one.

"Child, I'm sure you done heard this before, but I need to go ahead and say it again. Your head was made for more than sitting on your shoulders, looking pretty. You got to think. And you got to think way ahead of the other fellow or at least try to. Some things don't call for you to be nobody's genius. They be standing right before your eyes as plain as daylight. I know that I ain't your Mama. And I ain't trying to over-step my bounds. Baby, I ain't trying to come down hard on you, but I ain't trying to Shugar-coat this thing either. When you see somebody in the fire, you don't hand them a cookie, a soda pop, and a can of gasoline."

The thought of the outcome of that made Flossie Mae shiver a little.

"Don't git me wrong. I think that every one of us ought to want something out of life. Honey, those folks down yonder, at that Club ain't doing a thing except using you up. What you getting out of hanging 'round that Club half the night? I know they pay you a few dollars and you're able to buy yourself a few store-bought rags? But I got to believe that you came way up here for more than that. Eventually, they'll end up pulling you down. You knows that, don't you?"

Flossie Mae looked as though she was uncertain as to how she should answer if given the opportunity to answer.

"When I first laid eyes on you, you looked like a young school girl. In the short time that you been here, you done put on some age and you done shed a few pounds too. You didn't have none of those to lose. You won't much bigger than half a minute to start with. And that jack-legged, so-called, sorry excuse of a man you got ain't doing nothing except sifting you for every nickel and dime that he can get his filthy hands on. If you ain't mighty particular, he'll mess around and try to snatch everything you got 'way from you that he can get, including, your good name. But like I said before, 'I know I a'int you mama.' I tell you these things so you won't have to go through what I had to go through.

Now, there's a heap of things I could say about this Walter man you done told me about, but I won't. One thing I done learned for sure, the surest way to run a body into the arms of another body is to talk against them. But I will say this, if you intend to carry on with this fellow, I believe your troubles may be just getting cranked up."

"I don't," Flossie Mae began. She reasoned within herself that it was best if she just allow Miss Francine to have her say, not that she needed her permission.

"Honey, the more my folks talked about that man I got myself all tangled up with, the more I wanted to be with him. Then, when I had him, I didn't know what in the world to do with him. Like a plum, natural-born fool, I believed every word that came out of his mouth just like it was coming straight down from heaven. By the time he shredded his skin and I got to see the real him—the snake that he was—I didn't like what I saw. I was far away from home, didn't know nobody, and didn't have no sense. Cause if I did, I would have never left with him to start with. Folks got a habit of promising you the moon when they can't even give you so much as a grain of sand. I learned from it though. Believe me when I tell you, it was one of the hardest things I ever had to face. It's no easy thing to learn that somebody you supposed to be close to don't care no more for you than they do a bedbug. Child, no matter how bad the situation, there's always something that we can be taught by it. Even from a ditch bed, we can learn something about ourselves, life, and other folks. You see, life ain't picky 'bout who it picks on. So if we don't like waddling in the mud, we git on up from yonder, and clean ourselves up. And one thing this old woman done been taught is how to git up."

Flossie Mae continued to hold her head down. She

listened, but she would not look up at Miss Francine.

"Honey, you might as well hold your head up. You ain't the first one and you won't be the last one. Just between you and me, when I was your age, I didn't even know half as much as you do. I knew a whole heap 'bout washing and ironing and mopping floors, but I didn't know enough about life to fill up a hollow tooth. While I was home, mama and papa taught me all they could. They watched out for me, took care of me and all. Once I came face to face with the real world, I found out that things were a whole heap different out there than they were whiles living up underneath my folk's roof. We don't like hearing it, 'specially if we want to believe different, but most folks, most of the time, ain't looking out for your best interest. They be looking out for their own self. Child, I ain't one of those womens who don't have no use for a man, but these mens 'round here don't mean you no good. Honey, most of these mens looking for some gal simple-minded enough to believe that they got good sense. They after somebody who's gonna look up to them as if they're somebody's savior.

Flossie Mae smiled for the first time.

"But if we would ever allow our brains to think for us every once in a while, we could keep ourselves out of a whole heap of binds. There just ain't no telling us nothing when we think we in love." Miss Francine said.

She was tired of talking and had just about ran out of things to say. She could tell that all of her talking had bearly made a dent in Flossie Mae's thinking. She could just sit and hold her hand until she went off to sleep or something. She didn't need to be alone. She needed to know that she could do just fine and be even finer than that without being somebody's whipping post or floor mat.

"Shug, you might not believe it, but when I was your age, I was a tiny, little something. I didn't look half bad either, if I must say so myself. When that Negro I called myself marrying ended up leaving me, I didn't have no idea how I was gonna take care of myself. Talk about somebody scared. I found myself in the dark in more ways than one. Don't think I been talking just to hear myself talking either. I knows what it feels like to be tossed to and fro. I don't be telling this 'less I think it's gonna keep somebody from landing in the same ditch I had to crawl my way out of."

Flossie Mae listened in silence. She wondered what more Miss Francine could have to say?

"Child, after being freed from one fool, I messed 'round and got myself tangled up with an even bigger fool. His words were sweeter than honey dripping from the honey comb. They were everything I needed and wanted to hear except they didn't have a bit of truth nowhere about them. One thing went wrong after another. Without taking you all through the woods, trying to get to the forest—for six long years, I was one of those gals who do mens' favors for money. That was the hardest six years of my life. There won't one night that came or went that I didn't get sick or cry myself to sleep—when I could sleep. But one day, I got sick and tired of being sick and tired. I was more than ready to git myself up, out of that ditch. I promised myself, the Good Lord, my mama who didn't have no idea what was going on, and my papa who would have come and dragged me home by my ears that I wouldn't keep laying on my back, using myself up. I was fixing to git myself up and make something good come out of what I had done been through."

Flossie Mae tried to imagine Miss Francine as one of those "ladies of the evening." but couldn't. Nonetheless, it was her story. She doubted that she would make up a thing like that in an attempt to make her feel better. Then again, she had seen ladies come into the Club that men referred to as their "companion for the evening".

"Honey, you might not be laying on your back, giving mens' favors for a few dollars here and there, but just as sure as you born and keep allowing other folks to use you up, it'll mount up to the same thing. Folks will use you, if they can, if you let them. And when they gits tired of you, they 'll throw you out on the trash heap as quick or quicker than last week's garbage. I knows I done 'bout talked your head plum off. Child, don't think I'm gitting no kind of pleasure out of having to say this. I try to keep the past dead and buried. Just the same, I figured if it can help you, I can stand to drag those dry bones out one more time. The very same things I'm telling you today, somebody had to tell them to me yesterday. I didn't like hearing them probably no more or a lot less than you do right now. Still, I needed to hear them, for my own sake. Shug, everybody won't stand up in their truth or take up time telling you the truth. Some folks could care less whether you make it or not. And some folks will laugh at you and help to kick dirt in your face when they see you down and out. Then when you kick the bucket, they will come to your funeral service just to make sure you dead. Except for the Lord, nobody can love you

better than you can love yourself.

"A little, old woman named Miss Addie taught me that. She was the one who helped to pull me up out of the ditch that I was in. She was a peculiar acting woman. From the outside, she looked like the sweet, grandma type—if you rubbed her the wrong way—she would give you a run for your money. Miss Addie cussed worse than ten drunken sailors. But, she helped me just the same. If it won't for her, I don't know if I would have had the courage or the good sense to see that I was worth something, something far more valuable than what I was putting myself through. She would say, 'Honey, we can allow our troubles to shape us or break us down, but you are not your troubles. And as long as you governing yourself according to what you standing in, it's gonna mess around and swallow you up. Your mind and your heart got to start singing something other than, 'Poor, old me'. Cause if you sitting 'round here expecting trouble to turn you a loose, you'll be waiting 'til hell freezes over.'

"Miss Addie ran a boarding house over on the east side. She gave me a job doing the house-keeping. Now, keeping up a house is something I knew how to do real good. My mama taught me that. I knew how to work hard too. I learned that from my papa out in those 'bacca fields. I learned a lot from Miss Addie. The rest, life taught me, but mostly, the hard way. She took me under her wings and showed me how to run a boarding house. She paid me ten dollars a week plus room and board. Out of that ten, she taught me how to put a few dollars away every week. She would say, 'Gal, if you ever intend to have anything, you got to learn how to hold onto a dollar.'

"Sometimes, Miss Addie kept at me so much, I felt like my ears were gonna fall clean off, but I listened anyhow. Never did get sassy with her. She was trying her best to help me. But, I tell you, Miss Addie was something else," Miss Francine said.

She laughed, but Flossie Mae saw that her eyes were filling up with tears. "I best git on out of here and let you git yourself together. I know I done 'bout talked your ears off. But I don't believe a bit of it have been wasted on you. I know the day will come when you'll have to pass on something in order to help somebody else. Miss Addie use to say, 'Child, you ain't going through this just for your own self. One day, you will come across somebody that'll need your wisdom to help them to make it through.'

"Child, if there ever was a 'somebody', I believe, you got to be the one. And just as sure as the wheels of life keep on turning, I know the day will come when you'll past on something to help somebody else too. Just as sure as we need air to breath, if we keep living, we'll have to make it over a rock or two. Sometimes, we may have to duck a few. We may have to crawl out from under a couple of them too. But, I think—the worse thang we can do to ourselves is to wallow 'round in self-pity. I know, with the help of the Lord, we gonna make it anyhow. Ain't we, shug? "

Flossie Mae could hear it as plain as day—as if her mama had just came in and stood up in the room with her. 'We're gonna make it anyhow, with the help of the Lord.' That's what she always said whenever things got real heavy or real rough.

She hurried up and put it all out of her mind. She didn't have time to be thinking about nothing except getting ready to go to the Club. Like her mama, Miss Francine had a whole heap to say when she took a notion to say something. However, she didn't see how she was letting other folks use her when she was the one getting up on that stage singing. And she was getting paid good money to do it. After all, that's the reason she had come to the City.

—◦—

CHAPTER TWENTY TWO

Augustus Atwater failed to show up for work. Mrs. Baker went on and on half the night about how she was in a bind. She had looked at Flossie Mae real strange when she told her that she didn't have no idea where he was. And she didn't. But there was nothing strange about that. The only time she could be sure of where he was, was when she had him in full view. Even then, it's possible to be visible and still not be present. She believed that she could write a book on that.

Walter Saunders came into her dressing room. She was fixing her hair. He bent over and kissed her neck. She did not do as usual, turn around so he could plant a quick one on her lips.

"Hey Baby, what's wrong?" he asked.

"Nothing," she answered, without looking in his direction.

"No. It's more than nothing. I know you," he said. It aggravated Flossie Mae when folks went around supposing that they knew her. Still, she didn't offer him any further explanation.

He took her by the hands and pulled her to her feet. "Baby, what's wrong?" he asked again.

Sometimes, it got on Walter Saunders nerves when he had to coax her into telling him something. At other times, he liked it when she pouted like a spoiled child because he got the chance to make her feel better.

However, she intended for this not to be one of those times. She would see to that. "Well, if you must know, it's female troubles. That's all," she claimed.

"Oh, that!" he said, full of disappointment as well as relief. He knew that 'that' would put a definite halt to any plans he may have had for later. Nonetheless, he was glad Rue hadn't said or done anything to offend her.

It wasn't the first time Flossie Mae had blamed her mood on female troubles. She doubted if it would be the last. She told herself, in a sense, she hadn't lied. She was having female troubles, just not *that* kind. Nor had it escaped her how quickly he had let go of her hands.

She and Walter Saunders seemed to spend the biggest part of their time together, hidden behind closed doors. Sure, he was always telling her how much he loved her. And he gave her lots of things, flowers, cards, clothes, and such. She knew that their *love* had to be carried on in secret due to the fact that she was a married woman. She also knew that neither of them had any rights to that love.

Flossie Mae had determined in her mind that things would be different. She wanted him to take her out in the open. She wanted to do more than lay on her back for somebody who would be gone before daylight. If he really wanted her like he said he did—he would have to *really* show her.

She had done a heap of thinking in the space of a few hours. Won't nobody gonna use her up and then throw her out on no trash heap like yesterday's garbage! Not even Walter Saunders!

In spite of everything going on inside as well as outside of her, Flossie Mae managed. On stage, she was able to push it aside, at least for a little while. As usual, her singing was the only thing that really satisfied her. It gave her comfort, allowed her to be herself and go beyond herself to a place that was sweet like her sister Betty and divine like all of that goodness her Mama talked about so much. As far as she could see, for her, singing was like being born again and again and again.

When she was on stage, she was Miss Bettye Devine. Up there, folks could call her whoever they liked, but she knew who she was. Off stage, she only had a good idea of who she wanted to be. It was like living two separate lives.

"In the cool of the night—
The breeze blew through my window.
In the cool of the night—
The breeze blew through my window.
But you came to me and made everything all right.

You warmed me up with your good loving—
You took the chill away.
I said, you warmed me up with your good loving—
You took the chill away.

It might be thirty-eight degrees outside—
But in here—
It's got to be one hundred and eight." She sang.

She looked over at Walter Saunders. He grinned worse than a hound dog that had just caught its' first rabbit. Most likely, he thought, it was her way of apologizing to him for giving him the cold shoulder earlier. He could think whatever he liked, but the song won't about him or no other man. It was just a song. She had noticed how quickly he had backed away when she told him that she had female troubles. He had acted as if she had suddenly turned into something poison . Nevertheless, two could play that game.

La'Rue Baker was standing by the bar. She glanced over at Walter Saunders. She then glared in Flossie Mae's direction. She rolled her eyes and went up to her office.

Augustus Atwater stopped reporting for work at the Club altogether. Flossie Mae didn't know what had become of him, if anything. Sadly, she didn't much care. Besides, him not showing up suited her just fine. And if he was missed by anyone else, you sure couldn't tell it.

La'Rue Baker seemed more than pleased to replace him.

"Sonny" as everybody took to calling him appeared to take the boss' ways in stride. He was real quiet, took in a lot. Flossie Mae doubted if he was even as old as she was, but he acted more mature than half the folk she knew. He didn't drink. He didn't smoke. He just worked there to make some money to help his mama out with his brothers and sisters.

Some of the menfolk around the Club tried to give him a hard time, but he took that in stride too. As far as she could see, the man came to do a job. When it was done, he got his jacket from the back room and went home. That is, up 'til he took a notion to start poking his nose into her *affairs*.

"Ma'am, I don't mean to be poking my nose in your business, but if I had seen you in some other place, I would have figured you to be a school teacher or somebody like that," he had said one night.

"Why would you figure a thing like that?" Flossie Mae asked, curious, yet sort of flattered.

"I don't know ma'am. You just don't look like you belong in a place like this," he answered, looking at her as if he knew something about her.

"Well, you are right about one thing, you don't know. And I would thank you to keep your nose out of my business!" she said, strutting off in a huff.

On one hand, Emmanuel "Sonny" Putton thought Flossie Mae would be pleased and highly flattered by his compliment. On the other hand, her anger sort of tickled him, especially when he thought about Mrs. Graystone, one of his grade school teachers. She was nice, but she was also about as plain as an unused cotton ball. But, that was not what he had meant, not at all.

On another night, Flossie Mae saw him leaning on the broom, eyeballing her like he was trying to figure something else out.

"What in the world? What you looking at?" she asked.

"I ain't looking at nothing!" he answered.

"You best be getting that floor swept before Mrs. Baker come in here and catch you loafing around," she said.

"I ain't scared of her. Besides, I do the job she hired me to do. Everybody can't say that," he said.

"You sure do have a lot to say about other folk's business, don't you?" she asked.

"Not really. I can't help what my eyes see. If folks don't want me to see, they ought to close the door," he said, putting his hands into his pockets.

"Folks like who?" she asked, not sure she really wanted to hear the answer. However, she was sure of two things, Mr. Putton had seen something. And he was getting on her nerves.

"I rather not say, but there sure is plenty to see. As long as I work around here, I don't ever have to spend no money at the picture show," he said.

Flossie Mae liked and disliked Emmanuel Putton at the same time. Still, couldn't he have found somebody else's nerves to pluck? He was always watching and figuring and poking his nose into other folk's business. She couldn't help but wonder what he knew? And what he had seen?

Though she tried to avoid him like the plague, he always seemed to find his way to where she was before the night was over. If she hadn't known any better, she would have thought that he was smitten with her. Except, a man who is trying to win your affections don't usually say things to a woman that might cause him to get smacked all the way to kingdom come.

"Is old man Saunders really your boyfriend? Or are you just fooling around with him because you don't know any better"? he asked.

Flossie Mae was mad enough to swear. She had learned plenty of cuss words since she had been singing at the Club. She hadn't taken up the habit because she didn't want to. The time or two that she had tried, Augustus had laughed at her. Besides, she had sounded foolish even to herself. She had better ways to get her point across other than making herself look foolish.

"What did you just say?" she asked, glaring at him so hard it's a wonder she hadn't burned a hole in his clothes.

"I asked you if old man Saunders was your boyfriend? Or if you are just fooling around with him because you don't know no better?' he repeated, ignoring her glare.

"Boy, you sho' nuff got a lot of gall! You best stay out of my doggone business 'fore you wish you had!" Flossie Mae fussed.

"I was just wondering why such a pretty lady like you wouldn't be taken with fellows your own age?" he said, unruffled and as if she hadn't said a word.

"There you go again—meddling! I done seen some nosy folks in my day, but I believe you take the cake," she continued to fuss.

"My grandma used to tell my sisters to watch out for the rooster that struts before all the hens. Cause ain't a one of them gonna ever be but so special to him. He's more concerned with his own self. He just want a post to roost on," he said, walking away.

"And while they were at it, somebody should have told you that your nose was meant for smelling and not for poking!"

That was the beginning, the nature of, and the extent of Flossie Mae and Emmanuel Putton's relationship. He tried to steer her into places she didn't want to go and point out things she wasn't ready to see. She sassed him. At the end of the night, they gladly went their separate ways.

Walter Saunders continued to keep company with Flossie Mae. He still loved her, but for him, some of the fun had seeped out of the relationship. For such a young woman, she had become so serious about everything.

He didn't know what she expected out of him anymore. Hadn't he shown her how much he loved her? Hadn't he told her over and over again? Why did she think he was showering her with all of those flowers and gifts? There seemed to be no way to please the girl anymore.

For him, things meant love and love meant things, lots of things. Appearances meant more than actualities. Now, it appeared, she was trying to hold him down to all of those promises he had made to her in the heat of passion. At the time, he had meant every one of them.

Flossie Mae reminded him of Lillie, her hair, her lips, and the curve of her body. Like Lillie, there was a certain something about her that was innocent, yet cunning. She was childlike, yet womanly. She was so sure of herself, yet so uncertain. The problem was, she was not Lillie.

As he saw it, marriage was the final blow. It was the one thing he felt would deadbolt his freedom. There had been only one woman who had had the ability to lure him to the altar. After a while, a long while, it had been his pleasure to be a husband, to come home to his *wife*.

Lille had helped to make their house a home. She had helped to make their life together a pleasant one. Actually, she was the main source, the force, the focal point. Without her, it would have been just another structure with four walls, a roof and a door. All of that pleasure came to a sudden halt when he had to say good-bye to his dear, sweet wife and his only son who they had agreed to give the name Quentin. It still saddened him to think about all of the wasted time, all of the times he had taken that love for granted as if it would last forever.

The loss of his wife and son caused a kind of hurt he never ever wanted to bear again. Life had allowed him so much and then snatched it all away without so much as a second thought. It had taken him a lot of years to get through it. He suspected getting over it entirely was far too much to ask. He had no desire nor did he want to risk getting caught in that painful position again or repeating that experience.

Sometimes, it just hurt too much to really love someone. There was no doubt in his mind that he had loved Lillie. A part of him still did and always would. And he believed, just as sure as the sun rises and sets, Lillie had really loved him too. He was so happy when she told him that he was going to be a daddy.

It seemed a cruel act of fate that he should lose a wife and a son on the very same day. Lillie never got to see or hold her son. Quentin never got to see his mother, at least, not down here. Though he hadn't seen the inside of a church in a long time, he knew that there was a God up there somewhere. It gave him satisfaction to believe that his family was in Heaven. He consoled himself with the thought of God choosing two special angels for Himself.

Walter Saunders wanted to believe that he was in love with Flossie Mae too. It was just a different kind of love than the love he had shared with Lillie. But whether he ever would or ever intended to marry her was another story.

La'Rue Baker struggled daily to come to terms with the situation between her and Walter Saunders. As far as he was concerned, there was and had never been a situation. His friendship with Teddy was the only thing between them, the only thing binding them. However, she told herself that he might be out of reach, but he was definitely not out of mind.

For now, perhaps, he didn't see her in that way, the way a man sees a woman he longs for. Therefore, waiting was the only choice she had in the matter. She sure wasn't about to force her love on somebody who was too foolish to accept it. When he touched her, regardless of how innocent, she got goose bumps like a school girl. If she hadn't learned anything else during her time of despair, she had learned how to wait. And she was determined to wait for Walter Saunders to come around.

Flossie Mae continued to make money for the Club. She had always drawn a good crowd. Perhaps, she was even the Club's main attraction. That fact alone kept La'Rue Baker from sending her on her way. However, she was no longer *just* an employee. As La'Rue saw it, she had also become her competition. And she didn't like losing to anyone or anything.

"Miss Lady, are you sure that old man Saunders is in love with you? And how can you be so sure?" Emmanuel Putton blurted out without the benefit of a "how-do-you-do" or anything else that would have given the notion or the appearance that he had even a sprinkle of manners.

"Listen Boy!" Flossie Mae started.

"Okay, Miss Lady, I'm listening. As a matter of fact, I'm all ears," he said.

"What me, and Mr. Saunders to you, is or is not is none of your cotton-picking business!" she said, angrily.

"Well, I'm supposing you can't answer that because you don't know for sure," he said, not deterred in the least by her command.

"Not that it's any of your business—if you must know—yes, he does!" Flossie Mae insisted.

"Did he tell you? Do he really mean it? Or is he just using you for as long as he feels good about having a woman as pretty as you hanging on his arm?" Emmanuel Putton asked.

"Why are you worrying about us? Are you writing a book or something? Cause you got more questions than the law allow. But while you're busy worrying about me, you need to be worrying about your own self!" she fussed.

"Oh, I ain't worrying about you! I was just trying to figure something out. If old man Saunders is so head-over-heels in love with you, tell me why he's been all snuggled up with someone else?" he asked, being more blunt than he had intended.

"Hush up your mouth! You ain't seen no such thing and you know it!" Flossie Mae shouted at Emmanuel.

"I know what I saw. And you know that I saw it too. But, you don't want to know. Sometimes, women can be like that," he said, calmly.

"Women! I bet the little you know about how a woman is can fit inside a thimble! What you do know is how to spy on folks when you ought to be working!" she continued to fuss.

"Don't believe me. Ain't no skin off my nose. But in time, you will," he said, pushing the broom down the narrow hallway. Then he looked back, adding, "I know more about women than you think I do."

While Emmanuel remained unperturbed, Flossie Mae was just short of having herself a tantrum. Emmanuel Putton made her sick! Always running his mouth! Acting like he knew everything! He didn't know one doggone thing about her or Walter Saunders!

"He is, he is a bald-faced"

"There is not one drop of truth to"

"He is making all of this up," she thought over and over again, but could never quite bring herself to call Emmanuel Putton a liar.

In the time she had known him, he had gotten on her nerves more times than she cared to think about. He had poked his nose into her business without an invitation. He stood around, staring at folks like he was a lunatic or something. And he bad-mouthed Walter Saunders before her. But she had never known him to lie. Could he, at times, be too truthful? Yes indeed. Did she consider him to be a liar? No.

Flossie Mae wanted to ask him about the who, where, when of what he had seen or thought he had seen, but she feared the answer would be something that she didn't want to hear and really didn't want to know. Perhaps, there was some truth in what Emmanuel had said. Maybe she didn't really want to know. Nevertheless, she would have to keep her eyes open.

CHAPTER TWENTY THREE

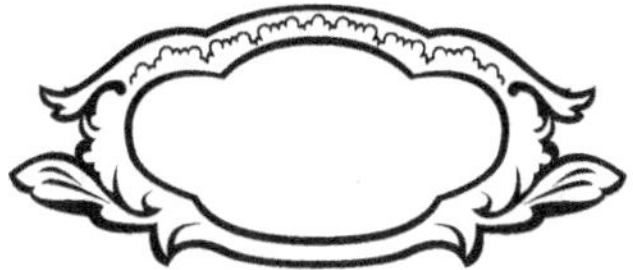

One morning, almost two months to the day that Augustus Atwater had forced himself on her, Flossie Mae woke up to the smells of sausage, fried potatoes and onions, scrambled eggs, buttermilk biscuits and fresh brewed coffee. Much like her mama, Miss Francine knew her way around the kitchen. As the saying goes, "She put both feet, her heart and her elbows into everything she cooked."

Instead of basking in the aromas that drifted up to her room and looking forward to making her way downstairs for breakfast, she ran in the direction of the bathroom. She felt as if she was about to heave her insides clean out. She was light-headed. And she was weak in the knees. She wondered if she was coming down with a bad case of something. It was about all she could do to make her way back down the hallway and onto the bed. She had *never* felt like that before—*ever!* And she never ever wanted to feel that way again. Of that, she was certain.

"Gal, ain't you gonna eat something this morning?" Miss Francine asked, knocking on the door. "Child, breakfast is on the table. You best git down here before it gits cold. And you know, once Luther sits down, he ain't bulging 'til he done tried to eat up everything in sight."

"I ain't hungry," Flossie Mae said as loud as she could manage, as loud as her voice would allow. Her words bearly came out in a mumble.

"Now, I done told her time and time again that she got to eat! She eats less than a sparrow! A body can't live off nothing! And it sho'nuff needs a heap more than love to git it through the day," Miss Francine fussed as she made her way down the back stairwell, talking to no one in particular.

After getting through several days—weeks of what she described as feeling worse than something the dogs had just dragged in from the alley, worse than someone who'd just been washed in muddy water and rung out as tightly as possible, worse than being hung out to dry in the scorching sun between a rock and a hard place. Of course, there was really no comparison between her hard place and the one she supposed or exaggerated. Thankfully, by evening, she usually felt like herself again.

One morning, Flossie Mae sat up in bed as though she had a spring hitched onto her backside. "Oh, my gracious!" she said, remembering how her sisters had suffered with sickness when they got in the family way. She thought back to the last time she had seen *anything*. She had been so busy, she hadn't taken notice that her 'visitor' hadn't shown up at all this month nor had it the month before.

Flossie Mae went from sickness to nervousness to fearfulness. "She won't! She couldn't be! How could she be? Surely, she won't expecting no baby! " she told herself.

However, it didn't take Miss Francine long to figure things out. Apparently, she and Emmanuel Putton had noses made for sniffing out trouble. As sharp as Butch's sense of smell was, she doubted if her papa's old hound dog could sniff out a rabbit faster than those two could smell trouble. And neither one of them bothered with beating around the bush or trying to fix up their thoughts so they wouldn't fly out of their mouths and knock you over the head.

"Gal, have you done messed 'round and got yourself in

trouble? You can bearly take care of your own self! Tell me how in the world can you see after a baby? When it gets here, do you plan on dragging it down yonder to that Club too?" Miss Francine asked without bothering to wait on an answer, as usual. "I'm here to tell you, the more you talk, the sooner folks go out and make more trouble for themselves. It don't make a lick of sense to me why a full grown or *thank* she grown woman can't look after herself no better than that. I told you that that man won't doing a thang except digging a ditch and waiting for you fall in it. What he say when you told him about this here—'bout you being in the family way? Bet he didn't say nothing close to what you thought you was fixing to hear! Peoples is more interested in tending to their own pleasures than they are in doing the right thing!"

"Miss Francine, I'm not sure that—I mean if I am expecting, it might not be Walter's baby," Flossie Mae said, trying to explain.

"Gal, don't tell me you done allowed another one of those no-good weasles down there at that Club to fool you up!

"Oh! No ma'am! It ain't that!" Flossie Mae said, sounding more like a small child than a woman.

"Well, I been on this here earth a mighty long time. I done heard all sorts of things. And from what they tell me, there ain't never been but one miracle birth where a natural man didn't play a part in it," Miss Francine said.

"I believe. I believe this is Augustus Atwater's baby. Since that day at the apartment—after he forced himself on me—I—I been pretending to have female troubles. I didn't have any relations with Walter Saunders for more than a month." Flossie Mae stuttered, hoping to assure Miss Francine, but really trying to convince herself.

"Honey, that's like saying that you got six in one hand and half a dozen in the other. Either way you look at it, still adds up to a baby. And either way, you'll be the one left to figure this thing out. You know that don't you? Except, there ain't a whole heap to figure on. In six to seven months, you'll have yourself a young'un to see after. You fixing to be some child's mama. Lord, have mercy on you as well as that poor, little child. You'll just have to do the best you can by them," Miss Francine said.

Flossie Mae didn't say nothing. She just cried.

"I declare. I done seen mosquitoes with more sense in their little, tiny behinds than some of you gals got in those great, big heads of yours'!"

If Miss Francine had any sympathy for her or her delicate condition, you sure couldn't tell it. "Child, no use in crying now. You best save them tears, git on up from yonder, and start looking after yourself. Cause you will need all the strength you can muster. You might as well swallow something down even if it ain't no more than a soda cracker."

Whether she wanted to admit it or not, Flossie Mae knew that Miss Francine was right. She would have to do a heap more than lay up in that room feeling sorry for herself. She had some figuring to do. And if she was really carrying a little young'un inside her belly, she had to do a heap more than figure.

When she stood up, she viewed herself in the mirror. She rubbed her middle. There was a slight, a very slight bulge. As much as she had come to despise Augustus Atwater, she already felt some sort of attachment, a different kind of affection toward *her* child. The feelings were strange to Flossie Mae whose focus had mainly been on herself, what she wanted, and how she aimed to get it. She wondered if what she was feeling was anything like that *motherly love* she had heard about for all of her life. Though she was scared and plenty scared, she reasoned to herself that they would make it with the help of the Lord.

Walter Saunders noticed how peculiar Flossie Mae had begun to act, but he wasn't the only one. Emmanuel Putton and La'Rue Baker had noticed too and all of them were trying to figure out why. Though she knew that she should probably tell Walter Saunders about the baby, she wasn't in a hurry to do so. The little bit of experience she'd had with men assured her that one of two things were bound to happen. He would either embrace and accept *her* child or he would want no parts of them. But she knew before she did or said anything, she needed to check with the doctor as Miss Francine had said.

"Child, there's no sense in gitting your feathers all ruffled up for nothing. All's well and good if you ain't started baking something in the oven. But from the looks of it, you fixing to have some bread in your basket. Honey, I believe there's a young'un on the way. And if there is, all will still be well and good. So it's best to check with the doctor to make sure. Could be, you done just wore yourself out with all of that late night rambling and juggling you been doing."

Every now and then, Flossie Mae allowed herself to suppose. What if it ain't true? What if there's no baby on the way? What if it's something else altogether? Sometimes, especially in those times when the fear of it all tried to take over—she even hoped that it wasn't true. Out of everything she had hoped for, had planned for, a baby never entered her mind. Conceiving, carrying, bearing, caring for, or rearing up a child was never a part of the equation. Nor had she planned for so many of the things that had happened. She wondered, did she, in all of her admittedly selfishness even have enough love in her to give to a child?

The doctor's report assured Flossie Mae. It also resolved her doubts while at the same time, confirmed her fears. And Miss Francine Black encouraged her in her own way that everything was going to be all right.

"Gal, you done messed around and craved yourself out a place up in here," Miss Francine said, patting her abundant chest. "And since you done got the word for sure, it's high time you start to think 'bout yourself in different terms. You're somebody's mama now. You got to see after yourself better than you been doing. Some of that other mess that's done took first place in your life, it's time to give it a back seat or put it out altogether. I come to tell you, you won't have the room for all of it. So you might as well make up in your mind which a way it's gonna be. Cause one thing for sure—you can't make no apple pie with 'taters."

On her days off and whenever she felt up to it, Flossie Mae began to put a few things together for *her* baby. She made things that could be easily used for a girl or a boy. Neatly folded in the top dresser drawer were little yellow diaper shirts with matching booties, green ones, and white ones trimmed in green or yellow began to appear. She had also purchased several pieces of pink clothe and two yards of blue along with the matching trim and yarn, but decided to save them until after the baby came.

—◦—

CHAPTER TWENTY FOUR

After a long and trying Saturday night at the Club, Flossie Mae had a thoughtful, restful, and peaceful Sunday. On Monday, she awakened with a come-what-may attitude. For whatever reason, she felt that it was the right day to tell Walter Saunders about *her* baby. Besides, she realized that she wouldn't be able to hide it from him or anyone else for much longer. Surprisingly, there was no morning sickness. She read a Scripture from the Bible her mother had given to her. Afterwards, she got dressed, straightened up her room, and went downstairs.

Miss Francine did a double-take when she saw Flossie Mae walk into the kitchen. "My mercy, child, look at you! I ain't seen you look this good in a month or two of Sundays! Come and sit yourself down right over here. Let me fix you something to eat."

Flossie Mae ate those scrambled eggs and two biscuits spread thick with strawberry jam like it was her last meal. Miss Francine smiled. But it was much more than the smile of someone who took pleasure in watching other folks enjoy her cooking. She was happy that after suffering the misery of morning sickness, "her girl" could finally sit down and enjoy some food for a change.

She waited. Nothing happened. Everything—every bite and every swallow stayed put. She felt full. She felt good. She felt strong enough to face the task that was before her.

Though there was a telephone at the Boarding House and though Walter Saunders also had a telephone, Flossie Mae didn't bother with calling. She did as usual. She just showed up at his door.

She had never needed an invitation before. Nor did she have to make her intentions known beforehand. And he had always seemed glad that she had come. Except, that was then and this was now. Things tend to change. Sometimes, they change, seemingly faster than shifting winds. Most times, things seem to change faster than we can keep up.

As she climbed the three steps leading up to the short walkway, Flossie Mae tried to gather her nerves as well as her thoughts. She knocked on the door several times, but there was no answer. His car was in the driveway. Therefore, he was at home. He and his car never got too far from one another. She knocked several more times. Finally, he answered—abruptly.

"WHO IS IT?" Walter Saunders asked. He sounded highly agitated.

"It's me," Flossie Mae answered.

"ME WHO?" he asked.

"Walter, open the door. It's me. Flossie Mae," she answered. She was puzzled. And she was becoming slightly annoyed.

"OH" was all he said.

Still, he did not open the door immediately. She figured, he was just trying to put his pants on or something. She had certainly seen him pant-less before, so she didn't understand why that would be a great concern. Now was no time to be bashful, especially with her standing outside in the cool of the morning. When he did manage to open the door, all he said was, "I wasn't expecting you."

"I know. I just needed to talk to you about something real important. If I wait, I'm afraid it might be too late," she said.

He looked nervous. And he kept looking toward the bedroom door as if he had left something of himself behind.

"Walter, I hope I didn't wake you," she said, half apologetically. "But I remember you telling me that you are an early riser."

"You didn't," he said without really looking at her. "Can I get you something?"

"No thank you. I'm fine," she answered. It occurred to Flossie Mae that she and Walter Saunders were being as cordial as two strangers who had just met on the street.

"Well, you might as well have a seat," he said, laying his overcoat on the back of the sofa. The invitation was as uninviting as someone offering you a plate full of breadcrumbs, then telling you to, "Help yourself".

As she sat, her eyes canvassed the room. It had been a couple of weeks since she had been there. Not much had changed in such a short period of time—nothing much. Except for the two half empty glasses on the bar, the scarf lying on the floor next to the barstool, a scarf that she recognized as belonging to La'Rue Baker.

Suddenly, Walter's coolness, his nervousness made sense. There was a woman in the bedroom. Of that she was sure. And she was just as sure that she knew who she was.

"Shug, can we do this another time? Can it wait until— maybe later today or tomorrow? I got a terrible hangover. I had a little too much to drink last night. I probably need to sleep it off or else get hold to a hair of the dog that bit me," he said, trying to force a laugh out of himself.

But Flossie Mae neither laughed or smiled or bulged from her seat. She just sat there for another moment or two, speechless, staring at those glasses and that scarf. At some point in her observations, she realized that things would be easier than she thought. She no longer felt the urge or the need to tell Walter Saunders anything about her or *her* baby.

"You're right," she forced herself to agree, "we can do this another time. No hurry. Go back to bed and get yourself some sleep. Hope you get hold of that old dog soon—so you can feel better—before it gets the chance to bite somebody else.

"Glad you understand," he said, trying to kiss her. "Oh, believe me, I do understand," she said, turning so that his lips bearly brushed her cheek.

She stepped outside the door. She heard the click of the lock and then the rattle of the chain. As she stood fastening her coat and readjusting her scarf to guard her against the brisk morning air, she heard footsteps and then voices.

"I thought you were going to tell her about us!" the female voice said.

"I am." he said, calmly.

"WHEN!" the voice exclaimed.

"Rue, give me a little time. Will you just trust me?" he asked.

Her suspicions were confirmed. He did have another woman in his house. And it was La'Rue Baker. "Yea, La'Rue, just trust him," Flossie Mae said aloud, as she stepped from the walkway onto the sidewalk. "While you're at it, why not trust a skunk not to spray you and a porcupine not to stick you?"

Howbeit, she was not as heartbroken or as disappointed or sad as she thought she would be. Nor did she hold any feelings bent on hatred, jealousy, or envy toward La'Rue Baker. After all, she had done the very same thing. She too had got caught up in the claws and clutches of Walter Saunders. He was that kind of man, the type of man a woman could easily fall for even when she knew better.

There were no tears, no fits of anger. She just felt numb. Yet, she also felt relief that it was finally over. She knew that she had been hanging onto the wrong things for the wrong reasons. Nonetheless, she was concerned about her job at the Club. How was she, how were *they* going to make due. It was, had been and forever would be—only with the help of the Lord. Flossie Mae walked the remainder of the way as if she didn't have a care in the world.

When she entered through the front door of the Boarding House, Miss Francine was sitting, mending slip covers. "Honey, did you git that business of yours taken care of?" she asked.

"Yes, ma'am, I did," Flossie Mae answered before going up to her room.

She flung herself onto the bed, but just as quickly sprung back to her feet. "I refuse to do this to myself. And I refuse to allow anyone else to do it to me. He—They ain't worth me shedding another tear or losing any more sleep over! No more, Flossie Mae! No more!" she scolded herself.

She wasn't necessarily feeling rejected or hurt or self-pity. She had become accustomed to things working out pretty much in her favor. Lately, her plans seemed to go whichever way they happened to take a notion to, leaving her behind to play catch up or risk being left behind.

There's nothing like having the truth look you square in the face when you're a woman full of child instead of a young gal full of wide-eyed dreams. She was left with no other choice except to look back. And the more time she spent viewing things as they really were, she found that she could reach no other conclusion. Nothing much had become of her plans. Sure, she was singing at the Club. That was the reason and the purpose for her coming to the City.

However, the closer she got to the truth, the more she realized, she was too anxious to leave home, but she didn't have any direction. She had left the entire matter up to Augustus Atwater, except, he didn't know where he was headed either. She had not heard from him nor did she know where he was. As far as any of it truly making her happy—it didn't. It hadn't. It couldn't.

The only times she felt anything close to true happiness was when she was up on the stage. But no sooner than she stepped down from it and returned to her dressing room, she felt the same old way again, lost and in betwixt and always in between.

She had hoped to fit in, to be one of them, but she won't and never would be. All of her trying had gained her very little. She had become someone she was not. In hopes of becoming a great, big *star,* she had allowed her head to be turned, had compromised herself, had went against her upbringing, and worst of all, she had managed to deceive herself.

She could call herself, "Miss Bettye Devine" or anyone else 'til the cows came home, but deep down inside, she was and would always be Miss Flossie Mae DuPont. Though by way of another foolish mistake, and according to the law, she was Mrs. Flossie Mae Atwater.

She realized one more thing. She was now in the unfortunate position of needing that singing job at the Club far more than it needed her. And now that La'Rue Baker and Walter Saunders' relationship had advanced to another level, her position was most uncertain at best.

If it had been left up to La'Rue Baker, "Miss Bettye Devine's" singing career would have been cut shorter than the life of a fly caught in a spider's web. The patrons of the

Club loved her. Or at the least, they spent more money on the nights she sang than when she didn't. For that cause alone, La'Rue Baker decided to tolerate her a while longer.

However, Flossie Mae couldn't help but notice the change of attitudes around the Club. Even Emmanuel "Sonny" Putton had changed. She still caught him watching her every now and then, but he didn't engage in conversations or accusations anymore. A nod or a half smile was about as much as he offered.

Needless to say, Walter Saunders became as absent from her life as a snowflake in July. Gone were the seemingly endless requests. No longer was she invited to sit at his table. And gone were the nightcaps, forced smiles, and pretense. She didn't miss the flowers or the gifts or the late night visits to her dressing room. . She now realized that it had come with a high cost. She had basically sold herself for a few minutes of attention and some meaningless trinkets.

In regards to Augustus Atwater, he could have been on the moon for all she knew or cared. However, a small part of her, and a very small part at that, knew that he was the Papa to the baby she carried inside her belly. And even if she couldn't stand him or never laid eyes upon him again, she had decided not to bad-mouth him before *her* child no more than she would bad-mouth her own self or her own doings. After all, they both had hit their own share of necessary as well as unnecessary bumps in the road. She had come to the City looking for one thing and found something she hadn't bargained on.

The sooner she realized that all of the things her Mama and Papa had taught her about life were true, the sooner her eyes would open, really open—perhaps, for the first time. And the sooner she accepted that what Miss Francine had been telling her about folks was for her own good, the better off she would be.

"Honey, folks will use you up, if they can. When they gits done, they will throw you out on the trash heap quicker than yesdiddy's garbage," she had said.

Flossie Mae was determined that that was not going to happen to her.

CHAPTER TWENTY FIVE

Mrs. Bertha got up earlier than usual. She went into the front room, sat down in her rocking chair, and folded her arms. The chair creaked as it slowly moved to and fro. She began to hum. Her actions were a for sure sign to anyone who came into the room that she was having a talk with the Lord.

Although it had been more than twenty years since she had carried Flossie Mae in her womb, she could feel her. She was kicking about, restless. Something was the matter. She didn't know what, but she knew Who did.

Mr. Frederick Douglass DuPont had heard his wife ease out of the bed. She hadn't slept much—so neither did he. He knew that she wouldn't mention what was troubling her if she could help it. At least, not before she had done talked it over with the Lord.

He didn't like to see his Bertha fretting over things. For the past year or so, it hadn't been about the what, but the who. They hadn't laid eyes on their baby gal for more than three years. She sent letters regular telling them how good she was doing up in the City. She always sent along a few dollars to help out which she didn't have to do, but insisted upon nevertheless.

It was plenty enough for him to know that she was doing all right for herself. What she didn't know, they hadn't spent a single dime of that money. He and Bertha had been getting along just fine without it. He had learned a few things about life—Just as sure as summer comes, winter won't be too far behind. And though he wanted things to turn out for Flossie Mae just the way she had planned in her head, he also knew that they might not.

She had hitched herself up with somebody who didn't hardly know which way was up much less how to get there. She had left home full of dreams and big ideas—going off to meet up with somebody full of hot air. But it seems, they got up yonder and found their way. He won't too proud to admit when he was wrong. According to Flossie Mae's letters, "That Boy" was doing right by her. However, when it came to Mrs. Bertha and her chirrens, she was seldom wrong. Usually, whenever she got a feeling that something was the matter with one of them—it was.

"It sure would be nice if Flossie Mae could come home for a visit. Wouldn't it?" Mr. DuPont mentioned at the breakfast table.

"Amen to that!" Mrs. Bertha replied.

"Those folks up yonder keeping her so busy, singing and all, but maybe she can take a little time out one of these days," he added after seeing his wife's eyes light up like two stars shining in the midnight sky at the mere mention of their baby gal coming home for a visit.

"I didn't git much sleep last night for thinking 'bout her," Mrs. Bertha admitted.

"I know. You tossed and turned half the night. And you were up early, long before the rooster even crowed," Mr. DuPont said.

"I don't know what, but I'm telling you, something's the matter with our baby girl, Frederick. I can feel it in my bones. She ain't sick or nothing, but things ain't been going as good for her as she has been saying in those letters of hers. Like I said, I don't know what, but something or another is going on that she ain't telling," Mrs. Bertha said with certainty.

The tears welling up in her eyes brought him as much pain as the sparkle in her eyes brought him joy. He was at a loss for words. All he knew to do was hold her. Then the words started pouring out of him. He too listened as if someone else spoke them.

"Oh, Dear Master, if You see fit to bring our child home, we ask You, if You would please do it, Sir. Lord, we ask You to please fix whatever the trouble may be. We knows that it's in Your power to do all things. We done trusted You over these many years to take care of us and our chirren. And we ain't about to stop trusting You now. Lord, we can truly say that You ain't never let us down."

"Never, Sir," Mrs. Bertha agreed, her voice bearly above a whisper.

"Father, we knows our chirren are of age now and it's not our place to be trying to tell them what they ought and ought not to do. They got to make their own way and live their own lives. But we do know that we done trained up every last one of them in Your way. We done showed them right from wrong. Lord, we know that You will do Your part just as You always have, but if we done errored along the way, please show us. We ain't saying that we have been perfect. You knows for Yourself that we are far from it. If we done somehow, in doing the best we know how, done something or another to cause this, we wants to git it right. Master, Sweet Jesus, please keep our chirren in Your care. Please give my Bertha back her good night's rest. And help us to mount up on eagle's wings while we wait. We put this and all other matters in Your hands. Amen."

When Mr. DuPont's prayer had ended, Mrs. Bertha rested her head on his shoulders and whispered in agreement, "Amen. Amen. Amen."

Then Mr. DuPont kissed his wife hard. She kissed him back. There was nothing left to do except eat, go out in the fields and try to put in a good day's work. Compared to the wait, that would be easy. Man, he included, tended to want everything fixed right now. But he knew that God has His own way and His own time for doing things. No matter how long He took, they trusted Him to do it.

"I need to see you before you go in the back," Mrs. Baker said to Flossie Mae as she entered the Club.

Flossie Mae turned on her heels. She knew that it had to be something mighty important. La'Rue Baker hadn't said no more to her than what was necessary since the day she had went to Walter Saunders' place. And if she had had an inkling of doubt as to whether it was really her in his bed, her attitude toward her further confirmed her suspicions.

"After tonight, I—we, won't be needing you to sing on Wednesday nights anymore. From now on, we will be doing what we call, "The Wednesday Night Special". *We* have a young man we would love to introduce to our customers. And *we* believe they will find him to their liking."

"Sure," was about all Flossie Mae had to say. Actually, it was about all she could say. At least she tried to say it with a smile which was more than La'Rue Baker had done.

La'Rue Baker began to walk away without another word, but turned to add a final comment, "I've been meaning to mention something to you about a larger dress size. If you aren't careful, before too long, you are going to spill out of the other ones. I guess all of that country eating got you sprouting like a sack of potatoes."

She felt herself glaring at her boss. Oh, she could show her country all right. It wouldn't take much for her to chunk her as if she was a sake of potatoes. Her citified behind didn't know nothing about the country or what she ate or did not eat. On second thought, she realized that she had more than herself to be concerned with. She had a baby steadily growing inside of her. Besides, La'Rue Baker nor Walter Saunders was worth the effort or the discomfort the anger rising up in her might cause.

During all of her daydreaming about city life, Flossie Mae never visualized that city folks had their own share of problems just like country folks. At times, it appeared they may have had more.

When she walked out on stage, she believed that she had the perfect song.

> *"I got the hard times—I got the hard time blues—*
> *I got the hard times—I got the hard time blues—*
> *I got the hard time blues—way down in my shoes—*
>
> *There ain't been no sunshine—just a many cloudy day—*
> *I said, There ain't been no sunshine—just a many cloudy day—*
> *So many clouds—they done took my clear skies away—*
>
> *Oh, I got the hard times—I got the time blues—*
> *Oh—I got the hard times—I got the hard time blues—*
> *I got the hard time blues—way down in my shoes—*

Flossie Mae, "Miss Bettye Devine" whenever she was on stage, stepped aside. The band played. As she looked out, into the audience, she saw folks swaying back and forth. She glanced toward Walter Saunders' table without meaning to, possibly out of habit. He had his head down.

Because his head was so big, he probably thought she was singing about them. She was. However, not as in he and she, but them as in most of the folks she had come across while living in the city—a City that she had wanted so much to be part of. Folks, who in her own mind, she had held up over her very own Mama and Papa. She had been so wrong for so long. But, it was too late now.

The Blues she sang belonged to her. It belonged to the Band. It even belonged to Mrs. Baker, as well as Augustus Atwater and Walter Saunders. But more so, the Blues belonged to Marlene, a waitress at La'Rue's Place. She waited tables, enduring the pinches and pats of young men and old men alike. She learned how to bear it all with a smile–in spite of the lewdness and the rudeness involved. She managed and withheld when their hands tried to reach beyond into forbidden places as if by her taking and delivering their orders seemed to mistakenly signify that she was also available for much more.

Flossie Mae had seen Marlene, on many a night, crying in the back room because she was tired of pretending that it was all right to be disrespected, to sell pieces of her dignity for hopes of a bigger tip—a dollar or two—maybe. She was just trying to serve them, to do her job the best she knew how. Night after night, she endured for her children at home who still needed a roof over their heads, bread in their mouths, shoes on their feet, and clothes on their back.

Marlene cried for her children who needed their father. She cried because she needed him too. She needed him to help her to provide them with all of the necessities of life which included his love. She wanted to stand by his side, love on him. She wanted to be the wife and mother her family deserved instead of the fraction of a woman she often felt herself to be. Whenever her feet didn't hurt, her heart ached. At times, she was either too worried about ends not meeting to rest or too tired to keep her eyes opened.

Still, long gone was Jerry Templeton with his big dreams and high hopes which excluded, "Being tied down to a nagging woman and a house full of hollering babies!" How many times had she heard him say it? How many times had he threatened to leave? If she had a dollar for every time he had dared to utter those words, she and her children could be sitting on Easy Street.

Yes, the Blues belonged to Marlene. She had lived it out. She knew those songs though that was never her intention. They had become her life despite her expectations. She had loved J.T. with a kind of passion that only comes along once in a lifetime. But now, that same love made her feel unloved and abandoned. It left her trying to make due. Yet, while still trying to do right by her children. And she tried to uphold him in their eyes even when her head told her that he had taken the cowardly way out. Marlene often thought how she should have given more credence to J.T.'s threats to leave and far less to his confessions of love.

On Wednesday night, although her head told her to stay in and get some rest, she got dressed and went to the Club anyhow. Her decision to go was mostly to satisfy her own curiosity about "The Wednesday Night Special" and partly to avoid having to answer Miss Francine's questions about why she wasn't at the Club?

She sat in the corner booth farthest away from the stage. She had come in somewhat unnoticed, which was her intention. "Club soda," she had said when the waitress came over to take her order. She kept her head down when she returned with her drink. No doubt, she knew who she was. Still, she didn't acknowledge her.

The lights became even dimmer. La'Rue Baker walked onto the stage. "Ladies and gentlemen, due to uncontrollable and an unforeseen circumstances, Miss Bettye Devine is unable to be with us on tonight," she announced.

Flossie Mae had an urge to stand up in protest and expose La'Rue Baker for the liar she had become, but just as quickly decided against it.

The crowd booed.

"However," La'Rue continued, raising her hand slightly, "we have tried to take this unfortunate situation and turn it into an opportunity to present someone who, I promise, will have you begging for more."

The crowd sat in a wait-and-see silence.

"Ladies and gentlemen, I am pleased to present to you, Mr. Smooth himself, Mr. Sonny Putton!" she announced. The crowd clapped politely.

In momentarily disbelief, Flossie Mae repeated what she had heard—"Sonny Putton?" She sat with her mouth open, stunned as if she expected any more or any less from La'Rue Baker. She didn't even know that Emmanuel "Sonny" Putton could sing.

"Sonny" walked onto the stage grinning from ear to ear. He took a bow. He then kissed La'Rue Baker on the cheek. She patted him on the shoulder with one hand and acknowledged him to the crowd with the other. Then she walked off the stage and stood at the end of the bar. The expression on her face could have very well been that of someone who had just won the raffle at the County Fair. La'Rue Baker was very proud of herself.

Sonny Putton opened his mouth and began to sing.

Flossie Mae could not come to terms with her feelings. He could sing. Of that, she would willingly admit. But her real struggle was whether he was a singing fool or just a fool singing?

She slipped out before the end of his set, before she could reach a conclusion.

Sonny Putton did not see his singing as an insult or an injury to Flossie Mae. He just saw it as business, plain and simple. Period. He had no intentions whatsoever of sweeping and mopping all of his life. He saw La'Rue's Place as a stepping stone, a very small stepping stone in his climb to the top. As he saw it, everybody had to start somewhere.

He had been singing since he was about six or seven years old. He had been told that he might've been even younger than that. His Grandma use to call on him to sing every chance she got. He quickly grew out of his shame. He credited that to all of those quarters his uncles gave him afterwards.

After his daddy got sick, he no longer spent or according to his grandma, wasted his money on childish things. He soon learned that a few quarters could go a long way. They were better spent on things like bread, milk, and kerosene.

When they had to move out of their house to a tiny government apartment—in the projects, away from family and familiar surroundings—every quarter, dime, nickel, and/or penny that he could get his hands on was needed. He had worked since he was twelve years old. Of that account, there was no lapse in his memory. He had delivered groceries for McSwain's Corner Market. After his daddy's passing, he became the *man* of the house. And his mother had reminded him quite often.

It was a much too heavy responsibility for such tender shoulders, but he tried to manage nevertheless. He was determined that his sisters nor his brothers would ever go hungry. And one day, his mother would not have to work her fingers to the bones. One day, they would have a real home again, a home surrounded by family and friends. If singing helped to afford them the privilege—good! If he happened to step on a few toes, so be it. As he saw it, his family came first.

Just as La'Rue had promised, the crowd did beg for more, but mostly, the ladies. And just as expected, "Sonny" Putton had delivered.

La'Rue Baker was more than pleased. And so was Walter Saunders. He was more than willing to sit back and allow Rue to do his dirty work for him. Weeks had passed. Still, he had not bothered to offer Flossie Mae an explanation of any sort as to why he had broken off their relationship so suddenly. Nor had he stated that he actually had. Though they both knew that it should have never existed.

He avoided her all together. He avoided making eye contact with her at the Club. He avoided talking or even speaking to her. And he avoided taking part in any decisions that involved her. He knew that La'Rue planned to get rid of her, eventually. That would make things a lot easier on him, but it would not necessarily be best for her. Neither was he totally convinced that it would be best for the Club. "Miss Bettye Devine" had raked in a ton of money for La'Rue's Place. Most of all, her removal would help to remove some of his guilt. She was so young, so naïve, so vulnerable, so hopeful.

Had she not shared some of her dreams with him? Hadn't he known how much singing really meant to her? He could chalk the whole matter up to nothing more than a bad business deal. But, he knew for her, it was much more than business. Singing was her heart.

Sure, he was willing to accept a small portion of the blame for what happened between them. She was full of zeal, but she wasn't completely innocent. And that so-called husband of hers, he had to bear his share of the blame too. There was no way that he would have knowingly walked his bride into harm's way and then left her there.

They were Mrs. Fame and Mr. Fortune. She had come to Philly with her eyes full of star lite, searching for fame. He, on the other hand was a fool for money. If it meant getting his hands on a few dollars, he probably would have sold his own Grandmother to the wolves.

Walter Saunders felt, if there had to be someone else, she was better off with him being that somebody. At least, he had treated her with kindness, gave her things that she would not have had otherwise. If some of those other jokers he knew had gotten hold of her, there's no telling what would've become of her. Reassuring himself that it had, in the long run all been done for her good helped to ease some of his guilt. He hoped a strong drink or two would help to drown out the rest.

Besides, as much as his manhood hated to admit it, Rue was more his speed. Flossie Mae was a young woman full of desires and expectations. With her, you never really knew exactly where you stood. At times, she was also very moody, spoiled, and unpredictable.

But even so, there was something in him that did not

want to settle down or be tied down to any one woman for any extended period of time. It wasn't just Flossie Mae. It was him, him with any woman, including La'Rue Baker.

Since Lillie, he had gone through women like a child in a candy store. He touched, desired, picked up and put down. Sometimes, his eyes had gotten bigger than his appetite. He had on many occasions, for many different reasons, bitten off more than he was able to chew. He had also gotten stung a time or two. He had used. And he had been used in return.

To say that he had always come out even would have been a lie. The fast life had taken its' toll on him in ways he didn't care to dwell upon. It didn't take long for him to find out that men were certainly not exempt or immune from the pain of failure, not even the strongest of men. Trying to drown your pain in someone or something else seldom works to one's advantage.

He had his own set of troubles. Flossie Mae was a young girl. She would eventually meet someone more suitable for her and her dreams. She didn't need him. Though in the beginning, he needed her. Or at least he needed to be needed by her. It may not have been his place, but he wanted to rescue her from her fool of a husband. In the beginning, that had been his intention, that and nothing else. Howbeit, even the best of intentions can potentially get out of hand.

Flossie Mae figured that even a blind alley cat could smell a rat in its midst. She won't blind or feline, but she smelled something that won't right. La'Rue Baker was planning to get rid of her sooner or later, probably sooner. Until then, she had no intentions of walking 'round on egg shells or pins and needles. And neither was she fixing to waste up her time fretting over it.

La'Rue Baker was the next to the last person in the world she wanted her young'un to take after. Carrying around a bunch of hatred in her heart wouldn't do a thing but mock her young'un. Then, every day for the rest of her life, she wouldn't be able to forget about that woman—and have herself to thank for it.

Though it may have been just an ole wives' tale or just another suspicious notion, it was still a chance that she wasn't willing to take. Undoubtedly, she might not ever get around to loving her, but she wasn't going to waste precious time hating her either. In a roundabout way, La'Rue Baker had actually done her a favor.

She remembered a story she had heard for most of her life about a woman who decided to take a stroll through the woods. The woman was with child. When she came to the bend, a huge bear jumped out from behind a grove of trees. With claws raised, the bear growled. They say, "The bear was so close, the woman could smell its' foul breath." Needless to say, the woman ran and screamed her way to the clearing. There some hunters stood and brought an end to the bear. Unfortunately for the bear, it ended up on the hunter's table. And unfortunately, for the woman and her babe, every time the child cried, his cry reminded his mother of the bear's growl.

It would be bad enough if her young'un had to come into the world looking like its longheaded pappy. That part couldn't be helped. But some way or another, she could help the other.

She had made her mind up. She was just gonna abide her time. Her thoughts toward La'Rue Baker were about to turn from vinegar to sweetin' water. And in her heart, she had bid Walter Saunders good riddance. He won't, never was, and never would be hers to have or to hold or to keep. Neither was he hers to give or to take. If La'Rue Baker wanted him, she could surely have him.

CHAPTER TWENTY SIX

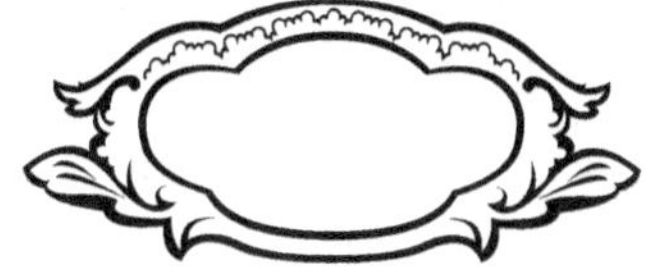

"Gal, are you up?" Miss Francine asked, knocking on the door like the house was on fire or something far worse. "Your sister, Betty is on the telephone!"

Flossie Mae scrambled to her feet, pulled on her house coat, and ran downstairs.

"Child, you know better than that! You fixing to mess 'round and break your neck! You running down those stairs just like you done gone and lost your mind!" Miss Francine fussed, shaking her head at what she saw as Flossie Mae's carelessness.

"Betty! Betty!" Flossie Mae said, her voice caught somewhere between a laugh and a cry. "Is everything all right? How is Mama and Papa?"

She held her breath. She waited. She dreaded hearing the answer.

"Everything's fine. I just wanted to hear your voice. It's been a while. We miss you," Betty said, not bothering to mention that she was all their Mama had talked about at Sunday Dinner.

"I've been writing regular just like I promised," Flossie Mae said.

"I know. I know. It's not the same though. It would be even better if I could see you. But your singing been keeping you too busy," Betty said, mostly repeating what her sister had told her several times before.

"Maybe—I will—one of these days," Flossie Mae said. "How is that brother-in-law of mine?" she asked in an effort to change the subject, knowing that Betty could not and would not give up a chance to talk about him.

"He's doing just fine. He's been treating me like a plum queen since he got my belly looking like a plump, watermelon," Betty answered, laughing,

"Your belly is what?" Flossie Mae asked, excitedly, her voice bearly below a squeal.

"My belly done started looking like I done swallowed a good-sized watermelon, maybe even two. I can't see my feet no more," Betty laughed. "Mama, says, 'It's a little gal for sure'. We're kind of hoping for a boy though. But, we will gladly take whichever bundle of joy the Lord decides to bless us with."

Flossie Mae could tell that Betty was real happy. She was happy for them. Nonetheless, she didn't utter a word of her news. She didn't know how. She could never lie to Betty.

The operator came on the line. It was time to put in more coins.

"Well, Sis, I got to go I wish we had more time to talk, but I don't have to tell you that this is long distance," Betty said.

"Hug Mama and Papa for me and tell them I'm doing just fine. Give the rest of the family my best and tell them to hug you for me too," Flossie Mae said, sounding a lot more cheerful than she actually felt.

"We love you, sis," Betty said before ending the call. She held the telephone close to her bosom before returning it to the cradle.

It took Flossie Mae quite a while to pry herself from the spot she was in. She wasn't ready to pass by the kitchen door, not yet. She always cried after talking with Betty. She cried after she sealed up a letter to her family. She cried whenever she was homesick which had started to happen more and more often. She also cried whenever she thought about how she couldn't go back home.

"How's the family?" Miss Francine called out from the kitchen.

"Everybody's doing just fine," Flossie Mae answered.

"Shug, they can't help but miss you. I know if you were my young'un or a sister of mine, I would miss you," Miss Francine assured.

"I miss them too," Flossie Mae said, taking another step forward.

"Well—Child, why don't you git your bones back on that bus and take yourself home?" Miss Francine asked.

"I can't," Flossie Mae answered.

"No such thing! Why can't you?" Miss Francine asked. Flossie Mae sighed.

"Because I—Because I done—" Flossie Mae fumbled for an answer.

"Why? Do you think you can't just because you done messed up? Who in the world hasn't at some time or another? Child, your peoples love you. Even I knows that. They ain't gonna hold this thing against you," Miss Francine said with a great measure of certainty.

"It ain't that. I done wrote to them, telling them how good I been doing and all. They don't know that Augustus and me done busted up. They don't know that I'm fixing to have a young'un. And they certainly don't know 'bout me and Walter Saunders. I done fibbed to them 'bout everything," Flossie Mae cried.

"Honey, if you think you done pulled the wool over your Mama's eyes, you got another think coming. You done painted a rosy picture for her and all, but I doubt if you done fooled her like you think you have. I don't have no chirren of my own, but one thing I know, Mamas be knowing their chirrens. She knows 'bout life. And she knows that you ain't waltzed yourself way up here in the city and escaped all the troubles of life. I suspect she been praying for you more since you been gone than she did in your whole, entire life."

Flossie Mae stood silent. She knew Miss Francine was speaking the truth.

"Let me tell you something, everybody don't git the chance to go back home. I thinks it's a blessing that you are one of the ones who can," Miss Francine said.

"Miss Francine, you ain't trying to get rid of me, are you? Sounds like you wanting me to go," Flossie Mae finally said.

"Look here, Girl. I only wants what's best for you. This here city life ain't done you no favors. And if the truth be told, you ain't seen nothing but trouble since you been here. There can be a steep difference in what we hope for and what we actually git," Miss Francine said.

After a long pause, Flossie Mae said, "I'm a little tired now."

"You go on and lay down a while. Git yourself some rest before supper," Miss Francine said.

She knew Flossie Mae wasn't quite ready to hear or face the truth. She was still in love with singing. She still wished that things had worked out for her better than they actually had. But, they hadn't. Won't no need in helping her to fool herself. Besides, she had come to love the child like she was her very own daughter.

Just as soon as those folks down at that Club caught whiff of her being in the family way, she wouldn't have no more singing job anyhow. And if Walter Saunders suspected that he's the daddy, he might be forced to show his real self. Mens' like that won't looking to accept responsibility for their actions. He was seeking pleasure for himself and nothing else. Waiting 'round to find out which a way that ill wind might blow is the last thing she needed to be doing.

Even if she decided to stay, what in the world was she planning on doing with her young'un? Was she gonna drag it around, all over creation? A baby needs a family. They need their Mama and Papa. They need their Grandma and Grandpapa, aunts and uncles and cousins too. They needs to be surrounded by folks who love them, not folks who gone pass them by without even seeing them. Children don't need folks who won't even care enough to remember their name from one day to the next or folks who look on them more as a burden rather than the blessing they are.

It won't her place, but she had a mind to help the girl whether she wanted her to or not. Sometimes, folks won't take a step on their own. You got to hold their hands and help them to put one foot in front of the other until they see that they can walk all by themselves. But how could she help Flossie Mae to see that she didn't need those folks down at that club to git to where she needs or wants to be.

Flossie Mae laid across the bed, but she didn't go to sleep. Instead, she thought about her talk with her sister, Betty. And she thought about what Miss Francine had said. One thing Betty had said replayed in her mind like a badly scratched record, "Mama said it's gonna be a little gal for sure."

She could picture her Mama's hand on Betty's fat belly. She, no doubt, had been praying for her grand-young'un ever since she heard the news. No doubt, she had already made up a couple pairs of booties by now. In her mind, she could picture the family making a big fuss over Betty, especially Ophelia. She could see Joseph Avery grinning from ear to ear every time somebody so much as mentioned the word, "Baby" or he thought about how he was about to be a Papa. And she could also imagine her Papa out in the barn making something or another, finishing it up just in time for the little one's arrival.

But it didn't take no imagination at all for her to picture herself miles away from home, except for Miss Francine, going through her time alone. Won't nobody praying for *her* baby or making a fuss over her or grinning from ear to ear or taking the love and care to make him or her their first and very own piece of furniture. All her baby would have was her. Though she won't sure if she would ever be enough.

Flossie Mae buried her face in her pillow and cried, again. Her tears seemed to have a mind of their own. They came whether she wanted them to or not. She told herself that she would get up and wash her face good before Miss Francine called her down for supper.

Miss Francine couldn't help but notice Flossie Mae's red, puffy eyes when she came into the kitchen. That child had been crying! She had been crying hard too. Didn't nobody have to tell her 'bout crying. Couldn't nobody fool her when it came to crying either. Eyes that done slept hard is a sight different from eyes that done cried hard. Her mind was made up. She was set on doing everything in her power to see that that child got back home where she belonged.

Flossie Mae spent more time pushing her food around on her plate than she had spent eating it. Miss Francine watched 'bout as long as she could stand.

"Gal, you knows you got to eat something! You 'bout to mess 'round and make yourself sick!" she said. "After supper why don't you write to your folks. It might help you to feel better. I'll see that it gits mailed first thing in the morning. I'll pay for the postage myself."

Mr. Simms said, "Francine, why come you ain't never volunteered to send no mail off for me?"

"Man, you better hush-up! If you can't walk your old, rusty, crusty behind downstairs to mail your own mess, it don't need to be mailed!" Miss Francine fussed with Mr. Simms.

Flossie Mae didn't pay him no mind though. He and Miss Francine carried on like that all the time. She believed Mr. Simms sought of liked her, but according to the way she talked to him, it sure won't no two-way street.

He looked over at Miss Parker, laughing and said, "I told y'all, 'That gal is in love with me'."

"Well, if she is, I sure don't ever want none of that kind," Miss Parker said, laughing until she cried.

As Flossie Mae looked around the table at the faces of the people, listened to them carrying on with one another as usual, she realized that she was surrounded by strangers. Sure she knew their names, bits and pieces about their lives, but she felt no real connection to them. Miss Francine treated her good and had said that she looked on her as she would her very own daughter. Although she had a fondness for her like she had for no one else in the City, she was not her daughter. And she could never see her as her Mama.

Life was puzzling. She wondered why we try to cling to folks who don't have their arms out to us? And why we try to push folks away who try to embrace us? She was sure that she won't the first one to ask those questions or the first to look for the answers. One thing she did know, the answer was out there somewhere—waiting to be found out.

Flossie Mae had seen them time after time. She could hardly help it. There was a Club This, That, and The Other on nearly every corner. They all featured a band and/or a singer. There certainly didn't seem to be a shortage on either. She wondered how many young girls had made their way to the City in search of that pot of gold at the end of their rainbow?

After her experience in the City, she didn't believe that there was anything to be found at the end of her rainbow except someone waiting to hand her another pot full of trouble. She didn't want to feel that way. She wanted to hold onto her dreams, to become somebody, to show her folks that she had made it.

Augustus Atwater, La'Rue Baker, Walter Saunders, and Emmanuel Putton had all turned out to be snakes in the grass. Had it not been for Miss Francine, she would have judged all city folk unfairly and measured them all with the same ruler.

Because it appeared to be a day for honesty rather than self-pity, Flossie Mae was forced to admit to herself that in the beginning, she had used Augustus Atwater just as much as he had used her. He had been her ticket to the City. It was her own foolishness that helped her to get tangled all up in the mess she was in.

How she longed to put her head in her Mama's lap and hear, "Gal, everything's gonna be all right. You just wait and see." How she wished that she could sit on the front porch with her Papa and have one of their talks. She even missed Ophelia and her fussing. She wanted to go home.

She put her hand on her growing belly. She had felt something move on the inside of her, something that appeared to be no more than a slight flutter. Still, she waited. She hoped that it would happen again. In her wait, she thought about all the reasons why she should go home. With them also came the many reasons why she shouldn't. It remained unanswered in her head. Would the voice of reason out-weigh her fears?

CHAPTER TWENTY SEVEN

When she walked in the door of La'Rue's Place, Flossie Mae got the same feeling she had been getting for weeks. Lately, she had begun to feel like she was trapped inside a cage, depending on the same folks who helped to shut her up in it to help free her from it. She was tired of crying. She was tired of being used. She was just tired. Period.

As she combed her hair and fixed her face, she asked herself if any of it had been worth it? Then she heard the Band playing. It was almost time to go out. She put on her best face, took a deep breath, and prepared herself for the stage.

"Ladies and gentlemen, Miss Bettye Devine!" La'Rue Baker announced.

In spite of outside appearances, La'Rue Baker was about to boil on the inside. She had mentioned to Walter Saunders that *they* needed to fire Flossie Mae after she finished with her sets. He had said, "No". They got into it. She had accused him of still having feelings for her. One thing had led to another. Before they knew it, they had said too much. He had strutted out of her office, puffing like a bull. She threw her ash tray, breaking it, making a mess for her to clean up. Afterward, she had blamed the whole mess on none other than Flossie Mae.

When Flossie Mae began to sing, her load felt lighter, but she knew that it was only temporary. The feeling of contentment and freedom would be over just as soon as she stepped off the stage.

The patrons made a lot of fuss. They cheered. They called out requests. They sung along. They clapped. They danced. But as she looked out into the audience, she felt lost. She felt something she could not explain. She didn't want *this* anymore was all she knew for certain. She stopped. She backed away from the microphone. She looked around. But she knew that she was not quite through. Not yet.

The Club went silent. La'Rue Baker stood with her hands on her narrow hips. It was hard to tell whether the puff of smoke was coming out of her nostrils or from the cigarette that hung from her lips. Walter Saunders sat silent. He stared at Flossie Mae on stage, wondering what in the world had come over her? Had Rue went ahead and said something anyway? He glanced at her. He saw that she was just as puzzled as he was. They both sighed in relief when Flossie Mae "Miss Bettye Devine" walked up to the microphone again.

Flossie Mae's facial expression changed, not only that, her whole being seemed to change right before everyone. She opened her mouth and began to sing. The Band was lost. They just followed as best as they could.

She began to sing.

> *"Oh, Lord, have mercy— Please, have mercy on me—*
> *Oh, Lord, have mercy— Please—have mercy on me—*
> *And help me to get back home—home to where I belong—*
> *I came to the City, trying to make a big name for myself—*
> *I said, 'I came to the City, trying to make a big name for myself'—*
> *Instead, I got chased through the jungle— with the wolves on my trail—*
> *Oh Lord, have mercy. Please, have mercy on me—*
> *Oh Lord, have mercy—Please, have mercy on me—*

And help me to get back home—home to where I belong—

I know my Mama prayed—she done prayed both night and day—
I said, 'I know my Mama prayed—she done prayed both night and
day—'
For You to be with her child and help her along life's way—

Oh Lord, Lord, Lord!
Lord—please have mercy on me—
Oh Lord, Lord, Lord!
Lord—please have mercy on me—
And help me to get back home—home—where I belong—
And help me to get back home—home—where I belong—
Please help me to get back home—home—where I belong—

Flossie Mae felt that there was nothing else left to say. She walked off the stage, went into the dressing room, gathered her things, and prepared to leave.

"You can't do that! You can't just walk off the stage like that!" La'Rue Baker shouted, pointing her discolored finger toward Flossie Mae.

"Who the devil do you think you are?" Flossie Mae asked.

"I know who I am! You're the one who has forgotten who you are!" La'Rue Baker said, her husky voice pitched about as high as it would go.

"Believe it or not, I know who I am. I may have forgotten for a time, but believe me, I know now!" Flossie Mae assured her in no uncertain terms. "And by the way, I won't be singing here no more," she added.

"If not here, you won't be singing anywhere. When I get through, won't nobody hire you to clean their toilets much less sing on their stage!" La'Rue Baker threatened.

"Lady, you can do as you please!" Flossie Mae said.

As she walked out of the dressing room and into the narrow hallway, she brushed up against Emmanuel "Sonny" Putton who stood, propped up on the broom, getting his ears full for free. She kept moving, not even slowing down long enough for him to say one word to or about her.

Walter Saunders stood at the back door. He grabbed Flossie Mae's arm at the elbow. "You sure you want to do this?" he asked.

"I'm as sure as I've been of anything in my life. Now take your hands off me!" she answered just before walking out and away from the Club.

Unbeknownst to her, he had just warded off another encounter, rather an accident waiting to happen, in the form of and better known as Chester "Shugarfoot" Horton. Saunders had seen him come into the Club with a *lady* on each arm. They had sat about mid-way between the bar and the stage. Though the lights were dim, still, he could see that "Shugarfoot" Horton was up to no good.

Chester Horton had been meaning to take time out of his busy schedule to see what La"Rue Baker was putting down. He had heard a while back that she had become a Washed-Up-Has-Been, but he reckoned—like so many things, it was just a rumor. La'Rue Baker wasn't his type, but she looked good. As he looked around, he saw a few things that he would probably try to lure over to his camp. He had seen a few other things that he would probably add to enhance his already thriving business.

Everyone in the business, who knew or had heard of "Shugarfoot" knew that his Shugar won't always sweet. Many had begun to call him, "Bad News" Horton. He was known to supply a little something to his people that would take the edge off. Unfortunately, for Annie "Lil' Red"

Tatum, it had done much more than that. Afterward, her recording of, "Uptown After Midnight" had become a hit. Sadly, she was no longer around to benefit from or bask in her fame. She was often imitated, but there was only one, "Lil Red".

Horton had also gotten the word that there was trouble in La'Rue Baker's camp. He had come in to take a peep at Miss Bettye Devine for himself. Apparently she was already spoken for. The way Saunders had guarded that door told him more than he needed to know. He didn't want to take any unnecessary chances. Walter Saunders was sneaky, hard to figure, and too quiet. He could keep Miss Bettye *Devine*. Sonny Putton would have to do. His *man* had reported to him that Sonny could "blow" and that look in his eyes told him the young man was real hungry for the limelight.

The brisk night air gave her a chance to clear her head. Something had happened to her on that stage. Something had given her the courage to do what she could not do alone. She not only walked away from the Club and singing—she had called on the Lord to help her to do it. The same Lord she had had little use for in the past.

In her mind, she thought that she had her life under control. She had made plans and expected everything to work out as she had hoped. Yes, she wanted to go home. But she questioned, How? How could she ever face her folks again when almost everything she had written in her letters had been a lie? How?

Flossie Mae tried to tiptoe down the hallway to her room, but there won't much that got past Miss Francine. However, by the time she had eased The Good Book down on her bed and pushed her feet into her slippers, she heard the door to Flossie Mae's room close. She only wanted to remind her to leave the letter so she could mail it to her folks in the morning.

Miss Francine sat back in the chair beside her bed, reached for the Bible and finished reading Psalm 37. For some reason or another, she had read it several times over the past few days. She would be the first to admit that she hadn't always done right and still, sometimes didn't. But one thing she did do, she believed in God's word. And she trusted Him to do whatever He said that He would do. She read the very last verse aloud. "The LORD shall help them, and rescue them from the wicked and save them because they have put their confidence in Him".

When she had finished reading, she closed the Bible, sat it on the bedside table, and began to pray. "And Lord, I knows that I ain't one to talk, but that child in yonder needs You pretty bad. I needs You too. I don't want to make a wrong turn and run her off from here. She ain't got no place else to go 'less she goes back home. Course, I ain't sitting here, trying to tell You nothing that You don't already know 'bout. But, she sure don't need to go back to that knuckle-headed boy or those folks down yonder at that Club. They ain't meant a thing except trouble to her ever since she laid eyes on them. Lord, I knows if You got me out of the mess I was in, surely, You can do the same for her. I believe her folks would welcome her back home with open arms. I remember reading in Your Good Book about the young man who took what his Papa had to give him, went off and spent it all up, living the fast life. After he done lost everything he had, he realized that what he needed was right there at home. When he was on his way back, his Papa ran to meet him and took him in with outstretched arms just like nothing had happened. His Papa went so far as to kiss him on the neck, put a ring on his finger, and put a robe on him. I'm figuring that's how it will be with Flossie Mae. Can't nobody convince me that her folks don't love her. And I don't believe they'll look down on her for any mistakes she done made. She just got to give them the chance to show her. Lord, show me how to help her. It's been a long time since I've allowed myself to get close to somebody like this—much less go 'round sticking my nose into their business. And I don't recall ever praying for somebody else 'less there was something for me to gain by it, like the money they owed me for the rent. But this time, I ain't concerned one bit 'bout the money. Besides, she sort of stubborn and prideful. She keeps insisting on paying her own way. Money or no, I would be willing to give her a place to stay for as long as she needs it. With all of that being said, at a time like this, she needs her family. A young gal like her don't need to be bringing no young'un into the world all by her lonesome. 'Course, I'm willing to do all I can for her, but she needs her Mama, and though she might not come right out and say so, I believe she wants her too. Right now, she don't know how to make the first step. Please help her, Lord. And save her from herself if need be. I know I don't talk to You as often as I should. I'm trying to do better. I really am. I owes this here Boarding House and *everything* else I got to You. And I thank You, Sir. In Jesus' name, I pray. Amen."

Afterwards, Miss Francine turned her covers back, kicked off her slippers and laid down. No sooner than she had got herself all situated, she had to get up. As much as she enjoyed it—that cup of hot tea that had become her habit before bed, oftentimes caused her to make water half the night.

On her way to the bathroom, she heard a noise coming from Flossie Mae's room. "That gal is in there crying," she thought to herself. She wanted to knock on the door and ask, "Why?" But decided against it. Probably for the same old reasons—hurt, disappointment, loneliness, confusion, regret, and/or just plain old tired of being sick and tired. There sure won't no shortage of that going 'round.

Most likely, she figured Flossie Mae was in there wrestling with her own self. Far too often and for many reasons, we choose the bad over the good and then waste years of our lives learning from, living with, and lamenting over the difference.

On the way to her bedroom, Miss Francine knocked on Flossie Mae's door. "Shug, don't forget to leave the letter to your folks so I can mail it in the morning." There was no reply. No sound. Only silence. Then, there was only the flip-flop sound that Miss Francine's slippers made on the waxed linoleum covered floor as she walked back to her room.

Flossie Mae lay across the bed, listening for the sound of Miss Francine's door shutting. As much as she appreciated her help, she just won't in the mood to be hearing how everything will work out all right. How?

In some ways, Miss Francine reminded her of her Mama. Half the time, they talked like the answer to your troubles was fixing to drop straight down from heaven. They seemed to see rainbows while everyone else saw storm clouds. No matter what, they always looked for the brighter side.

Seemed about all she could do at the time was wallow in her troubles along with whatever feelings she felt behind them, fear, anger, hurt, disappointment, shame, guilt, and so forth and so on. That's where she was and that's all she could see. She didn't have the strength to look for much else.

CHAPTER TWENTY EIGHT

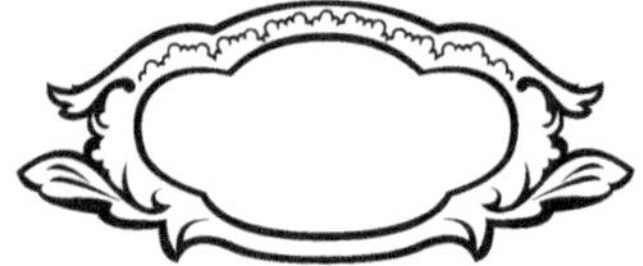

Miss Francine didn't go 'round quoting Bible verses all the time, but she knew some Bible. Some of that knowledge was a result of what her Mama had taught her. And some she had learned on her own during hard times and through hard trials and tribulations. As she pulled the covers up over her round shoulders, she said, "You may suffer weeping in the darkness, but child, you will see joy when your daylight shows up!" And that she knew to be the truth from personal experience.

According to the clock on Flossie Mae's bedside table, it was three-thirty. Everything seemed to be quiet. Everyone appeared to be sleeping, except her. She had just finished writing the letter to her folks. As usual, she had written telling them how well things were going for her. For whatever reason, (perhaps and because she felt like a failure and believed that they would also see her as such) she couldn't bring herself to tell them the truth.

Besides, everybody was jumping for joy over Betty and her soon-to-be-born baby. The last thing they needed was for her to dump her troubles in their laps. "I miss you all a whole lot" was about the only thing she hadn't tried to fix up. She then sealed the letter, took it downstairs and laid it on the kitchen table where Miss Francine would be sure to see it.

Knowing human nature a heap better than she claimed, after picking up Flossie Mae's letter, Miss Francine figured that it probably was filled with more of the same.

"I'm doing fine."

"Everything is fine."

"I love y'all."

"And give everybody a hug for me."

She knew because that's how her letters use to read. Half the mess she had gotten into could have been avoided if she had had enough guts to admit the truth to herself and to her folks. That's why she wrote down Flossie Mae's home address.

"Lord, I ain't got a bit of business poking my nose into this child's business like this here, but I sure wish somebody had done it for me. It sure would have saved me from many a headache and licks upside my head," she thought.

She would leave much of the telling to Flossie Mae, when she gits home. In her own due time, she should be the one to decide to who and what to tell. At least, she would get the ball rolling. She could hear footsteps upstairs. Generally, she would be preparing breakfast, but had decided that breakfast could wait. Her letter couldn't. So she returned to her room and began to write.

Dear Mr. and Mrs. DuPont,

> *My name is Francine Black. Your daughter, Flossie Mae has been staying at my Boarding House. I know it ain't my place to be writing this letter, but I done took a liking to her almost as if she was my very own. And that's why I took out this time to write to you even if I ought not to be poking my nose where it don't belong. Flossie Mae don't have no idea that I'm doing this. If she did, I'm sure she would pitch a plum fit. I don't need to tell you how stubborn she is. First, let me say that she ain't sick or*

nothing like that, but the City is a mighty big place. There ain't nothing like having a family who cares about you even when things don't go as well as you had hoped. According to what I done heard from your girl, I believes that's the kind of folks you all to be. Anyways, with that being said, I thinks your child needs to be around her family right now. I don't know what all she's been telling you, but knowing her as I believe I do, she done painted you a real rosy picture. Sir/Ma'am, I ain't never seen a rose bush yet that didn't have its' share of thorns. Your girl loves you all a whole heap. She misses you all something awful too.

> *Yours truly,*
> *Francine Black*

Afterward, Miss Francine wrestled with herself over whether to send the letter or not. It didn't take but a minute or two to convince herself that she was doing the right thing. Before doubt could try to twist her arm again, she folded the letter, put it into the envelope, sealed it, and put the postage stamp in place. There was no turning back now. And she sure wasn't about to waste three cents worth of postage.

During the early morning hours, Flossie Mae had managed to fall asleep, but wished she hadn't. She had dreamed about Augustus Atwater. He had come back from who-knows-where. His mouth was still full of lies. But that won't nothing strange. With his every breath and every step toward her, she drew her baby closer and held onto it tighter.

Then parts of the dream began to turn it into a nightmare. He kept saying that he was ready to be a father to their child and a true husband to her. Then he took the baby, walked out the door, looking back at her grinning one of his up-to-no-good grins. She woke up tired and scared.

Augustus Atwater had no right to *her* baby! She believed him to be capable of such a horrible act, especially if he saw it as a way to hurt her. She didn't put anything past him.

Right then and there, she decided that she didn't want him near her. Even more than that, she didn't want him to know there was a baby. The more she tried to convince herself that it was just a dream, the more she feared the possibilities. Though she hadn't seen hide or hair of him in months, like most snakes in the grass, he was subject to rear his old head at any time.

She didn't know it and probably never would, but Augustus Atwater wouldn't be showing himself to anyone on this side ever again. The Howard Brothers had done him in for good.

That sweet, young thing that he was messing with on the other side of town, unbeknownst to him, turned out to be one of the daughters of the elder brother. Besides being a *business man*, he had made quite a reputation for himself as a ladies' man. He suspected that he had fathered about sixteen children, give or take a few. Though he publicly acknowledged only four, the four he and his wife, Connie had born and raised.

It appeared that every which a way Augustus Atwater turned, life just seemed to outdo him. Of all the women he could have picked out of the hundreds, even thousands in the City—why did he? How did he manage to pick the daughter of one of the Howard Brothers?

At first glance, he thought that Frank Howard was coming after him over money again. The most he expected was to have his nose, his arm, his leg, or some other vital body part broken in two.

"Man, I'm going to pay you all of your money just as

soon as I get it," he promised. "I done run up on some hard times, a little snag, but I'm working on this deal. It's about to come through for me. When my ship comes in, I'm going to give you what I owe and then some. Man, you know I'm good for it."

The more Augustus tried to explain, the madder Frank Howard got. The madder he got, the harder he punched. He didn't stand a snowball sitting up on a hot, tin roof in mid-July of a chance. This giant of a man with his six-foot, three-hundred and twenty pound frame tossed him about as if he was a rag doll. If he hadn't caught him with his pants down, at least he could've and would've had a chance to run.

When Frank Howard got tired of whipping him, he pulled out his pistol. Then he looked down at him and said, "Man, this ain't 'bout no money this time, it's 'bout family! This my blood you messing 'round with!"

The last sound Augustus Atwater heard just before Frank Howard fired a bullet into him was the cry of young Gardenia screaming, "Daddy, no!!!!!" The last face he looked into wasn't one of an angry *business man*. Instead, it was one of an angry father. How unfortunate for him, the last *woman* to lay in his arms just happened to be the daughter of a Howard Brother. And the last breath he took, he took without knowing that he would soon be a father himself.

Perhaps, if Augustus had known—perhaps, he would have changed. No one will ever know, least of all, Augustus Atwater. Howbeit, he should've known that if we continually play with fire—eventually, we will get burned.

Mrs. Bertha was looking out the kitchen window when the mailman came. She stood watching the cloud of dusk he left behind drift toward her bedlinens flapping on the clothesline. "That po' man drives through here like he's racing to a fire," she said out loud.

She wiped her hands in her apron and walked out to the end of the road to check the mailbox. The new Sears catalogue had come. It was no more than a wish book except for the things she was able to pattern her Sunday dresses after. Then she noticed the two letters. The writing on one she recognized right off. It was Flossie Mae's. She didn't recognize the writing or the name on the other. Still, it was addressed to them, Mr. and Mrs. Frederick DuPont.

Mrs. Bertha sat down in her rocking chair. She stared at both letters for a long while, without opening either. "Why would somebody from the City who we don't know be writing to us?" she asked herself. "Well, you won't know 'less you read it," she answered herself.

First, she opened Flossie Mae's letter and read it. As usual, everything was fine and she missed them. And as always, Mrs. Bertha cried. Time hadn't made this thing no easier. She missed her young'un. And she wanted her to come on back home.

As she read Miss Francine's letter, her heart grew even heavier. It was more from what was not being said than what was actually said. Something was the matter with her baby just like she had suspected. The writer of the letter said that she wasn't sick or nothing. So what was it? Mrs. Bertha knew there was more than one way to be ailing. She asked herself, "What is That Boy's part in all of this?"

She tucked the letters into her apron pocket and walked out to the barn where Mr. Frederick DuPont was sharpening the plows' blades.

"A letter came from Flossie Mae today," she began.

"Did? What she have to say?" he asked, with a slight

smile. "Is she fixing to come home for a visit?"

"The way she keeps telling it, everything is just fine," she answered, a bit more skeptical than usual.

"Babe, that's a good thing, aint it? You sounding mighty doubtful," he said.

"I always wanted to believe that things were the way Flossie Mae said, but this here letter came in the mail too," Mrs. Bertha said, taking the letter out of her apron pocket to hand over to her husband.

"Why don't you read it to me, Bab," he asked. "I don't have my specks out here with me."

Mrs. Bertha gladly obliged him, knowing the true reason why he had asked her to read the letter had little or nothing to do with his specks. As a child, her Frederick had worked so much just to help keep the family going, he didn't have much time for proper schooling. He could read about as well as their young'uns could in the second or third grade. He could scratch out his name and a few other things if he had to, but much of that was self-taught.

She would never utter a word about him going out to the barn with the chirrens' school books. He didn't think she knew, but she did. There won't much about him that she didn't know. She knew how shame he was over his shortcomings as far as his education was concerned. With all of that being said, she felt that he was still one of the smartest men she knew. She was real proud of him and told him so every chance she got.

After Mrs. Bertha had finished reading the letter, Mr. DuPont stood silent for a time. Then he said, "Babe, you know she got to come back home, don't you? She done went there and tried life on for size. Although we didn't want her to go, we stepped aside and let her do things her way. But I can't see a young'un of ours out there sinking in deep waters and we don't do something or another to try to pull them out . Flossie Mae is coming home even if I have to drive up yonder myself to git her."

Mrs. Bertha didn't say much that would add or subtract from what her husband had said. She just put the letters back into their envelopes. "I'm going back up to the house to finish looking my greens," she said.

"Woman, you ain't seen me all the morning. You 'bout to waltz off, just like that, without even giving me some Shugar?" he teased.

"Frederick Douglass DuPont, I declare, you acts just like we still courting." Mrs. Bertha flirted.

"Ain't we?" he asked.

"Sho' is," she laughed, planting a big one right on his lips, then switching off.

"Gal, I love to see you coming, but I declare, I sho'nuff love to watch you go!" he laughed, slapping himself on the leg.

She laughed in that way she had whenever they were being frisky with one another. She then gave him something to look at all the way back up to the house.

As usual, her Frederick had managed to take her mind off trouble, but no sooner than the screened door had shut behind her, she was thinking about how they could get Flossie Mae to come back home short of dragging her. One thing she was certain of, it sure wouldn't be easy. Nothing with that child had been easy—starting with the day she come into the world. There was something about her that caused her to walk the long way around rather than take the short cut.

In and of its' self, there won't a thing wrong with that.

The problem was, all the things that were bound to come up against you along the way. The longer the walk, the more chances there are to stumble. A body couldn't help but get more than its' fill of lumps and bumps and bruises. Thankfully, with the right love and care, those were things that would eventually heal.

It appeared, Flossie Mae had run up on more than her share. But like her Mama used to say, "A hard head makes way for a mighty sore bottom."

Still, they had to find a way to get Flossie Mae to come back home.

In the meanwhile, Miss Francine who was seldom shaken by much, jumped every time the phone rang. She figured the DuPonts had gotten her letter by now. The day was sure to come when they would call Flossie Mae and tell her about it.

She won't expecting no big fireworks behind it or nothing like that. If Flossie Mae pitched a fit, she could handle it. But, what she was afraid of was, losing her trust. The girl needed somebody to talk to, somebody who cared enough about her to tell her the truth. Miss Francine was determined to fill the gap until she could get back home to her Mama. That's who she really needed, her Mama.

CHAPTER TWENTY NINE

Sunday dinner at the DuPont's house hadn't missed a beat since Flossie Mae's departure. But, this particular Sunday's gathering was very different. Everyone could tell that something was lying heavy on Mrs. Bertha's heart. And when Mr. DuPont blessed the food, he was unusually long-winded.

The table was spread with fried chicken, field peas, turnip greens, candied yams, rice and giblet gravy, corn on the cob, buttermilk pies, a six-layered chocolate cake, and iced tea. Mrs. Bertha had done all she could to satisfy the likings and the appetites of her family. She intended to bring her family together every chance the Good Lord gave her even if she had to do it with the help of fried chicken and greens. And if the food didn't get them, Mr. DuPont's ending prayer would certainly give them something to think about.

After everyone had praised her on cooking such a fine meal and had assured her of their sincerity by eating 'til they were about to pop, Mrs. Bertha sensed that it was 'bout her turn to speak. She knew each and every one of her chirren as well as she knew the back of her hands. Ophelia, the oldest was real good at barking out orders, but when it came to doing, she had to be coaxed or pushed harder than the rest of them. She had just as many excuses for why she couldn't do as she had reasons for why somebody else should.

Since she and Buddy had the most dependable car

amongst them, in her mind, it stood to reason that they should be the ones to go. But, of course, she won't about to overstep her bounds. She had never been a conniving sort of woman, but as Mrs. Bertha sat and watched while Buddy Washington ate like it was his last meal, reared back in her chair and patted his belly, she said within herself, "The seven or eight years of Sunday dinners he done ate ought to be more than enough to cover the cost of the trip." However, she and Frederick were more than willing to pay.

She kept her hands busy while everyone else ate their fill and beyond. Mr. DuPont continued to sit at the table. Usually, he and the other menfolk went out on the porch while the womenfolk cleaned up, packed away food, saw to the babies, chatted and/or whatever else caused them carry-on as they did when left to themselves.

As soon as Buddy got ready to push his chair back, Mr. DuPont cleared his throat. "We got a letter from Flossie Mae the other day," he began, "and Miss Black, the lady she rents from, she sent us a letter too."

"We got them on the same day," Mrs. Bertha added.

"Well, the lady seems to think that your sister needs to come home," Mr. DuPont continued.

"Is something wrong?" Betty asked, her eyes stretched wide with concern.

"Only thing she needs to do is git her end back on that bus and bring herself on back home then!" Ophelia interjected.

"Ophelia, if it was that easy, I'm sure she would've come back home by now," Mrs. Bertha said.

"Mama, every last one of us begged that gal not to leave 'way from here! What she want us to do now, beg her to come back?" Ophelia asked, looking at Buddy who was nodding his big head.

"Tell me, which one of y'all wouldn't want us to do all that was in our power to save you? If and when you was to ever find yourself out in the middle of nowhere and something had come up and grabbed a hold of you, wouldn't you expect your family to try to help you? Ophelia are you saying that you would want us to leave you be, let you fend for yourself, let you make it the best way you can? Wouldn't you want us to grab hold to something and go after you? Or would you rather we just stand on the edge and holler to you that you ain't had no business out there?" Mrs. Bertha asked. Though her questions were directed at Ophelia, she was talking to each and every one of them. And they all knew it.

"All I know is, some peoples don't ever learn 'less they go by things the hard way," Ophelia said, trying to stand her ground without realizing she didn't have any ground to stand upon.

"Well, seems to me, if Flossie Mae is tired of life in the *Big City,* all she got to do is git herself on the bus and come back home just like my wife said," Buddy added, about to point his finger.

Ophelia looked at her husband. Her big, stuffed to brim husband with his big feet still underneath her Mama and Papa's table, acting beside himself. There was a great, big difference in her talking 'bout her sister and him talking 'bout her. She knew how far to go.

Mr. DuPont thought about how he had a remedy for that finger if it ever gits pointed in the wrong direction. He loved his son-in-law, but he felt that Buddy Washington, at times, was as full of himself as he was of the Sunday meal he just ate.

"Mama, I'll call Flossie Mae and tell her that we can

come and get her at the end of the month," Betty said.

"You'll do no such thing! Child, you ain't got a bit of business out there on that road in your condition. Whiles you out there, trying to help somebody else, you libel be the one needing help your own self!" Ruby said.

"Helping somebody else? Flossie Mae ain't just somebody else! She's our sister! And she needs us!" Betty said, close to tears.

"Hold your wagons in the road!" Mr. DuPont commanded. His tone of voice left no doubt that he meant for them to hush up their fuss!

Mrs. Bertha just sat in silence, looking from one of her gals to the next.

"Mama, you know that we ain't able to go, but we'll do what we can to help out. I can fix a box so whoever goes can have something to eat on. And we'll be glad to give a few dollars for gas or whatever else might come up," Mable said.

"Now, Mable—you knows if there's any cooking to be done, Mama wants to do it herself," Ophelia butted in before Mrs. Bertha could answer.

"No, I say, "if Mable wants to do it, she should do it. Thank you, Shug," Mrs. Bertha said, looking in Mable's direction, smiling.

"Well, we can help with the gas too. Old Betsy does good getting us around Coley's Corner. I'm afraid, much further than that and she'll put us down for sure. No sense in taking no unnecessary chances out there," Joanne said.

"That old mess won't even git y'all 'cross the bridge and back much less all the way up to the Phillie-del-fee-ia," Buddy said, grunting afterward like he had just said something noteworthy.

Isaiah reared up. Joanne patted him on the arm. It was hard to get use to Buddy Washington even though they'd had years to do it. He had the means of a poor man, but the mouth of a rich man who was accustomed to rubbing other folks' nose in his money. Trouble was, the means never managed to catch up with the mouth.

"We will take that old truck out yonder and go git her ourselves 'fore we allow y'all to start squabbling over this!" Mr. DuPont said. Though everyone knew if he meant that truck parked out in the yard, they would never make it. But, no one dared to utter a word, not even Buddy Washington.

For a minute or two, everyone sat in silence. Then Betty spoke, "I believe I know what our trouble is, Flossie Mae had the nerve to go out and do something that we have only dreamed about. She left home in search of her dreams. Maybe things didn't turn out the way she had hoped, but least she tried. If the truth be told, every last one of us done thought about or talked about leaving Coley's Corner, someday. Flossie Mae went further than any of us had the nerve to. She did it. And if we're mad about anything, let it be because she got to come back home."

"Nah, that ain't what I'm mad about! And I'm just gonna go 'head and tell it!" Fanny fussed. "Ever since the day she was born, Flossie Mae ain't done a thing except twist Mama and Papa 'round her   finger. Whatever Flossie Mae wants folks act like she 'pose to git it. We took our ends out in the fields and worked like hired field hands instead of daughters."

"Huh! We worked out yonder like menfolk," Ophelia added, "had to."

"But, not Flossie Mae! She always thought she was too good to git out yonder and sweat 'long with the rest of us.

She done it, but she complained every step of the way," Fanny continued.

"Not only that—she complained 'bout everything from having to walk to school to wearing hand-me-downs to living in Coley's Corner. Everything!" Ruby chimed in.

"Only thing that gal thought she was 'pose to do was sing in the choir and sit 'round looking pretty," Joanne said, adding yet another voice to the tirade.

Mrs. Bertha and Mr. Frederick sat, listening. They had said within themselves that these things were good to know. It was a good thing to hear out in the open what had been hidden in their chirren's hearts for years.

"What I want to know is, what she coming back here for? If she hated being here so much and couldn't wait to leave, why she coming back? Ain't one thing done changed in Coley's Corner, not one thing!" Ophelia said. Then she added, "Ma, y'all know we love Flossie Mae and everything but,"

"But nothing!" Mr. DuPont interrupted. "I'm surprised at y'all. We're family. And family loves one another. That love keeps right on loving in good times as well as the bad. You gals are doing a whole heap of talking 'bout your sister and all, but in my mind, the thing is already settled. Your sister is coming home—with y'all's blessings or without them. We ain't fixing to sit here and wait 'til she's lying in a pine box to bring her either. If it takes every breath in my body, I'll see to that!"

Truth was, Mr. DuPont had looked 'cross the table and seen the disappointment on his Bertha's face. He felt steamed enough to take on a bear!

"Papa and Mama DuPont, y'all ain't got to worry 'bout this no more. We'll make arrangements so Flossie Mae can come home. Me and Betty will see to it. I'll drive. I need Betty to stay here with y'all 'til I come back. And then I'm gonna need one of the womenfolk to ride with me," Joseph Avery said, trying to ease the tension as well as the DuPonts' minds.

"I'll go!" Ophelia said.

"Who will cook my" Buddy Washington started to ask.

"Buddy, now you know that you and the chirrens always have more than a plenty to eat! Besides, this trip can't take more than a day at the most. Ain't that right?" Ophelia asked, eyeballing Joseph.

Understandably, Joseph was looking at Betty who was looking at her Mama. She wanted her to do something, to say something. The last person they had expected to speak up 'bout going was Ophelia. And won't nobody in the mood to be hearing her mouth all the way to the City and back.

"Before this here thing goes any further, I want to have my say," Mrs. Bertha began. "Ophelia, you're the oldest. I expect you to act like the oldest. Don't go up yonder, rattling off at the mouth like an empty wagon. You ain't going so you can point fingers and such. Your job is to git in that car, ride up yonder, git your sister and bring her back home. That's all you got to do. Don't let me hear tell of you trying to chastise her. Can't a one of us see past sunset much less way down the road into next week. Don't none of us know what next year holds for us. If we did, we might not want to git ourselves out the bed."

"Mama, I" Ophelia started.

"Hush up and listen to me!" Mrs. Bertha commanded.

"Ain't a one of us above making mistakes. All of us have at some time or another. If we keep on living, we bound to make some more. We can't afford to walk around being all high-minded and so quick to speak against somebody else, so unforgiving. It will sooner or later show us up for who we really are. My Lord was the Only Perfect One to walk this earth. He lived a blameless life, yet, He didn't look down on nobody. The Good Book that I read tells me that all of us fall short. All of our righteousness is like filthy rags. And I can't see where one dirty rag got room to be speaking against another dirty rag. And if you leave a dirty rag lying 'round long enough, it'll sour and soon start stinking. You might not be guilty of what I'm guilty of, but we're all guilty just the same. What our Lord done for us while He hung up on that Cross is what makes the difference. Sin had done us in. Every one of us was born into it, but thanks be to our God, we don't have to die in it. It behooves every one of us to be careful 'bout how we run other folk down. But for grace, it could have been you and me too. I ain't got much more to say except this here. Y'all find room in your hearts to love your sister. You love her and let judgment be God's. He's a just God. He sees and He knows the whole of a thing when we only know or think we know in part."

Everyone sat, looking down into empty plates. Ruby's baby girl broke the silence when she woke up hollering.

"And let the church say, 'Amen', " Mr. DuPont said.

Folks left the table quicker than bear feet can make their way across a hot-tin roof. Ruby was glad to go see to her baby—much gladder than she had been in a long time. Four babies in five years was taking its' toll on her body and her nerves, especially when her old man acted as if his only responsibility was to call her name each and every time he heard them cry or need changing or anything else.

Mrs. Bertha went into the kitchen. Mr. DuPont followed close behind. "Gal, I believe you done missed your calling," he said, laughing.

"Frederick, sometimes, your chirren—your been-grown chirren acts just like lap babies! I had to say something less I be forced to remind them of a few things! They wouldn't want folks to point out or hold up their faults for the whole world to see!" Mrs. Bertha was stewing worse than a pot full of red, ripe stewed tomatoes.

"You done preached that fine sermon and all. I believe *'our chirren'* have seen the error of their ways. If they don't, a few more of your sermons Reverend DuPont and they'll all be changed," Mr. DuPont said in an attempt to bring a little calm to the storm that was stirring up, inside of his wife.

"Won't nothing new said in yonder. Those gals of *yours* been hearing that same talk all of their lives. And it don't seem like a bit of it done sunk in. Here they are, trying to raise up babies when they still acting like babies their own selves!" Mrs. Bertha said as she continued to stew.

"Well, I'm goin' out on the front porch," Mr. DuPont said. He knew when his Bertha spewed steam like a boiling tea kettle, it was best to leave her be and let her cool off on her own.

"Grandma" Mrs. Bertha heard.

Suddenly, Ruby's oldest son, James was gripping her about the legs. She was about to tell him to go on back outside with the others when he said, "Grandma, thanks for cooking that good food. I love coming to your house."

Mrs. Bertha bent down and gave him a big hug. "Baby, I love you coming to my house. And I love you too," she said.

She couldn't help but smile. Chirren have a way of stirring up something on the inside of you. And they also have a way of melting that something. "Shugar, I sho' do thank you for coming in here. You gave your old grandma just what she needed." Mrs. Bertha said, patting James on his head.

"Grandma, do you still like peppermint sticks? " he asked.

"I sho' do —Do you?" she asked.

"Yes ma'am," he answered. His eyes began shining brighter than two brand-new fifty cent pieces.

"Well, you take one and tell the rest of them to come and get one," she said as she reached into the candy jar.

What she did for one, she tried to do for all. That's the way she had raised up her chirren. That's the way she tried to be with her grands too. Needless to say, every child's shoes didn't wear out at the same time. Nor did every child get a belly ache at the same time. And neither did every child need lifting up or sitting down at the same time. She didn't favor one over the other. She loved all of her chirren—from Ophelia to Flossie Mae. She called each and every one of them out to the Good Lord. Her tears flowed as freely for one as they did for the other.

CHAPTER THIRTY

Betty and Joseph had a telephone installed. She didn't have to go to the store to use the pay phone anymore, but she did. Party-lines left little room for privacy when you had folks sharing the line who were bent on not minding their own business. What she had to say to Flossie Mae was of no concern to Mrs. Bennett or Mrs. Hardy. But that never stopped them from listening in before. She and Joseph's ring was two long ones and then a short one. Other than that, they didn't bother with picking up the telephone.

"Hello," Miss Francine said.

"Hello, Miss Francine, this is Betty, Flossie Mae's sister. Before you call my sister to the telephone, I want to thank you for writing that letter to my folks. I would love to meet you one day. I believe you really do care about my sister's well-being. And I want to tell you that we sure do appreciate everything you've done for her."

"Child, I ain't done a thing I wouldn't want somebody to do for one of mine if I had any. She can be mighty stubborn when she wants to be. But, at the same time, she got a great, big heart. I best git her to this phone 'fore this call puts you in the po' house," Miss Francine said.

They both laughed. Then she called out to Flossie Mae in a voice almost loud enough to raise a body from their eternal rest.

"Hello" Flossie Mae said in a sleepy voice.

"Gal, you still sleeping? Half the day is 'bout gone. The City done spoiled you rotten," Betty said, teasing.

"Betty! Is everything all right?" Flossie Mae asked.

"Everything is fine, sleepyhead," Betty answered, searching for the right words to say.

"Did y'all get my letter?" Flossie Mae asked.

"Listen sis, I got just a few more minutes left so I best make good use of them and come right out and tell you why I'm calling. Flossie Mae, Joseph and Ophelia are coming to get you at the end of the month. Mama and Papa says that it's time for you to come home. We all miss you so much. So please don't say , "No". Just come for a visit. Then, if you must go back, we'll understand. But, I must tell you that Papa is ready to drive his old truck up there if need be. None of us want to see that happen," Betty said.

"I would love to, but I" Flossie Mae began.

"I got to go. I'll call to let you know the day they'll be coming. Love you, sis. See you when you get here," Betty said, pretending not to hear what Flossie Mae was saying.

By the time the call ended, Flossie Mae felt like she had a belly full of butterflies. Betty had said that they were coming to get her at the end of the month. She couldn't go home, not in her condition. Neither was she ready to hear them say, "I-Told-You-So". Just the thought of having to ride all the way back home, listening to Ophelia was enough to prick anybody's nerves.

When she came to the City, she came on a bus with nothing but a handful of promises to go on. She didn't know where hide or hair of Augustus Atwater was. She hadn't heard from him nor had she gone out looking for him.

"Gal, you look like you done seen the boggy-man or something. What in the world wrong with you?" Miss

Francine asked.

"Nothing," Flossie Mae answered as she turned her face away from Miss Francine and continued to walk back to her room.

"Child, I don't want to pry, but I can see as plain as daylight that something is troubling you." Miss Francine insisted although she already had a good idea what that frown on her face was all about.

"Betty says that her husband, Joseph and my oldest sister, Ophelia are coming at the end of the month to take me back home," Flossie Mae explained.

"And what did you say to that?" Miss Francine asked.

"She didn't give me a chance. She said that she would call to let me know when they'll be leaving," Flossie Mae explained.

"Are you going?" Miss Francine asked.

"I don't know. How can I?" Flossie Mae asked, her voice breaking as fear and shame tried to get the best part of her.

"Look-a here, gal, you ain't the first one who done found yourself in a fix and you best believe, you won't be the last. This here world is full of folks who done tried their hands at one thing or another and failed. But one thing I can say 'bout you, you stayed up on that bucking pony longer than I would have. Some folks ended up in a pit, but it turned out to be the best thing that could've happened to them. Honey, I done seen you look like you was plum lost and didn't have no good idea where to turn in to. I done seen your eyes full of homesickness and longing for family. Life tried to break you, but you held on. And what life couldn't do to you—you tried to do to yourself. I done told you time and time again that I done come to love you like one of my own, but Shug, you don't need me. You need your mama and papa. You need your family 'round you. You ain't got a bit of business staying up here, trying to raise that young'un on your own when there's so much love waiting to be poured out on you," Miss Francine advised.

"Miss Francine, it ain't just that," Flossie Mae began. "Before I left home, I said some things to my Mama 'bout how we were living and all. I even talked about the Lord just like I didn't need Him no more. My eyes were all fixed on leaving home and making a big name for myself. And when I left home, I didn't love Augustus Atwater a bit more than a farmer loves a drought. Here I am now, 'bout to have his young'un and I don't know where he is or where to look for him and wouldn't care if I did. I done had plenty of time to be honest with myself. All I seen in Augustus Atwater was a ticket out of Coley's Corner. I knew Papa would never hear tell of me just going off to Lord-Only-Knows-Where by myself. I figured he wouldn't be able to stop me if I was following after my husband. Up 'til the night I walked out of the Club, I longed for that kind of life with everything that was in me. Singing was the only thing I wanted to do. I wanted to be a *star*. I wanted folks to look up to me. But I came to Philadelphia and made a big mess of my life. After all I done been through, that's all I got to take back home with me to show for all the time I done wasted—a great, big, old mess."

"It's true, on one hand, you going home with a lot more baggage than you left with. But on the other hand, you going back with a lot less. I know how it is to get the big-head and feel like home ain't got nothing more to offer to you. You feel like you done been squeezed into a tight spot and you can't see no way out. Everywhere you look, things keep going on just like they did the day before. You screaming, but don't a soul hear you. Everybody except you seems content with the way things are. So you keep peeping 'cross the fence. And you do it for 'bout as long as you can stand to—'til you see an opening. But when you finally get over yonder, you find that the other side ain't a bit better than where you were—it's just different. And Baby, that's what you got to take back home with you, you got everything you done learned whiles you been over here on the other side. You done learned some lessons for yourself as well as for that young'un you carrying in your belly, 'long with any more that might come along. Every road we allowed to travel, we travel for a reason. Don't think that it's no mistake that you happened to come this way. Sure you might've made a few mistakes 'long the way. Hindsight done let you see that you probably could have found a better way. But, you show me a man who claims to have never made a mistake and I'll show you an old, big, fat lying fool. Whatever you have done wrong or believes that you could have done better, for whatever mistakes you done made on this pathway called, "Life." Baby, you got to forgive yourself. And then, you got to forgive those who you believe done wronged you. That's the only way you gonna keep that thing from hoovering over you like yesterday's dark and gloomy, rain-filled clouds. Otherwise, it will keep you stuck and drenched in the misery of the valley called, "Could-a, Would-a, Should-a. "

"But how can I look my folks in the face?" Flossie Mae asked. "They don't know 'bout nothing except how good I been doing. That's all I ever told them in my letters."

"Your folks ain't about to hold you to that. They may have never set foot in the big city before, but I bet they know enough about life to know that no matter how lovely the rose may be, the stem is still full of thorns. Rain comes in everyone's life. It comes in various degrees, for any number of reasons. After you done lived a while, you learn that it's coming. You just don't know when or whether you're git a sprinkle or a downpour. Child, life don't pick out no special people to pick on. It happens to us all. As for the Lord, you saying how you didn't need Him no more didn't move Him in the least. He knew that you did. He knew that you would. And He knows that you will. He knew that sooner or later you would have an occasion to call on Him again. And He knew exactly when that day would come. So He loved you enough and had patience enough to wait on you. That's how your folks did too. They willing to make the first step and come for you. They probably know that your stubbornness or pride or shame or disappointment won't allow you to. That right there tells me that they ain't through loving on you. Gal, if I was you, I would go on back home and grab up all the love I can."

"But I" Flossie Mae began.

"But you can swallow that pride of yours or you can choke on it," Miss Francine said. She was done with babying Flossie Mae. "I'm gonna let you go on. I done had my say. I got to git myself down there to that bank 'fore all of us be out the door. All I ask is that you think about what your folks are trying to do for you."

Flossie Mae went up the back stairway, to her room. She sat in the chair by the window and laid her hands across her belly, "What a surprise you'll be," she said.

CHAPTER THIRTY ONE

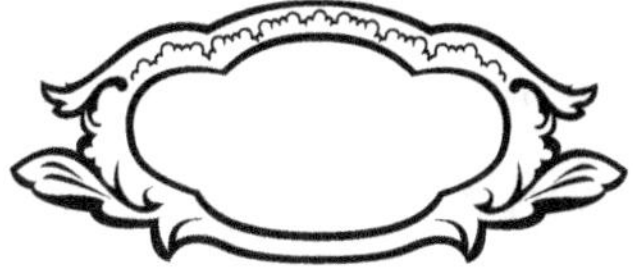

Joseph Avery was on his way home when he spotted Odell White standing in front of the General Store/Bus Depot. The smell of diesel was still in the air. Odell White waved with one hand and lifted his duffel bag with the other. He had enlisted in Uncle Sam's Army and was home on leave.

Joseph had bearly stopped the car before he was out and shaking Odell's hand. They had been friends probably since the first day they laid eyes on one another which was further back than either of them could remember. Folks used to say, "If you see one of them, you'll see them all". Them, included, James Russell. They were like three peas in a pod.

As it so often does, life eventually changed them from young boys full of mischief into young men. Joseph Avery married Betty. Odell White went into service. And James Russell moved to Bridgeton where he had landed a job working at the Bridgeton Textile Mills.

Odell put his duffel bag in the back. "My Mama will be surprised. She didn't know I was coming. I can't wait to sink my teeth into a piece of her fired chicken," Odell said, laughing as if he could already taste it.

"How you doing, man?" Joseph asked, reaching over to pat Odell on the shoulder.

"Life is good! The Army ain't quite what I expected. Then again, it's more than I expected. All of that training sort of cleared my head," he answered.

"Me and my wife got us a baby coming soon!" Joseph announced, grinning from ear to ear.

"Knucklehead, you mean, you fixing to be somebody's daddy?" Odell teased.

Joseph's grin got even wider. "Yeah man, I sure am," he said, baring the look of a proud, soon-to-be papa. Had he not been driving, he probably would have strutted around with his chest stuck out just like the proudest rooster in the chicken coot.

Then Odell's look grew more serious. "How is Betty and the rest of the family?" he asked.

"Betty is doing fine, considering she done got as round as a ball. But I ain't complaining. That just gives me more of her to love. And the rest of the family is doing fine to," he answered.

"How is Flossie Mae? You know it almost tore my heart out when she married that—what's his name? You know—I been in love with that girl ever since we were in the fifth grade. I done everything I could, but she wouldn't have no parts of me," Odell said.

"I thought you said all of that Army training had done cleared your head. Don't seem all that clear to me. Your mind is just as fixed on Flossie Mae as it ever was," Joseph said, stopping the car in front of "The White House" which was the childhood nickname they had given to Odell's house.

"I still think about her every now and then. But I know she's a married woman now. There's no hope for us. Never was. Flossie Mae likes city boys. Maybe we can get together 'fore I head back. We can look up James Russell or something," Odell said, grabbing his duffel bag from the back seat.

"We'll do that, but I'll have to let you know. Babies come whenever they get ready or so Mama DuPont says. And just in case anybody's interested, I'm supposed to be driving up to the City next week to get Flossie Mae," Joseph said.

"Odell leaned into the car, acting way too interested, especially for somebody who done professed to have gotten over somebody. "Flossie Mae is coming home? You sure, man? You got a load? Do you need another driver?" he asked.

"It's just me and her sister. You remember Ophelia don't you?" Joseph asked, smiling.

"Oh Lord! Not Ophelia, Miss-Mouth-Almighty herself! 'Miss Yall-Better-Git-On-Back-Down-The-Road-Somewhere -Cause-Ain't-Nobody-Courting-'Round-Here!" Odell mocked.

Both men laughed.

"Too bad Betty can't come. It's too close to her time. Otherwise, it would be like old times—me and Betty, you and Flossie Mae. And the only one who won't know that y'all ain't a couple would still be you," Joseph teased.

Odell laughed, but still, the thought stung him a little. He was in love with Flossie Mae. His affections for her were real. If she had given him a chance, he would have done right by her. Before he could express any of this to his friend, his mother came out on the front porch.

"Boy, you better git yourself on up here and give your Mama a hug!" Miss White called from the front porch.

"How are you doing, Mrs. White?" Joseph asked, getting out of the car to speak.

"Just fine and you?" she answered, then added, "Saw Betty the other day. That gal is as big as a tick!" she laughed.

"Don't forget me, man," Odell said before running up to where his Mama was standing.

Joseph had to turn around and go back the way he had come. He'd gotten so excited over seeing Odell White that he almost forgot that he was supposed to pick up something from the store for his wife. "Pickles, coconut cookies, a pint of strawberry ice cream, and hair grease," he repeated aloud.

As Betty had promised, she called Flossie Mae to tell her that Joseph and Ophelia would be leaving early Saturday morning, before daylight. She didn't tell her that Odell White was planning to come along. In a way, she was hoping that he would change his mind. She felt that Flossie Mae needed time to herself and time for her family. Knowing that Odell White probably still had strong affections toward her sister, she didn't want him to get his hopes up. She couldn't recall Flossie Mae ever giving him the time of day. And although she hadn't mentioned him in a while, it was possible that Augustus Atwater could be somewhere in the picture, a strong possibility at that. But, seen or not seen, he was in the picture. He was her husband.

Mrs. Bertha readied Flossie Mae's room like she was expecting a newborn baby instead of a fully grown, young woman. She turned the mattress, changed the bedlinens, put on one of her best bedspreads, mopped and waxed the linoleum, beat the throw rugs, washed, starched, and ironed the curtains, opened up the windows, and any and every other thing she could think of.

Early Saturday morning before the rooster crowed or Mr. DuPont's feet could hit the floor, Mrs. Bertha was up, stirring around in the kitchen. In her mind, Flossie Mae hadn't been eating right and had probably turned into a puny, little somebody. One thing she knew for sure, the gal could hardly boil water without scorching it neither had she been interested in learning any different.

When Mr. DuPont came into the kitchen, she told him that she was just fixing Flossie Mae a little something to nibble on.

"Babe, it sho' is good to see your eyes twinkle like starlight again. Girl, I declare, this morning, you looking like that sweet, young thing I fell in love with way back when. If I had known it would make you look this good, this early of a morning, I would have went up yonder and brought that gal of ours home a long time ago," Mr. DuPont said, squeezing Mrs. Bertha from behind.

'Man, you better sit down and eat your breakfast 'fore it gits cold. Cause you the one walking 'round here with your eyes twinkling like they full of starlight. Frederick, I know that you been thinking 'bout Flossie Mae. But thanks be to God, our baby girl is coming back home where she belongs," Mrs. Bertha said, throwing her hands up in praise.

"Gal, are you sure you preparing just a nibble? Looks to me you're planning on a feast," he said.

"I'm only cooking fried chicken, field peas, turnip greens with corn meal dumplings, sweet tea and chocolate cake. And that's all I plan on cooking. No sense in making a great, big meal. We're still having that on Sunday," she said.

Mr. DuPont shook his head. He remembered everything on her list to be Flossie Mae's favorites. "Well, don't work yourself into a frenzy," he said.

He knew there won't no sense in saying much else. The way his Bertha felt about her chirren, especially one who had left and was now returning, he won't about to get in the way of that. He was just glad that they could eat off the land. Otherwise, the way his wife cooked, would put them in the poor house for sure.

Miss Francine was also up early. She intended on seeing Flossie Mae and her family off with a good, hot meal. If everything went according to plan, they should get there by eight o'clock. As hard as it would be to say, "Good-bye." she knew that Flossie Mae was doing the right thing. She saw a glimmer of light shining from underneath her door. She knocked. Flossie Mae was already dressed and packing her night clothes into her bag.

"Shug, are you sure you got everything? I don't want to have to hop on a bus to bring something to you," Miss Francine said, trying, but not really feeling up to kidding around.

"I believe I got everything, least everything that would fit. I gave some things to Miss Rosie. I don't think I'll be needing them no more," Flossie Mae answered.

Both women were doing all that was in their power not to break down. Then Miss Francine said, "What the heck, come on over here so we can get this over with." They held one another and cried.

"I will never forget you, Miss Francine. Thank you for all the talks and everything. If it won't for you, I don't know what I would've done," Flossie Mae cried.

"Child, you better not forget me. I won't let you. Don't think you done seen the last of me," Miss Francine cried.

They stood in silence.

In an attempt to lighten the mood, Miss Francine spoke, "Honey, we best get to moving. The wagon can't get loaded up with us standing 'round with our hands pushed down in our pockets. Can it?" With that, one sniffed—the other sighed;—both wiped away tears. Then Miss Francine left the room. Flossie Mae went back to her packing.

It was a good thing that Odell White had decided to come along. His army training had taught him a lot about map reading and following directions. Without him, Joseph had no doubt that they would have gotten lost plenty of times.

Ophelia wasn't much help. In fact, she wasn't any help. She slept during most of the trip which also proved to be a good thing. But it also meant that they had to listen to her snore worse than his Uncle Ned. He and Odell just shook their heads. Joseph was mighty glad that Betty didn't snore like that. He suspected that could be the reason why Buddy Washington was the way he was. The man probably hadn't had a good night's sleep in years.

After they'd parked in front of the Boarding House, they sat in the car for a few minutes, just looking around. The houses were so tall and so close together. And there won't hardly enough yard to shake a stick at.

"Huh," grunted Ophelia, finally waking up from her nap, "we here already?"

"Yelp. We made it," Joseph said.

"What we waiting for?" Odell asked.

"Wait a minute. Let me straighten myself up first," Ophelia said. "We been driving all the morning. I need to make myself presentable.

Joseph took notice of her, "We". He reckoned that "We" had also been sleeping too.

"We're here now! Why we still sitting in the car?" Odell

asked, opening the back door.

Joseph laughed. "Man, you on your way to put out a fire or something?" he asked.

"Nah! He probably trying to rush in yonder so he can go start up one. Don't think I don't know why you came. And I know you up to something. But I got my eye on you Odell White. You couldn't fool me then and you can't fool me now. Just remember, Flossie Mae is a married woman," Ophelia warned.

"It ain't like that. I'm just anxious to stretch these long legs of mine," Odell said, glancing in Joseph's direction. "I'm no longer that scared little boy and Miss Mouth Almighty you best understand that," he thought to himself. Yet, at the same time, he had to admit to himself that he was acting like one.

"Well folks, it's now or never," Joseph said, getting out of the car.

Odell opened the car door for Ophelia.

As they walked up to the door, Ophelia started, "I know one thing, that gal better not put up no fuss 'bout coming home or else I'm gonna,"

Joseph interrupted. "Ophelia, you know what Mama DuPont told you back at the house. Don't go to running that mouth of yours or else she'll take care of you."

Ophelia gasped. The nerve of this round-headed boy, trying to tell her what to do! Buddy Washington didn't even have that privilege and he was her husband. Before she could tell him so, Odell rang the doorbell. A sort of heavy-set woman with a great, big smile opened the door.

"Y'all must be Flossie Mae's peoples! Come on in here! My name is Francine Black! I sure am mighty pleased to meet y'all. Flossie Mae done told me so much about y'all. I don't feel like I'm meeting strangers. Now which one are you?" she asked, pointing toward Odell White.

"Ma'am, my name is Odell White. I'm just a friend of the family," he answered, extending his hand.

"I'm Ophelia Washington, Flossie Mae's oldest sister," Ophelia announced, stepping up to introduce herself. "And this here is Joseph Avery, my sister Betty's husband. Where's Flossie Mae?"

"I sure hope y'all ain't fixing to rush right off. I done prepared a hot meal and everything. Only thing missing is y'all sitting down at the table to eat it. Do anybody need to wash up or anything? The bathroom is down yonder, second door to your right," Miss Francine said, still not answering Ophelia's question.

"Menfolk, y'all can have a seat right in there. And Miss Ophelia could I please have a word with you in here ma'am. The food and Flossie Mae will be before you shortly."

Miss Francine and Ophelia stepped inside of a small, closed-in porch off the kitchen.

"I want to be careful not to over-step my bounds, but I think this bears saying. Your sister wants and needs to be with her family. She can also be as stubborn as a stuck door. It won't take much for her to dig her heels in and refuse to budge. Y'all needs to love up on your sister and let her know that y'all will still stand by her *irregardless* of whether she was able to make it in the City or not. And for now, she needs to be handled with care. What she don't need is y'all acting all high and mighty toward her like she is the only one who done ever tasted trouble. Y'all ain't got to whip her. She's been whipping up on herself enough for everybody. I knows you love her, so do what you can to make her feel like y'all welcoming her back home with opened arms. Do it as a favor to me. Honey, I sho' would appreciate it."

Ophelia DuPont Washington wasn't accustomed to allowing any and everybody to talk to her any kind of way. She didn't need nobody telling her how she ought to be treating *her* sister. She had known Flossie Mae all of her life. She had changed her diapers and wiped her snotty nose. This woman had known her for a couple of years and was talking as if she knew everything about her. But, Ophelia didn't say nothing except, "I understand". She won't about to disrespect somebody in their own house. Besides, she didn't want to have to deal with her Mama when she got back home. Whether she mentioned it or not, some kind of way, she would find out.

Truth be told, Ophelia didn't understand. She had no earthly idea what Miss Francine was talking about. What kind of trouble had Flossie Mae tasted? She won't about to worry with that now. There was plenty of time for that.

"Y'all needs to come on in here and eat this food 'fore it starts forming icicles. Just help yourselves. I'll go ahead and call Flossie Mae down here so she can eat too," Miss Francine commanded.

"Man, that woman put two feet and both elbows in this here! I believe she got some country in her," Odell said, smacking his lips and licking his fingers.

"Boy, you ain't been 'way from home five minutes and you done forgot all your manners! Ophelia began. "And ain't neither one of y'all blessed your food or nothing! I declare, y'all act just like a bunch of perishing, ill-mannered heathens! If I didn't know no better, I would think that you ain't had a lick of home training!" Ophelia scolded.

"Look here woman, I ain't fixing to take too much more of that mouth of yours. Buddy Washington might let you talk to him any, old kind of way, but I ain't Buddy Washington!" Odell fussed.

"And I done heard 'bout all I can take from both of y'all," Joseph said. "Let's not forget what we came here for. 'Fore I listen to any more of that racket, I'll leave y'all's behinds up here to get home the best way you can. I believe the bus usually runs through Coley's Corner 'bout Tuesday or Wednesday."

Ophelia smacked her lips and rolled her eyes, but she didn't say nothing, not one word. She didn't bother with saying too much to Joseph. He wasn't Odell White—somebody she could easily crank up. With Joseph, you never knew whether he was serious or just pulling your leg. And she was too far away from home to try him.

Everyone stopped eating about the same time and looked toward the doorway. Flossie Mae stood as if she wasn't quite sure if she should come forward or turn around and run in the opposite direction.

"Gal, you better git yourself over here and give your big sis a hug or something," Ophelia demanded.

"Ophelia ain't changed a lick. She is just as bossy as ever," Flossie Mae thought as she slowly walked over to the table.

Odell White sat, grinning from ear to ear. He didn't say nothing. He couldn't say nothing. Just being around Flossie Mae had always made him feel tongue-tied.

Joseph stood up. "Girl, we thought you had seen us coming and took off the other way," he joked.

"No. I've been waiting on y'all ever since Betty called to tell me that you were coming," she said. "I was just taking care of a few last minute things. I'm ready whenever y'all are."

Ophelia studied Flossie Mae hard. There was something different about her, something besides looking and acting older. She couldn't put her finger on it right then, but seldom did anything get past her for too long—or so she thought.

"Joseph, sit down and enjoy your food. Miss Francine got up early this morning just so we could be sent off with a good, hot meal," Flossie Mae said.

"And it sure is good too," Odell White finally managed to say. "This here food taste 'bout like my Mama or Miss Bertha cooked it. And Joseph, I sho' can't leave out Mrs. Emily. Cause your mama sho'nuff knows what to do with her pots and pans too."

"I done set most of my things by the front door. I'm gonna need some help with my big bags though," Flossie Mae said, pouring herself a glass of lemonade.

"Gal, you know that you ain't got to worry with lifting nothing. The *boys* can do that. Womenfolk don't have a bit of business struggling with no heavy bags when we got menfolk to do the struggling for us," Ophelia said.

"Flossie Mae, as you can see, ain't nothing changed. I won't call no names, but some folk are just as bossy as ever," Joseph said, laughing though he was quite serious. Flossie Mae wanted to laugh, but didn't. Odell White laughed and then added his two cents worth, "Some menfolk can't do the struggling cause their womenfolk wants to wear the pants. And let the church say, 'Amen'."

"Boy, you better quit that playing with the Lord! We should've left your narrow end back in Coley's Corner!" Ophelia fussed. It appeared, Odell White also had a pretty firm grip on her crank handle.

"I hope y'all ate a plenty. And if I can git anything else for y'all just let me know," Miss Francine said.

She had been trying to stay out of the way, but she had to come and check on Flossie Mae. She won't too concerned about the young men. Her sister, Ophelia gave her cause for concern though. She reckoned, being stubborn must run in the family . She'd seen how Ophelia looked at her when she was talking with her in private.

Flossie Mae was good and stubborn too, but she would listen. Her sister had a different kind of stubborn in her. She was used to running or trying to run the show and didn't want nobody telling her nothing. Miss Francine imagined that she was probably real familiar with trouble too.

"Miss Francine, we thank you for everything. The food was mighty good. I enjoyed every bite," Joseph said.

"If I didn't know no better, I would wrap a few of these biscuits and a couple pieces of this good, old ham meat up to take with me," Odell said.

"Honey, help yourself," Miss Francine said, smiling. She liked it when folks made a big fuss over her food.

"Now, that's a crying shame!" Ophelia scolded. "All of that food out yonder in the car and you in here begging like a half-starving young'un."

"That's all right. I don't say nothing that I don't mean. If I told him to help himself, that's what I meant. I done got too old and done seen way too much to be doing otherwise. Besides, it's my food. I bought it. I cooked it. And I can give it to whosoever I please," Miss Francine said.

Flossie Mae thought that Ophelia should just give up while she had the chance. Cause, there was no way she was gonna gain the upper hand with Miss Francine.

But Miss Francine almost looked forward to Ophelia trying to get the best of her. Many who were more apt than her had tried and failed. The family may have been too obliging to take her down a notch or two, but she won't. It appeared, she had gotten by for too long. Those young folks won't chirren no more. They needed to be treated as such. Like her Mama used to say, "Everybody got a place and they ought to learn how to roost or nest in it."

"Joseph, let me show y'all where my things are. I reckon we might as well get 'em loaded up," Flossie Mae said. "And Miss Francine, if you don't mind, I want to show Ophelia my room."

"First, they got to git over here and clean up their mess. Y'all acts just like y'all was raised up in the hog pen or something. Ain't nobody 'round here fixing to wait on y'all hand and foot!" Ophelia admonished.

Old habits die hard, especially when you don't see no need to change, ain't trying to change, and don't want to change. Much like her grandmother, Victoria DuPont had been, Ophelia was fine with Ophelia just the way she was too. It had served her well all these many years. She was the oldest. She would always be the oldest. And she planned on acting like the oldest. Period.

"Gal, what you got in here? Rocks?" Joseph asked, lifting Flossie Mae's larger bag.

"Just my clothes," Flossie Mae answered. She then added just as Odell White was about to pick up the other bag, "That's the one with the rocks in it."

Ophelia walked into Flossie Mae's room. It was a real nice room, but she would never admit it.

"How much was this setting you back every month? Why your room way back here? You sho' you was getting your money's worth?" Ophelia kept asking questions, without bothering to wait on the answers. Flossie Mae didn't understand why any of that was important now.

Flossie Mae really won't in a rush to go, but she was ready to get Ophelia away from there. She had said her goodbyes to the other tenants at suppertime, the night before. Now, all she had to do was make it through saying, "Goodbye" to Miss Francine again.

"We got everything loaded up. The boot is full and part of the back seat. We left just enough room for us," Joseph said.

"Well, I don't ride in nobody's back seat!" Ophelia said. "Y'all's bones are more limber than mine. I ain't fixing to be squeezed up in no back seat all the way back to Coley's Corner either!"

"What difference do it make who sits where as long as we all fit in the car?" Odell asked. Joseph wouldn't need nobody to remind him why he never wanted to ride in a car to anywhere if Ophelia and Odell would be riding in it too. Odell knew better than to follow up everything Ophelia said. If he was aiming to get Flossie Mae to finally take notice of him, she was noticing all right. Noticing how he was continuously drawn into the childish game of Tit-For-Tat with her sister, Ophelia.

Miss Francine stood, watching. Flossie Mae had already hugged her and said her goodbyes, but just before she got into the car, she ran back and hugged her again. Miss Francine couldn't help but cry. Flossie Mae cried too. Even Ophelia had to catch a tear or two.

"Gal, you better not forget to write me. I wants to keep up with how *everything* is going," Miss Francine said.

"I won't. I won't," Flossie Mae promised, getting into the car.

Joseph coughed then he started the car.

Odell cleared his throat. Slid in the backseat beside Flossie Mae and closed the door.

As they drove away, Miss Francine waved. "Y'all be careful out yonder on that road," she said.

Flossie Mae looked back until they turned the corner. She tried, but she couldn't stop crying. Odell White held her hand. He didn't mean anything by it. He was only trying to offer her a little comfort the best way he knew how. She didn't pull back. She just continued to cry.

Later, when she fell asleep, her head rested upon his shoulder. He didn't mind. She could lean on him whenever she needed to, for as long as she needed to. As soon as he laid eyes on her back at the Boarding House, he knew that he still had strong feelings for her. This time, it won't some schoolboy's crush, but feelings a grown man have toward a grown woman.

For now, he won't planning to do anything with those feelings except use them to hold her hand and rest her head. That's what she needed so that's what he would offer. But if she ever decided that she didn't need or want anything from him, he had to be man enough to let go. And as a man, he was willing to take that chance.

Thankfully, Ophelia fell asleep and slept for most of the trip back. Flossie Mae was happy about that. She won't ready for nobody to start asking her about Augustus Atwater. For one thing, she didn't have any answers to give them. She didn't know what had become of him. And she was certain his Aunt Lucy would ask. But her answer would be the same for her and everyone else. "I don't know."

CHAPTER THIRTY TWO

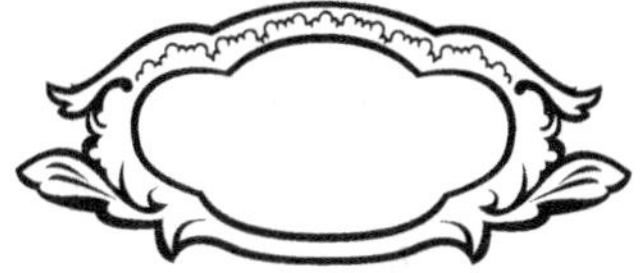

The closer Flossie Mae got to home, the more wide-eyed she became. Things looked so different. Though the cotton fields were still cotton fields and still went on for what seemed like miles and miles. And though Coley's Corner still appeared to be mostly made up of one corn field after another, still, it was home.

When Joseph finally turned onto the dirt road leading to her folks' place, the place that she had called, "home" for most of her life, she wanted to get out of the car and run to them. Being home had never felt so good—had never been appreciated so much.

After Joseph parked the car in front of the house, Mr. DuPont stood on the porch as if he was unable to move. He knew that he was wide awake. At the same time, he wondered if he was dreaming. It was almost eight o'clock in the evening which meant there was almost another good hour of daylight left. He was wide awake and waiting. Yet, he didn't see his baby girl.

After he was certain that Flossie Mae was in the car, he began to cry out, "Bertha! Bertha! Our Baby done come home! Flossie Mae is home!"

Flossie Mae ran up on the porch and hugged her Papa as if every bit of life she had left in her depended upon him hugging her back.

Ophelia stood on the other side of the car, looking toward the porch and mumbling to herself, "It's been quite some time since I've seen Papa carrying on like that. We come by here every single Sunday and sometimes we come during the week. Flossie Mae took herself 'way from here against their wishes. And now, he's over yonder 'bout to have a plum hissy fit just because she done decided to come back. She had no business leaving here in the first place!"

Joseph Avery and Odell White held their heads down as if the sight of what was happening up on the porch was about too much for either of them to take.

Betty had been asleep. She had come out of the back door and around the house. Joseph stretched out his arms to his wife. She snuggled up under him as they watched her Papa embracing her sister. To her, it was a wonderful, welcomed sight to see.

Mrs. Bertha continued to sit in her rocking chair, waiting for Flossie Mae to come into the house. She was mighty anxious to lay her eyes on her baby gal. But much like the day when she birthed her into the world, she had to wait. Over the years, she had learned—no matter how bad you might want a thing, at times—first, it has to get ready to come. And then, you got to wait until it comes.

So for her, Flossie Mae coming home was sort of like her rebirth. She had prayed and prayed to the Good Lord to take care of her child and do with her as He saw fit. And He had. The thing was out of her and Frederick's hands, but it won't out of God's hands. And neither was Flossie Mae out of His reach. Whatever winds had blown up yonder in the City and whatever choices her young'un made, He had kept her through it all.

When Flossie Mae came into the house, she saw her Mama sitting in the rocking chair, the very same rocking chair she had sat in the day she had left home.

Mrs. Bertha looked up at her daughter. She looked into her eyes. She looked at her plump middle. She knew almost immediately that her baby was in the family way.

She reached out her arms. Flossie Mae ran to her Mama and fell down on her knees. She laid her head on her lap and began to cry, "I'm sorry, Mama. I just wanted to be a star. I just wanted to be a star."

"I know, Baby. But in my eyes, you already were," Mrs. Bertha said, crying too. "In my eyes, you already were."

———◦○◦———

DREAM CATCHER
By M.J. Hart

Right in the midst of one of my sweetest dreams where
everything I ever hoped for lay at my feet,
I saw a "DREAM CATCHER" smiling at me.
It looked like an angel with sparkling wings which spread as far
as my eyes could see.
It's smile was inviting, filled with delight,
And when I reached out to touch it, I began to shine just as
brightly as the "DREAM CATCHER" I viewed.

"DREAM CATCHER, DREAM CATCHER, with wings all aglow,
please tell me your name," I sang.
"My name is Destiny," it sang back to me in a pleasant sounding
voice.
"And the light that you see is the purpose which God has placed
inside of you.
Through Him, you can accomplish anything.
He has given you gifts and talents. He designed you
wonderfully, fearfully, and uniquely."

"DREAM CATCHER, DREAM CATCHER with such beauty and
grace, please tell me why you have entered into my dream?" I
asked.
"I have come only to speak words of wisdom and to encourage
you, my dear," It answered.
At that very moment its' eyes became brighter than a zillion
stars.
They began to dance and twinkle with wonder and joy like a
trillion tiny lightning bugs.

And my eyes did too.

Its' words leaped forth and touched me deeply, but gently.
They filled every empty reservoir until I believed that I really
could accomplish anything.
I felt as if I was soaring high, the clouds my pathway to walk
upon.
"Your possibilities are as vast as the wide open sea," It said.
"Your future is brighter than the Northern Star. So catch on and
hold tightly.

Stay focused. Choose wisely.
Consider your tomorrows, not just the pleasures of today.
Don't stand by idly, allowing your dreams to slip through your
fingers or be stolen from you.
And don't linger outside of your dreams, waiting for them to
draw you in.
They are yours to have and to achieve.

But if you should fall short along the way, get up and catch hold
again, don't ever lose hope.
DREAM CATCHERS must keep on pressing in spite of the
challenges they may face.
Remember, no matter how slow or how swift you are in starting
out,
Or what obstacles you encounter while on your journey,
Be responsible, hold yourself accountable, always put your best
foot forward.

Your ultimate goal is to cross the finish line victoriously.
So above all else, choose life.
The blessings, and the abundance of God will encompass and

overtake you.
They will surpass all of your expectations.
Trust in the Lord. He is right there with you every step of the
way.
He is the Fulfiller of your heart's desires.

Its' light began to dim.
Its' voice grew almost silent.
It was rapidly fading from view.
I strained to hear the words that It spoke.
I wanted the DREAM CATCHER to tell me more.

"DREAM CATCHER, DREAM CATCHER, please don't go
away," I cried.
But It continued to draw further and further away from me.
Finally, It whispered, in a very soft voice,
"My dear, I'm only a reflection of the DREAM CATCHER in you."
And then I opened my eyes and saw that it was true.

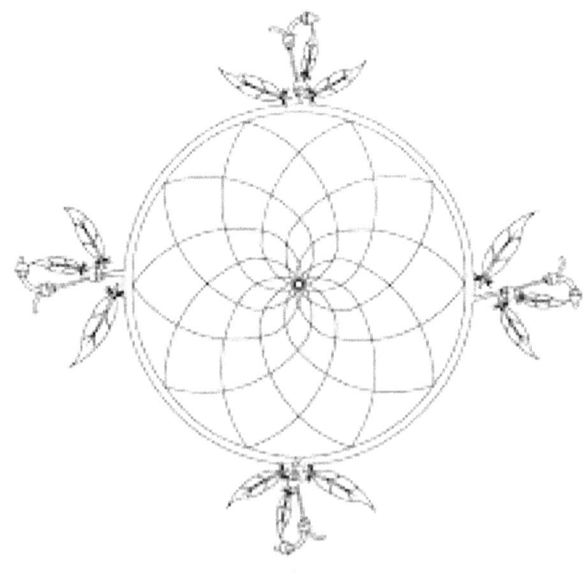

ABOUT THE AUTHOR

Mildred Juanita Poole Hart - native of Elizbeth City, NC. "Juanita" as she is most often called, is a cultural narrative storyteller, author and poet whose creative works spans over many generations of experiences shared from life and life's imaginations. THE REBIRTH OF MISS FLOSSIE MAE "BETTYE DEVINE" DUPONT is Hart's sophomore work. She has authored and published, THE PERFECTLY PAINTED PICTURE and author of the highly anticipated works, FROM THE JOURNALS OF MISS PEARLIE MAE FRESHWATER CRIPPINS. Besides church fellowship, Juanita enjoys reading, gardening, cooking, sharing with her siblings and on rare occasions, a sewing project. She still likes to get in her "Me Time" in a quiet place with a hot cup of tea and a slice of homemade cake. She has resided with her husband, James in Spring Lake for almost forty-six (46) years. She is a mother, grandmother and great-grandmother. M.J. says, "The more I write, the more I want and have to write. I no longer just proclaim that I am gifted and talented for it, but I am anointed for it! The more I write; the more grateful and humbled I become because I came to the realization long ago that I am not doing this on my own. To God, all the glory belongs. I pray that those who read and/or hear will be touched in some way by what He has given me to share." Writing for M. J. is much more than something she does; it is her passion. Hart fully understands and acknowledges the power of the pen as well as the power behind the pen. She has had the opportunity to share poems, readings, skits and plays in her community. She is very grateful for the encouragement from her broad family base, church, and friends throughout the years. Her husband, James is oftentimes an audience of one. "That's right" and a huge grin is his usual encouragement. She is affiliated with the South Carolina chapter of Pen of a Ready Writer Society.

ABOUT THE ARTIST

Alfreta Elanda Ross – Ross stumbled upon her gift and love for art when in high school, she needed one more elective to fulfill her credit requirements. She chose art without really considering she already had an eye, hand, or heart for the craft. Over the years, Ross had not fully utilized her gift, except on an occasional sketch. She, however after spending some time in her North Carolina home, her interest was rekindled.

She credits her inspiration to life in general: the people, the things, and events happening around her.

"I just want to draw a blade of grass; anything," commented Alfreta once when asked if anyone in the room could draw. Today she contends, "I didn't know that I would be given the opportunity to draw a pasture!"

For most of her adulthood, Alfreta have resided in Pennsylvania, and have five sons, two daughters, she's a grandmother, and is the daughter of storyteller and poet, Mildred Juanita Hart. Ms. Ross is also a member of the elite Pen of a Ready Writer Society and have published works in the PRWS 2014 Anthology, THE BREATH OF A FRESH WORD.